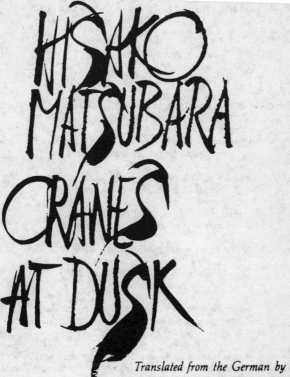

HISAKO MATSUBARA

CRANES AT DUSK

Translated from the German by
LEILA VENNEWITZ

Futura

Translator's Acknowledgment
I am deeply indebted to my husband, William, for the unstinting
help and advice he has given me in this tranlsation.
Leila Vennewitz

1

"I WONDER WHAT'S HAPPENED TO MAKE SHINAGAWA RUN like that?" said one of the old weavers.

The air was hot. It hung motionless in the lanes of the silk weavers' quarter.

The old weavers were sitting on benches on the shady side of the lane.

"He didn't even acknowledge our greeting," said one of them as he cooled himself with a round fan. "Not a bit like Shinagawa, really."

"I've never seen our area warden run like that," remarked an old woman who was leaning against the doorpost of her front door. "Something important must have happened."

"And what huge strides he was taking!"

"Did you notice? He wasn't even wearing his uniform belt, and his shirt was half hanging out of his trousers."

They all turned their heads toward the bend in the lane where, flailing his arms, Shinagawa had disappeared. Normally he wore army boots. This time he had raced by in his wooden getas. His steps were still echoing along the lane.

"I wonder where he went?"

"I saw where," announced a child who had run after him as far as the corner. "He went to the house of the staff surgeon's wife, that's where he went in."

"I see," said Nakamura the gardener, a look of concern on his face. "In that case it must be a highly official matter."

"It certainly won't be anything good," someone said. "Something's brewing all right."

Everyone looked up at the sky, which was radiantly blue and empty.

"Maybe we'll all be wiped out tonight," said a young woman who was sitting on the bench among the old people, nursing her baby.

"Yes, I also fear there's a threat in the air," commented one of the weavers as he nodded his gray head. "In fact I've been wondering for some time now why Kyoto hasn't been bombed yet."

"The Americans have forgotten about Kyoto," someone said, trying to joke, but nobody responded.

A child bounced a ball. Other children stood around him in a circle and sang in time to the bouncing. When the ball bounced out of time, another child was allowed to bounce it.

There was fear in the faces of the grown-ups that the end might come at any moment. Again and again the men and women looked up at the clear sky to see whether an American bombing squadron was already drawing its white vapor trails behind it. The children kept bouncing their ball. They laughed and sang.

Everyone knew that, apart from Kyoto, there was not a single Japanese city of over a million people that hadn't already been bombed. Tokyo, Yokohama, Nagoya,

Osaka, Kobe, Fukuoka . . . all the great cities lay in ashes, and something terrible had happened to Hiroshima and Nagasaki.

In Kyoto, life went on.

So far the food situation hadn't been bad. It was possible to buy necessities, although basic food items were rationed and often there was no fish, or it had already spoiled by the time it was delivered. Many people in the silk weavers' quarter had begun to grow their own vegetables, but the gardens of most houses were no bigger than pocket-handkerchiefs, so they sowed their vegetable seeds in flowerpots. The pots stood outside the houses.

In April a number of houses along the Hori-kawa stream had been torn down as a protection against possible fires. The people living in the neighboring lanes had lost no time in planting vegetables there too. The vegetables had flourished. The watermelons grew to such a size that many of the old people couldn't lift them alone. In June the beans had blossomed luxuriantly and were now slowly ripening. And there were tomatoes, eggplants, cucumbers, sweet potatoes, and spinach.

The demolition of the wooden houses had gone very quickly. First the shoji were removed from their grooves. Then the roof was taken off, and the tiles were carefully stacked. Finally a man came with a saw and cut through the main supporting beam. After that, all that was needed was a stout rope to tie round the beam. Twenty men and women would tug at it until the skeleton of the house collapsed inward. Each work column was headed by a municipal caller who would shout the order to pull the house down. *"Yoii-sho . . . yoii-sho,"* resounded the commands. Each column demolished a dozen houses a day, and all those who had lent a hand were allowed to take away as much wood as they could carry. The former occupants of the demolished houses would stand nearby, weeping or cursing, but resigned.

Even the municipal school administration had done its part in seeing that the remaining wood was removed as quickly as possible from the area of the firebreak. Boys and girls in the upper classes were let off school so that they could help to clear it away. Within one week, the broad firebreak had eaten along the Hori-kawa through the dense herd of houses, leaving behind only brown earth and rows of stacked tiles that were to be used during an air raid as a protection against shell splinters.

Almost all those who lived near the Hori-kawa were silk weavers, craftsmen with inspired hands. Their looms stood idle in the dusky interiors of their houses. Until the authorities ordered the looms shut down and ripped the metal parts out of their frames to be turned into weapons, they had produced the most beautiful silks in the world. Of the thirty thousand looms that had once filled the lanes of the quarter with their staccato clatter, less than ten thousand remained. Now all these stood silent too. Thus the lanes were pervaded by the stillness of a Buddhist temple, unless there happened to be children rushing out of the wide-open doors of the little wooden houses, shrieking as they ran along the yellow beaten earth of the lanes. The children were barefoot or ran around in their wooden getas. They wore only light clothes, shorts and dresses in the brightest colors. Their mothers were dressed in *mompeis,* the baggy gray trousers prescribed by the wartime government; they wore matching gray cotton jackets, like peasants. The women worked day or night shifts in the parachute factory that had been set up in the wooded side valley beyond the northern slope. There they wove the tropical-green parachute silk on looms and sewed it into parachutes.

Only a few men, all more or less elderly and no longer

required to serve in the Army, still lived in the silk weavers' quarters. Most worked in the precision-tool factories in town. There they produced compasses and delicate machinery and assembled telescopes, aircraft cameras, and other equipment needed by the military.

The very old people stayed home and took care of the children. Most of them had crooked backs from a lifetime of weaving. They often sat together on round, flat cushions on the shaded bamboo benches outside the houses. As the shade moved on, they would shift to another bench or go inside the house. From time to time they would open drawers containing samples of the silks they had once woven. The colors of the brocades surpassed memory. The silks would shimmer softly as if irradiated by an inner light. The roughened hands of the old weavers would pass gently over the chrysanthemum patterns, the irises, the asters; the leaf designs, the butterflies, the birds; over the endless variations of snow-capped waves, waterfalls, and cloud formations.

Beyond Kita-oji, where the streetcar went, the silk weavers' quarter bordered on the great Zen temple. Before the war, the muffled boom of the huge gong would sound from there every evening. The gong had hung in a pagodalike structure set on a tapering pedestal of big blocks of stone. It, too, had been claimed by the war to produce cartridge cases from its metal.

The grounds of the Zen temple, thickly wooded with immense pine trees, seemed even emptier than in peacetime. In the old days, processions of meditation students —all dressed in plain black, their bare feet in straw sandals—were often to be seen, escorted by one or more Zen priests likewise robed in black. Now only a few Zen monks and priests were left to care for the extensive grounds and the huge old temple buildings. They weeded under the pines, washed the white sand in the

Zen garden, pruned the shrubs, and used dry cloths and rice bran to polish the wooden surface of the singing walkways, a surface so shiny that the eaves of the temple roofs were reflected in it. Every step on those walks gave out a high, delicate note, not unlike the song of the nightingale. Depending on how fast one walked, on the rhythm of one's footsteps, and where one placed one's feet, a variety of tunes could be produced.

Sometimes old monks were to be seen walking along the lanes of the silk weavers' quarter in their black robes. They cared for the many small Buddhist temples hidden between the close-set houses. Somewhere or other the monks had hoarded a small supply of wax candles for their services for the dead. During the war years the candles had grown thinner and thinner because so many services had to be held and new candle wax was hard to obtain. Every day candles burned in the little Buddhist temples between the houses of the silk weavers' families. The fragrance of the incense wafted through the lanes, and from many houses came the high-pitched tone of the little brass gongs and the subdued murmuring of the mourners. When people think of death, they feel closer to Buddhism.

It was an entirely different feeling that bound the people to the great Shinto shrine situated high above the silk weavers' quarter on a hill, on a kind of terrace surrounded by trees. The houses crowded around the foot of the hill like a herd seeking protection. The hill reared up, its contours softened by the trees growing on its rocky slopes. The shrine on the summit, not visible from below, was hidden among these trees, in a silence usually broken only by the chirp of cicadas, the song of birds, the rustle of the wind.

Many people climbed the hill in order to visit the

Shinto shrine. When people think of life, they feel
drawn to Shinto.

The *Guji*, the shrine's high priest, was still young, not
yet forty, but was known to enjoy a great reputation far
beyond Kyoto. People treated him with a special rever-
ence that at the same time included affection and trust.
In the Guji's presence the many little meannesses that so
often plague daily life seemed insignificant. He gave everyone the feeling that life was much too important to be
filled with petty thoughts.

What was admired most about the Guji was his simple
way of talking. One could have a good laugh with him.
His laughter came from within and was devoid of all
affectation. The people of the quarter had a fine sense of
the genuine. When they walked up to the shrine and met
the Guji at the top, they felt no gap between themselves
and him, even though everyone knew the Guji was an
exceptionally well-read man and had already written
three books about the *I-Ching*. One could go to him with
one's troubles and questions. He uttered no moral exhor-
tations, the kind that sound lofty but constrict the heart.

From time to time Saya, the Guji's little daughter,
would accompany her father when he walked through
the lanes. He would hold her hand, and she would hop
along beside him. People smiled when they saw them.
The women weavers had given the little girl many colorful hair ribbons, red, white, purple, yellow. What Saya
liked best was to tie her hair with two bows of different
colors. Mi-chan, the pawnbroker's daughter and Saya's
favorite playmate, imitated her and also tied her hair
with bows of different colors.

Somehow or other, everyone in the silk weavers' quarter sensed that the war couldn't go on much longer.

"The war has grown old—like us," said the weavers, sitting on the benches in the shade of the houses.

"What's to become of us?" asked a young woman rocking her baby in her arms.

No one answered.

"The military government will go on fighting until Japan has been totally destroyed," said one of the old weavers, laying down his fan with a gesture of resignation.

They all remembered the statement that had been heard more and more frequently in recent days on the radio: "We shall never suffer the enemy to set foot on our sacred Japanese soil! When a hundred million Japanese souls rise up to heaven, it will be a fireworks display of a hundred million jewels—Japan will never be defeated—we would rather all die in beauty."

The air hung motionless over the valley. The sky was cloudless and dazzlingly blue. The afternoon sunlight was already turning a rusty yellow as if once again there were those strange smoky veils that had appeared after the fiery nights when Osaka had sunk into ashes. The south wind had carried the scorched smell through the length of the valley all the way to Kyoto. The smell had backed up behind the northern ridge of the mountains, and the heavy air had formed thin, horizontal layers of dirty fog. For a long time these veils had hung motionless over the city, gradually thickening into denser banks, turning the afternoon sunlight so brown that many people said the earth had turned upside down and was covering people and their houses with its shroud.

In Kyoto, as elsewhere, fire drills had been organized months ago. The fire-fighting units composed of neighborhood men and women were headed by Shinagawa.

Every week he had to hold at least one fire drill. The people living in the silk weavers' quarter were satisfied with their area warden.

"Shinagawa is all right," they would say. "He carries out the fire drills with a minimum of fuss."

Inhabitants of other districts were dissatisfied with the area wardens they had chosen. Many of them took their duties too seriously and with petty regulations made life miserable for those in their charge. One of them was said to have insisted that everyone hold the handle of the fire bucket in his right hand; those who were left-handed incurred his displeasure and were constantly being harassed with extra duties. Other area wardens took advantage of the opportunity to settle personal grudges. Since the area wardens were free to choose which house was to be used for the next major fire drill, some of them invariably picked the houses of their personal enemies and saw to it that plenty of water damage ensued.

"We made a good choice," said one of the weavers. "If we have to choose a new area warden, I'll vote for Shinagawa again."

"Yes," replied one of the others hesitantly, "provided we still need someone to carry out fire drills."

For a long time now it had been common knowledge that in Kobe and Osaka there was no way of combating the big fires. The enormous number of incendiaries falling from the night sky, combined with the speed with which the fire spread on all sides, defeated all attempts to put out the flames with pails of water. Moreover, the fire was said to have rained down from the sky as a burning, viscous mass, and wherever a drop of it fell a fire sprang up that couldn't be extinguished with water. Each drop on clothing had quickly eaten its way through to the skin and through the skin into life itself. Ever since it had become known that the Americans were capable of wiping out an entire city by means of one immensely powerful lightning-bomb from a single plane, it was almost impossible to look up at the sky without anxiety. The Americans had already unleashed their lightning twice, on Hiroshima and Nagasaki.

"I hear you shouldn't wear any black clothes," said one woman, "or you'll evaporate like a frog sitting on a lightning rod during a thunderstorm."

The children were amused by the notion of a frog evaporating.

"In a way it's a lovely thought," said Mrs. Yasumi, whose son had been killed as a kamikaze pilot, "if we should all die at the same time—like a gust of wind that whirls the cherry blossoms from their branches, carrying them up to the clouds." Since the death of her son she frequently recited the kamikaze poem that had been printed alongside the announcement of his death. She said that the souls of the dead kamikaze pilots had risen like a cloud of cherry blossoms into heaven, from where they protected their native land.

Everyone was silent, thinking of what would become of Japan if nobody should survive. "A sparkling fireworks display of a hundred million jewels rising up to heaven," said old Nakamura in a toneless voice.

"What a good thing it would be if we soon got a civilian government again!" someone said into the silence.

"But the military government was appointed by the Emperor . . ."

Once again everybody lapsed into timid silence. Only Mrs. Yasumi, who since the death of her only son was no longer quite right in the head, recited as if it were a death sutra the heroic poem of the kamikaze pilots:

Like white cherry blossoms
Borne by a gust of wind up to heaven,
So will the souls of heroes
Rise up to the clouds.

". . . rise up to the clouds," repeated Mrs. Yasumi softly, with a faraway look. "The Emperor has said so. . . . Now I am always glad to see clouds . . . but they have to be white clouds, white clouds sailing across the sky."

All those who heard her nodded in silence and looked away.

The one-legged pawnbroker came swinging up to them on his long bamboo pole. He had sharpened the top end of the pole to make it into a spear. A leather strap drawn through the shaft gave him support when he used his spear as a crutch.

"Here is the correct solution," he said. "There should be a lot more men who never leave their homes without their bamboo spears. It's the spirit that counts, the power of the spirit. It's the Japanese spirit that makes us invincible even when bombs rain down upon us."

He swung himself nimbly round his bamboo spear and with a loud guttural yell thrust it toward the sky.

During the last few months there had been frequent drilling with bamboo spears. Everyone with a home-guard uniform hanging in the closet, even women, had been trained in their use. It was with these spears that the sacred soil of Japan was to be defended should the Americans actually land. From every forest, from every hill, from every building and every home, bamboo spears were to be hurled at the invaders. Then, with the united power of the spirit, it would be possible to decide the war in favor of Japan.

Since the bomb had fallen on Hiroshima, however,

there had been much less mention of bamboo-spear drills.

"If we all have to die at once," said one man, "who'll be left to care for our souls?"

"I don't think it'd be a good thing either," said old Nakamura, "if the lightning were to wipe us all out together. If that happened, the whole city would be full of wandering lost souls."

The children had stopped playing with the ball. They had fallen silent, standing there wide-eyed and listening to what the old people were saying.

"Who will there be to carry on the memory of the dead and pass it on to the children?" asked a woman who had joined the group. "Who will put out rice and water every day for the souls of the dead?"

They all looked about them as if everything were already burned to the ground, as if the houses had disappeared, as if the familiar city, as if the valley in which Kyoto lay, had become an ashy desert devoid of human beings and inhabited only by wandering lost souls.

In a firm voice old Nakamura reminded them that the Guji of the Shinto shrine on the hill had said more than once that Kyoto wouldn't be destroyed and that Japan would lose the war.

"If the Guji up there"—he pointed to the nearby hill that loomed up darkly against the setting sun—"if he says something once, I believe him. Since he has said it twice, there's no room for doubt."

They all nodded.

"The Guji has never yet been wrong," murmured one woman.

"He told me, when my two oldest boys went to war," Nakamura continued, "that for both of them the circle of life would close out there. You all know that he was right. Unfortunately."

A look of tender sadness had appeared on Nakamura's gnarled face. He looked at his wife, who was standing a few steps away from him.

"Yes, that's right," she whispered hoarsely and nodded. "But Saburo, our third son, he'll come back, we hope."

"I am afraid to ask the Guji," said Nakamura, as if to himself.

When Shinagawa could be seen coming round the bend of the lane, everyone felt somewhat relieved that the waiting period was over. Someone walked toward him, and the rest hurried after.

The one-legged pawnbroker shouted, "Wait for me!" Cursing, he hopped along behind the others, making sure his bamboo spear got a grip on the pebbly surface of the lane. He arrived just in time to hear Shinagawa say that they were all to be ready by eight o'clock the next morning to empty out the old, stale water from all the fire buckets and fill them with fresh, new water. Next, all the air-raid trenches on the public squares were to be swept out and cleared of any stones that might have fallen or slipped down into them.

"So tomorrow's the day, is it?" said the pawnbroker breathlessly. "That's when they're finally going to drop their great flash of lightning on us?" Those standing around him motioned for him to be quiet.

"The sandbag walls," said Shinagawa in an official-sounding area warden's voice, "must be restacked wherever they have sagged. And the rows of roof tiles within the firebreaks need to be tidied up too. I've noticed a lot of weeds growing in between them. Those will have to be removed by noon tomorrow."

He looked narrowly at everyone, even the children, to make sure there was no misunderstanding.

"What's going on tomorrow?" whispered the pawn-broker to those nearest him.

"The Emperor is going to speak on the radio at noon tomorrow," someone whispered back.

Involuntarily the pawnbroker straightened up and tried to stand to attention on his single leg. He almost lost his balance and was supported by those next to him. In breathless awe the pawnbroker said in a loud voice, "His Majesty? Our Emperor . . . the Tenno? But that's impossible!"

People were exchanging bewildered glances. As far back as they could remember, there had never been any occasion when the Japanese Emperor had addressed himself to the population. Until that moment, the Tenno had always been a distant figure shrouded in the dignity of his high spiritual office.

"The Tenno is going to speak to us on the radio?" people whispered. "Impossible . . ." Their eyes held a mixture of awe, curiosity, and fear.

They knew that the Emperor issued decrees and that, according to the constitution, he was the Supreme Commander of the Imperial Armies; but that at some time or other he would descend from his mysterious remoteness and—in his own voice—speak to the nation was something nobody had ever dared to imagine.

"I feel like a man without a head," Shinagawa said, grasping his temples with both his big hands, "but the news is official."

The people nodded wordlessly, not daring to ask any more questions. They were busy with their thoughts and stood about indecisively.

The pawnbroker was still standing at attention. He reminded the others that in the early days of the war the Emperor had reviewed the military parade.

"He rode on a white horse and wore a plumed helmet," he said fervently.

"And a magnificent uniform," said one woman. "I saw it on the newsreel."

"But fancy him speaking on the radio," said old Nakamura with his gnarled face, "to us all, to the people."

"The news is official," Shinagawa emphasized again because they were all looking at him doubtfully. He tried to appear calm, but the excitement that had gripped him too was unmistakable. He looked down at his feet. "I actually ran out of the house in my wooden clogs," he muttered. "What must the staff surgeon's wife have thought of me?" He stuffed his shirt back into his trousers.

"Whatever the reason, we must be prepared for anything," said the pawnbroker. "Otherwise His Majesty, our Tenno, wouldn't be speaking to us over the radio."

Evening had imperceptibly descended. The hill showed as a black shadow against the reddening sky.

Shinagawa looked up toward the hill.

"Now I must go to the Guji and bring him the news," he said, wiping his forehead. He strode off on his wooden getas, flailing his arms as if they were fins. Before turning the corner he stopped and retraced a few steps. In a loud voice he called back out of the dusk, "Everyone must be informed . . . hurry to all the houses and spread the news." Before turning round again, he added, louder still, "But let no one in the area forget to black out his windows tonight! Otherwise I'll really be angry."

 **2**

No one quite understood the Emperor's words as they issued from the loudspeaker in a strangely distorted, high-pitched voice. The first reaction was therefore one of general bewilderment. For a while, people stood motionless, with bowed heads. Many held both hands over their faces to hide their tears. Something had happened that went beyond their comprehension.

The crowd filled the school playground, in the middle of which stood a large gray loudspeaker on a tripod. All of them, even the children, were aware that something of a staggering impact had occurred. Never before had the populace been allowed to hear the voice of the Emperor. Some of those standing close to the loudspeaker thought they had seen the Emperor's breath causing a vibration in the piece of cloth that covered its round opening.

After the Emperor had spoken, a normal radio announcer's voice monotonously read out a number of texts that were described as the Potsdam Declaration and presumably specified what the Emperor had just described as the unbearable that had to be borne. Nobody knew what Potsdam was. They knew such names as Roosevelt, Truman, Churchill, Stalin, Hitler.

To bear the unbearable, the Emperor had said. That was more or less the only thing the people on the playground had understood and all that had stuck in their minds from the strange long-winded speech of the Emperor.

So that's what his voice is like, many of them thought. They had imagined it differently, although they could not have said how. They had expected a more vigorous voice, more manly, more decisive, not as high and singsong as it had come out of the loudspeaker. Perhaps it was the fault of the radio, they thought, but the voice of the announcer after the Emperor's speech had sounded quite normal, almost embarrassingly normal.

When the voice of the announcer ceased, there was a stirring among the crowd. Slowly they lowered their hands from their faces and wiped their eyes. The scraping of feet on the gravel accompanied the stirring as it spread through the crowd. People were still not looking at one another. When their eyes happened to meet, they glanced away uncertainly and looked down again at the ground. Only those who knew each other well exchanged looks, wordless signs of understanding or query.

Until this hour there had been a kind of silent belief that the Emperor would, without the slightest doubt, appeal to the nation for a final struggle to defend the sacred soil of Japan. For that reason they had trustingly cleaned out the air-raid trenches again, filled all the fire buckets with fresh water, restacked the sandbag walls, and prepared themselves spiritually for death. Japan was to go down in beauty. Perhaps the final struggle had already begun, somewhere in the south on the island of Kyushu where, since the fall of Okinawa, an invasion by the enemy was said to be expected daily. Perhaps even now the enemy had already landed on the main island of Honshu or had assembled its "black fleet" outside the Bay of Tokyo, just as Commodore Perry had done ninety years earlier when he forced the opening up of Japan.

Now that the hour of the final struggle was at hand, each person was to carry within himself the readiness to die.

But strangely enough the Emperor had not summoned them to the final struggle. The term did not occur in his speech. As far as he could be understood, he had spoken of the suffering of the nation. He had said that what was now in store was unbearable, but that the unbearable would have to be borne.

"So we won't have to die?" piped a solemn-faced child. The clear voice broke the silence. The child's mother bent down, drawing it close so that it hid its face against her legs. Tenderly she stroked the child's hair.

Somewhere at the far end of the playground a child was crying. Many women covered their faces and joined softly in the weeping.

The ushers, recognizable by their white armbands, still had not relaxed their stiff military posture. Their eyes remained lowered, their lips unmoving.

Shinagawa said, "We should go up the hill to the Guji and ask for his advice."

He bowed before the Japanese flag as it waved from its pole. He also bowed before the loudspeaker from which the voice of the Tenno had come and which was now no more than a silent gray box on its tripod. Others followed his example, including the children. Then Shinagawa walked ahead, his head raised as befitted an area warden. People stepped aside for him, forming a passage to allow him to pass. The passage closed behind him, and the people followed. They were joined by increasing numbers. The narrow lanes of the silk weavers' district could hardly contain the flow. Finally a somewhat wider lane was reached that led in a straight line toward the great torii of bare wood that marked the entrance to the shrine. From there, under the shady oak tree, rose the steep flight of steps leading through many small torii painted vermilion red. Ferns stretched their fronds across the steps through which the roots of the oak tree had pushed their way. On reaching the old fox shrine at the end of the first flight, Shinagawa paused for a second or two with bent head. He hesitated before pulling the bell cord, but then he did. The high, resonant sound of the bronze bells drowned out the shuffling of the many feet on the steps. At the bottom of the steps the crowd now formed a solid mass.

"There's a whole lot of people coming up!" Saya called out to her father. She had heard voices and through the trees had seen the people climbing the steps from below.

Once again the Guji smoothed the paper lying in front of him on the table by passing the palm of his hand over the creases where it had been folded. He could feel the dense, fine-grained rice paper and remembered how it had soaked up the ink from his brush that December day four years ago when he had written on it. The news had just arrived that the war had started with a great Japanese victory at Pearl Harbor. Down in the city, triumphal processions had formed with military march music that had penetrated the protective screen of trees all the way up the hill. The maple trees then had been at their brightest red, the gold of cherry tree leaves had already fallen to the ground. At that time the Guji had written on this sheet of paper the prophecy that the war would plunge the country into deep night. He looked at the writing, the characters from the *I-Ching*. Before him lay the long brown envelope in which he had kept this sheet throughout the war. He had sealed it with a red paper seal. Today, before the Emperor had begun his address, he had broken the seal.

Saya poked her head through the open door. She waited until her father looked up at her.

"Shinagawa's on his way up and bringing a whole lot of people with him," she said. "He's already here."

She ran quickly along the passage that connected the shrine with the Guji's house. She wanted to stand in the passage beside one of the open shoji. From there Saya could look down onto the forecourt through a lattice of squares. When the sun was low in the afternoon, it shone through this lattice and threw shadow designs onto the floor of the long, narrow corridor. Then one could feel with one's bare feet the difference in temperature between the sunny squares and the darker frames. The floor of the corridor consisted of wooden planks, stained black and laid so close together as to make the joints invisible. Each day the maid wiped these planks with a damp cloth. Saya's mother made a point of having this work done very early in the morning, before breakfast, while, as she put it, the wooden flooring was still asleep. If the floor were to be wiped later in the day, when the day was already warm, then the wood would absorb too much moisture from the cloth through its open pores and the delicate, matte sheen of the floor would be coarsened. Her mother always saw to it that the maid followed her instructions exactly. The floor cloth had to be rinsed every day in clear, cold water and then wrung out twice. A proper cloth had to be used for wiping the floor of the corridor. Moreover, the wiping always had to be done in the proper direction, exactly in line with the grain of the wood so that any dust that might have settled between the grooves would be picked up.

The forecourt was already thronged with people. The

sun shone down almost vertically. The white rock supporting the Guji's house looked as if it were made of silver. The pine tree that spread its roots over the rock threw a bizarre, flickering shadow.

The shuffling sound of the many feet on the gravel of the forecourt died away as the Guji emerged from his study. He walked down the five steps from the house to the forecourt and said something to Shinagawa. Saya saw Shinagawa bow to her father. Then they walked side by side to the wide stone steps leading up to the shrine. There was movement again among the people. They followed her father and Shinagawa up the stone steps. Saya saw a few children from her school and others whom she knew from the silk weavers' lanes. All of them walked without saying a word, bent slightly forward. She would have liked to wave to old Nakamura and the vegetable seller, but no one looked toward the place behind the lattice window of the corridor, not even the children.

"Don't stand around like that," Saya's mother said sharply. Both the maids had been given the day off to visit their parents, and she had forgotten to soak the rice for lunch. The fish ration had gone bad again.

"What a day," she complained, covering her face with both hands.

"Do you want me to throw away the fish?" Saya asked.

"What a terrible day!"

Before the Emperor's radio speech, the Guji's wife had put on a silk kimono, dark blue with a woven pattern of many little yellow gingko leaves.

"I know it's not yet autumn," she had said, "but the Japanese nation will know how to die gloriously. This can only be compared to the falling of golden leaves in autumn, for Nature also reveals her true beauty only just before death."

Saya had helped her mother put on the wide obi. The heavy, stiff silk resisted being tied into a foursquare bow at the back. Her mother was not satisfied with her efforts.

"The leaf pattern on the obi has to be exactly in line with the pattern on the kimono," she said. "Do try a little harder!"

Saya also had had to put on a good dress, her best one. It was of thick cotton and much too warm.

"I don't want to hear any complaints from you," her mother said. "For the Tenno to speak over the radio is an unheard-of event. It can be followed only by the death of the entire nation. We must now all be prepared to die."

While the Emperor's voice was coming over the radio, Saya's father had sat with half-closed eyes, relaxed, almost smiling.

"You might at least bow your head a little," her mother had hissed at him. "What will the children think of you?"

Now everything had turned out differently. The Tenno had not called for the final struggle. He had not demanded that they die.

"Shall I slice the tomatoes?" Saya asked.

Her little brother Bo, who was playing on the dining room floor, crowed happily: "Tomato . . . tomato . . . tomato . . ." Saya had taken off the tight trousers their mother had made him wear. "May I take off my dress too?" she asked. "I'm so hot."

Her mother was still wearing her dark blue kimono. She sat with stooping shoulders at the dining table, her face propped in her hands. She had pushed up the sleeves of her kimono so they wouldn't lie on the table. She nodded at Saya without speaking. Saya quickly stripped off the hot cotton dress and took it to her room.

"Tomato . . . tomato . . . tomato . . . ," called Bo when Saya returned. In the kitchen she sliced the tomatoes and sprinkled them with salt. Bo came toddling over to watch her. He didn't yet reach the level of the kitchen table, so he grabbed the edge with his little hands and tried to stretch up as high as he could.

He hopped up and down with impatience and opened his mouth wide as Saya pushed a slice of tomato into it.

Meanwhile Ryo had come in and wanted to take all the slices. "Don't!" Saya snapped at him.

Ryo grabbed what he wanted and kicked Saya on the shin. At eight, he already regarded himself as a little samurai.

"Stop that quarreling," came their mother's tired voice from the adjoining dining room, "on a day like today."

"But Ryo is taking everything and making spots on the tatami mats!"

Ryo, both hands full of tomato slices, had run outside, leaving a trail of tomato juice behind him.

"You're a girl, after all," the mother said. "Wipe it up." She made sure that Saya took the right cloths—one for the tatami mats, another for the floor of the corridor, and a third one for the kitchen—that she kneeled down properly, wiped from shadow to light, and that she then took the right pail for rinsing the cloths.

"Everything has its deeper meaning," she said, "even removing spots. It's the little everyday things that give life its stability and its framework."

The mother sat down again at the dining table and stared with empty eyes at the wall. The ceremonial kimono she was wearing and her dejected expression showed that her mood hadn't changed since the morning.

"Isn't it nice that the war is over?" Saya said tentatively.

Her mother did not react. Her eyes remained fixed on the wall. Saya had often seen her with that vacant look and had always been scared by it. She wanted nothing so much as to comfort her mother, to conjure up a smile on that delicate, pale face.

Although Saya was only ten, she had long since learned that it was better to tell her mother very little or nothing of her own childish troubles. She could chatter away to her mother as if she hadn't a care in the world, allowing only what was cheerful and amusing to come bubbling out.

"Isn't it nice that the war is over and that we can all go on living? Just imagine if we were all dead now—even Bo."

She looked at Bo with wide, horrified eyes. "We're all still alive!" she cried and gave him a big hug.

Bo snuggled up to his sister. "Tomato . . . tomato . . . ," he demanded. Saya hurried into the kitchen to cut up another one for him.

"You see? Father was right," she called out to her mother from the kitchen. "He always knew Japan would lose the war and that even so nothing would happen to us."

"You don't know enough about that," said her mother in a tone of gentle reproach. "That kind of knowledge, and the deep emotion we must all feel for Japan, are utterly contrary to one another."

She covered her face again with her hands.

Outside the front door, footsteps crunched on the gravel, and a polite, singsong, feminine voice called out, "Anybody at home?"

Her mother raised her head. The somber mood had vanished from her face.

"The staff surgeon's wife," she whispered huskily to Saya. "Put some water on for tea." She jumped up, hurried to the door, and politely welcomed the visitor with "Oh, *what* a surprise . . . *what* a pleasure . . . !"

"I hope I'm not disturbing you" came the voice of the staff surgeon's wife.

"Oh . . . not in the least! You're most welcome."

Bo was playing with Saya's abacus, pretending he could count with the many wooden beads. "one, two, five," he counted, "a thousand, millions, a hundred . . ." With his awkward little fingers he shifted the counting beads up and down, "a thousand, millions, a hundred."

Now and again he cast a significant glance at Saya. "A hundred," he said.

The staff surgeon's wife was a member of her mother's circle. Both came from Himari and had known each other for a long time. The staff surgeon's wife was three years older. Since her marriage she had been living in Kyoto but was childless. As she lived at the bottom of the hill, not far from the great torii, she often came to see Saya's mother and have tea with her. Their afternoons together always started with a formal, lengthy exchange of greetings. Then, after discussing ikebana, they would often sit silently in a corner of the southeast room—the shoji opened wide so that they could gaze over the treetops at the city in the valley. The staff surgeon's wife would invariably say how beautiful the view of the city was from up here. Then they would often sit silently for ten or fifteen minutes in front of the vase that held her mother's flower arrangement.

"This one is no good at all," her mother would finally say. "When one contemplates it for a long time my imperfections become obvious."

"On the contrary," her guest would protest. "It is only when one contemplates it for a long time that one realizes the true balance of shape and color."

"Both my maids are away today," Saya heard her mother say. "Today is a special day, of course."

The kettle on the stove began to sing. Bo rolled the abacus back and forth along the grooves of the sliding door as if it were a locomotive. *"Shu-shu-tu-tu . . . shu-shu-tu-tu,"* he chanted.

Saya knew that her mother attached the utmost importance to serving the staff surgeon's wife the best tea in the best bowls, so she chose the box of tea that her mother would always take when there were special guests. With the proper cloth she wiped out the two ceramic bowls, then placed them on a black lacquer tray and carried them into the southeast room.

"With a pure heart I handed over my diamond ring," the staff surgeon's wife was just saying when Saya entered. "I firmly believed in Japan's victory."

"I knew for a long time from my husband that the war couldn't be won," Saya's mother replied casually. "As long as four years ago he prophesied that Japan would lose this war."

"But you never believed it!" Saya blurted out. "And you always scolded Father!"

An uncertain smile appeared on her mother's narrow face. She threw Saya a brief, disapproving glance and, turning to her guest, said, "Of course, in common with all those who love their native land, I wished for victory and banished any thought of defeat from my heart . . . just imagine for a moment . . . an enemy army on Japanese soil! In all our two thousand years of history such a thing has never happened—why should it be in *our* lifetime that Japan is to be occupied for the first time by an enemy army?"

"Quite right," agreed the staff surgeon's wife and sipped her tea.

"We all know," Saya's mother went on, "that every true Japanese heart weeps at the thought of our defeat."

"Quite right," assented the staff surgeon's wife. "We are living in unnatural times and must first get used to the idea of defeat. . . ."

"What we lack is historical experience," Saya's mother said. "My silly daughter doesn't know yet what it means to suffer a national defeat . . . a national disgrace . . . a child like that tends to talk nonsense. When I handed over my jewelry I did no more than my duty, knowing full well that we would still lose the war. . . ."

With a quick warning glance Saya's mother prevented her from saying anything else that might discredit her in the eyes of her guest.

"Come over here, sit down beside me," she said ingratiatingly to Saya. "You're a big girl now and can understand your mother's heart."

The tone of her mother's voice prevented Saya from leaving. She would much rather have stayed in the next room with Bo or run up to the shrine where her father was probably at this very moment standing before the altar. Maybe he was even speaking to all the people who had walked up there. Saya loved listening to him when he addressed a crowd. His clear voice carried a long way. It had a round, full tone. He never resorted to the verbal flourishes familiar to her from so many speeches at school. There everyone addressing the students from a raised platform—the principal, the teachers, the superintendent, men in uniform—spoke ponderously and with much clearing of throats.

Her father's speeches were always simple. He spoke to a hundred people exactly as he did to two, only louder.

It went through her mind that she could run through the woods and, when she reached the top, creep through the gap in the fence, which would enable her to get di-

rectly into the interior of the shrine. Two boards had
long been missing just where the sakaki bushes were
thickest. The gap was big enough for Saya to slip
through.

"What will the enemy do to our girls and young
women?" wondered the staff surgeon's wife. "It is terrible to think of all that might happen."

"Fortunately our daughter is only ten and too young
for that," said her mother.

"For what?" asked Saya.

"How sweet!" exclaimed the staff surgeon's wife, but
her mother said with a solemn face, "You're too young to
understand such things. You'd better go and play with
Bo."

Relieved, Saya ran out of the room. Bo was still playing with the abacus. He had placed a lot of little red
beans on the floor and said those were people who
wanted to travel in his *shu-shu-tu-tu*. He laid the beans on
the abacus and pushed it along the black wooden floor of
the corridor.

Once again footsteps were heard outside on the graveled forecourt. People were returning from the shrine.
They came down the wide stone stairway, singly or in
groups. Many of the women walked arm in arm, but not
the way they usually did. They were silent, sad. Saya
wondered why they weren't more cheerful. Surely the
war being over was a good thing? There would be no
more air-raid alerts now.

How often had her mother snatched Saya, Ryo, and Bo
from sleep during the night and by the light of a single
flickering storm lantern dragged them down into the
space under the house where they always hid during air-
raid warnings. Under the sky filled with the roar of many
aircraft engines, the nerve-racking howl of the sirens

seemed like a helpless scream. Saya's mother had to half drag, half carry Ryo. Saya, who was hardly awake herself, had to carry Bo on her back. Bo clung to her like a little monkey and immediately fell asleep again in the shelter. Ryo was scared of the confined, dark hole.

Their father had never come down into the shelter. He had always stayed outside under the roaring sky and walked up to the shrine. He had watched Osaka burn. From a distance of twenty-five miles he could see the bright bursts of fire shooting up into the sky. The highest column of fire came from the burning castle of Osaka. Tongues of flame overtopped even the shadowy line of the mountain range that bordered each side of the Kyoto valley toward the south.

"What happens if we get bombed like that here in Kyoto too?" Saya had asked anxiously.

"Kyoto won't be bombed," her father had often assured her. "You needn't be afraid."

Yuri-chan, a classmate of Saya's, was crossing the forecourt with her mother. When she saw Saya, she came running. She climbed up onto the rock outside and stretched up to the lattice window.

"The war's over!" she called gaily. "Really over!"

Saya imitated the voice of the Emperor as it had sounded over the radio, oddly constricted, very high and quavery. Yuri-chan gave a startled look through the lattice.

Both girls burst out laughing.

"Do it again!" begged Yuri-chan.

Saya went on mimicking the Emperor until Yuri-chan had to go back to her mother.

Bo wanted to look out of the corridor window too. Saya lifted him up.

"When's Oto-chan coming?" asked Bo.

"Soon," Saya told him. Together they looked out toward the wide stone staircase. By now, fewer and fewer people were coming down the steps.

"When's Oto-chan coming?" asked Bo.

Saya couldn't hold him up any longer and squatted down so he could climb onto her back. This made it easy for him to look outside and wave at the people passing by. Some of them waved back.

Their father was the last to appear at the top of the steps, and when Bo finally saw him in his priest's robe of shining white, he crowed with delight and slipped off Saya's back as fast as he could. With Saya running after him, he toddled the whole length of the passageway. Bo had to crawl backward down the wooden steps outside their father's study on account of his short legs. "One . . . two . . . three," he counted out loud. As a precaution Saya held on to the crossed shoulder straps of his little trousers.

Saya and Bo ran a race to cover the last twenty yards to their father. She took short steps to let Bo win. He laughed with glee at being the first to reach their father, who caught him on the run and swung him up into his arms.

3

MI-CHAN LIVED IN THE PAWNBROKER'S HOUSE JUST BEYOND
the bend in the lane. It was easy to recognize Mi-chan's
house by the broad white curtain hanging halfway down
across its front door. There were large black characters
on it indicating that good money could be had here in
exchange for pawned belongings. Those who had never
had to pass through this curtain looked a little contemp-
tuously at others who were known to have taken things
to the pawnbroker periodically. Because nobody wanted
to be seen lingering outside his house, everyone walked
quickly past that point in the lane, but Saya always ran
inside eagerly.

Whenever she slipped under the white curtain with Bo
shouting "We're here!," Mi-chan would immediately
come hurrying from the back room. Today was a special
day—the day of the *Jizo* festival.

"I'm not allowed to go out," Mi-chan told Saya wist-
fully. "It's too dangerous."

It was only a week since Japan had surrendered. The
pawnbroker was sharpening another bamboo spear. In

his little garden behind the house there were already a
quantity of them propped against the wall.

"I'll need them," he said, "we'll all need them when
the enemy comes. I'm going to run them through those
hairy monsters."

He was sitting on the edge of the wide wooden veranda, working away with his knife. Now and again he
would stop to rub the short stump of his leg, which was
sheathed in coarse army cloth.

"The typhoon season will soon be here," he said. "I
can feel it in my leg."

Mi-chan whispered to Saya that she would love to go
out with her into the lane to join in the festival. "But
suppose an American suddenly comes around the corner," she said, "what do we do then?"

She was convinced that Americans looked like demons
and that they ate little children just as the wicked monsters of the mountains and rivers did. "They have red
hair and green eyes," she said.

"There are also some with yellow hair and blue eyes,"
the pawnbroker called out from his bamboo-carving
place, "but the ones with red hair and green eyes are the
worst. When you get rid of a hundred of them in battle,
ten thousand new ones appear. They're not real human
beings."

"They have devils' horns too," Tama-chan, the pawnbroker's eighteen-year-old daughter, called out from the
kitchen, where she was cleaning vegetables. It was obvious from her voice that she was poking fun at her father's tales about monsters.

"You've never met up with them," he said, "but I have
—I've fought against them and lost my leg." He rubbed
his stump again.

Mi-chan, who was the same age as Saya, was the
pawnbroker's niece. After her parents had been killed in

Kobe in an air raid, he adopted her as a daughter. His wife had died of tuberculosis. Tama-chan managed the household and also helped in the shop, although during the last few months business hadn't been good. People didn't need much money, there wasn't much to buy.

The pawnbroker told them about the Americans he had fought on Guadalcanal. He was one of the few who had managed to get away, while it was still possible to slip through the naval blockade. He had been shipped out with the wounded after the first attack.

"But at that time," he said, "we had already eaten up all the coconuts and were living on nothing but grass and lizards, whereas the Americans were eating turkey with chestnuts three times a day. That was why they were growing bigger every day while the Japanese soldiers were shrinking. Toward the end our soldiers, when they saw a grasshopper flying by, thought it was an American airplane, and when a shoal of jellyfish drifted across the sea they fired their rifles until the magazines were empty because they thought it was the American fleet."

"And then?" asked Mi-chan, who had heard the story before but always wanted to hear it again.

"Then our soldiers all turned into flying fish," said the pawnbroker, "and disappeared into the vastness of the ocean."

Tama-chan called out from the kitchen, "Then there's no sense sharpening those bamboo spears."

"Be quiet, you're only a girl and don't know anything about our spirit," replied the pawnbroker testily. "It's our spirit that wins victories. We have to pin the hairy ones to the wall with our bamboo spears, then they won't be able to multiply any more."

"But that's all rubbish," said Tama-chan.

Bo stomped like a sumo wrestler along the floorboards of the veranda, holding his upright forefingers to his head to make himself look like a horned devil. He came toward Saya and Mi-chan and was ecstatic when the two girls fled screaming into a corner.

"That's why I'm not allowed to go out," Mi-chan whispered to Saya. "The Americans may come at any moment."

"But the Jizo festival . . . ," Saya said, loud enough for the pawnbroker to hear.

"The hairy ones may come at any moment round the next corner," said the pawnbroker. "They eat children, especially little girls." One could tell from his voice that he had no intention of letting Mi-chan out of the house.

"But that's nonsense," Tama-chan called out from the kitchen, and Saya said in a firm, clear voice, "The Jizos protect children."

"That's right!" called Tama-chan. "The Jizos protect children."

The pawnbroker rubbed the stump of his leg. He seemed to waver.

"Mayn't I go out with Saya then?" begged Mi-chan. "Saya will protect me too."

"Me too," cried Bo.

Tama-chan came out of the kitchen and stood between Saya and Mi-chan.

"It's quite true," she said to her father. "The Jizo festival comes only once a year, and today of all days you won't let Mi-chan. . . ."

"Well, take a careful look out the front door," conceded the pawnbroker.

Mi-chan shrieked in delight and was already running to the door.

"Wait, I'll help you put on a kimono!" Tama-chan called out after her. In honor of the Jizo festival, Bo and Saya were both wearing white cotton kimonos. Bo's had a pattern of blue diamonds, Saya's one of scarlet hibiscus blossoms.

Saya had to promise the pawnbroker not to take Mi-chan farther than Shinagawa's house and to come back at once if the hairy ones were to show up anywhere.

"Take good care, all of you," he warned them.

"Good care," said Bo and again stomped like a wrestler through the small room where Tama-chan was helping Mi-chan put on a kimono printed with red dolls. Saya tied Mi-chan's hair with two bows.

"Now I look like you!" said Mi-chan, hopping delightedly.

"Good care," said Bo, holding his upright forefingers to his head. *'Dong-toko-dong . . . dong-toko . . . dong . . .'*

The Jizo festival was already in full swing. The lanes of the silk weavers' quarter were thronged with children in bright summer kimonos. Wherever Jizo figures stood on their stone pedestals at street corners, surrounding them were quantities of morning glories twining up thin bamboo stakes that had been stuck into flowerpots. Other Jizo figures, the ones that usually stood in little wall alcoves or between two houses, had been assembled at various points where the children had gathered in large numbers.

Saya and Mi-chan ran with Bo to Shinagawa's house. It wasn't far, only two blocks away.

Shinagawa's house was built so that all the lattice walls screening the interior from the lane could easily be removed by hand. A platform that had been pushed up in front of the house took up almost a third of the lane. Reed mats covered the floor of the platform and the surface of the lane so that the children could all run around barefoot. Where the reed mats began there were many getas, big ones and little ones, some placed neatly but most of them tossed here and there. Children were constantly coming and going, slipping into their getas or looking for them to put on again. From the ceiling beam above the platforms hung a row of red paper lanterns strung so closely together that they touched. When the wind moved some of them, all the others swung too.

In a wide semicircle, on wooden bases, stood many little stone Jizo figures with clean red bibs and timeless childlike faces. Some wore caps as well, made of the same red material as the bibs. The Jizos from all the surrounding lanes had been taken to Shinagawa's house so they could watch the children's festival that is celebrated once a year in their honor. Each one had been freshly washed and scrubbed with a stiff brush. The oldest figures had been scrubbed year after year for centuries. Their contours had become blurred, and it was no longer possible to tell from their Bodhisattva faces whether they were smiling or sleeping.

Saya, Mi-chan, and Bo had to thread their way through the crowd of children. Sweet potatoes were being grilled over a charcoal fire beside the stage. The pungent smoke drifted through the lane. Shinagawa stood beside the fire distributing the grilled slices as they became ready.

"No," he would say whenever a child seemed too insistent. "You've just had a piece." With his long arms he would reach over the heads of the children crowding around him and make sure that those farther back received their slices.

"Watch it," he warned them, "they're very hot!"

Some of the wooden bases were wide enough to take several Jizos. They sat in the lotus position or stood with their heads slighty bent, as if looking down in benediction on the children. Some of the children offered their slices of sweet potato to the Jizos.

"For you," they would say softly, bowing before the serenely smiling figures of the old wayside deities, then popping the slice of grilled sweet potato into their own mouths.

When a child dies, the Jizos take it by the hand and escort it across the great wide river that divides the land of the living from the land of the dead. Children, it is said, are not yet strong or experienced enough to cross the river on their own, either on a raft or in a boat. Moreover, they might become absorbed in playing with pebbles on the riverbank. Slippery monsters might rise up out of the water. Then, if the Jizos don't watch out, the children will be devoured by the monsters.

Many of the children at the festival had brought along little colored balls made of cotton loosely filled with beans or melon seeds. They began to play with them on the platform, tossing them up in the air and catching them again. Other children squatted beside them, singing and clapping. Faster and faster grew the rhythm, and more little cloth balls flew through the air with ever-increasing speed. When rhythm and game became hopelessly tangled up, the children would laugh and change places so that those who had been singing before were now allowed to toss the balls.

Mrs. Shinagawa guided the game on the platform with a discreet hand, knowing just how to steer it so that each child had its turn. She was a little woman with darting button eyes, and she wore her graying hair combed tightly back and twisted into a knot. She came from Tokyo, as was evident from her accent. In forming her words, she used only her lips and the front part of her mouth; when she spoke it sounded as if children were spilling marbles onto the ground.

Her clear voice was heard calling out to her husband, "How many sweet potatoes do you still have?"

Shinagawa drew himself up to his full height and looked across to the platform. His broad face wore an affectionate smile.

"Not many," he called back. "The charcoal fire has almost gone out, too."

"That was a queer feeling yesterday," said old Nakamura, who had come to the Jizo festival with the two children of his oldest son, the one who had been killed in the war. "For the first time I heard the weather report again on the radio."

"So did I," said someone else. "Fine weather was forecast right away. As if to order."

"After four years, the first weather report. You can tell the war is over."

Someone asked if there would be looting when the Americans arrived, and everyone assumed an anxious expression, one that didn't seem quite appropriate to the gaiety of the children.

"What are the conquerors going to do with our young women and girls?"

Someone reported that the city administration had already prepared lists of the names of the women in the geisha quarter. An appeal had been made to the sense of national responsibility of these women and they had been told that much now depended on them. They must be spiritually prepared to satisfy the lusts of the conquerors.

"Are there enough geishas for that?" asked a youngish woman, drawing her blouse close over her breast.

"Well, there are also those around the railway station."

"But can one possibly offer the honored Americans those women?"

"Ah, yes, that's a big problem. The city will have to try and find a solution."

"I'm not worried about that," said an old man who had once worked for the city. "They've plenty of experience, and there'll also be an adequate supply of other women."

"It's not right," another man countered, "to think of our young war widows in this context. They don't deserve such treatment."

They all agreed, but also argued that the problem in this magnitude was a new one for Japan. Never in its history had foreign troops penetrated the country.

"And they are our enemies," said the youngish woman, tugging at her blouse again. "That's the worst part."

"It's a question of numbers," said the man who had once worked for the city, "not of whether they are enemies. Every enemy turns into a friend when he's given the right women."

The others fell silent. Only Nakamura said, "We must be prepared for anything, even the worst."

From another lane came the sound of loud male singing that drowned out the children's voices and was accompanied by what sounded like the banging of tin drums and saucepans.

"There they are again," said one of the old men, "come to annoy us."

Everyone turned toward the source of the racket and listened. One man who was hard of hearing raised his cupped hand to his ear.

It was common knowledge that the Koreans, who lived adjacent to the silk weavers' quarter, had been celebrating Japan's defeat since the day of capitulation. Some of them had been brought as laborers to Japan at the outbreak of war, but most had come thirty or more years ago, at a time when Korea was declared to be part of

Japan. All the same, they had never been accepted. Now they were putting on great banquets, marching in chanting, raucous groups through the streets, and appeared more and more often in the lanes of the silk weavers' quarter. When spoken to, they would reply only in Korean and laugh when nobody understood them.

"Hey, you there!" they would shout, loud enough for everyone to hear. "It's all over! Now *we're* on top, and it's up to you people to learn Korean!"

Shinagawa threw water on his charcoal fire and joined the others. There were still beads of sweat on his forehead. Mrs. Shinagawa brought him a towel. Shinagawa had to stoop quite low to enable his nimble little wife to wipe the sweat from his neck and forehead.

"I find these noisy celebrations disgusting," someone remarked. "Whose side are these Koreans on anyway? After all, basically they're Japanese."

"But not real ones."

"Nonsense," said Shinagawa, still stooping. "They're just banging away with their firecrackers. I haven't heard of any real shooting yet."

"But then where did they get their firecrackers?" Mrs. Shinagawa interjected in her rapid, marble-rolling accent.

The men stood silent and pensive.

"There you are," Mrs. Shinagawa declared. "You can't say the Koreans aren't dangerous. They have ammunition. They break open the cartridges and make firecrackers out of them. It's that simple."

Before anyone could reply she was gone again, reappearing shortly afterward on the platform, where she mingled with the children.

"I'm glad we had enough light bulbs for the lanterns," said Shinagawa. "You've all done wonders to make this festival an outstanding one!"

Even three days ago no one would have believed that it would be possible to extend the Jizo festival into the night. Everyone knew that the children loved it best after dark, when they could dance and sing under the lanterns, but as long as the blackout was enforced no one had been permitted to hang lanterns out in the lane. When the blackout regulations were lifted three days ago, the first thing Mrs. Shinagawa did was to fetch the forty-nine red paper lanterns from the storeroom at the rear of her house, where they had been lying for the last three years, wrapped in white oilpaper. Many of the light bulbs had been used up in the house to provide essential lighting. Light bulbs were precious, they were rationed. Those few that were available during the war were of poor quality and burned out quickly.

The chief electrician had strung the wires to connect the forty-nine lanterns and had also checked out the fuse box so as not to risk a short circuit.

"I've jammed in a coin," he had told Shinagawa. "I know it's not allowed, but it always works. For this once it'll be all right. Still, keep a few pails of water handy in case the wires start to smolder."

Shinagawa went into his house to switch on the chain of lanterns. Outside on the platform, his wife told the children to watch closely, something wonderful was about to happen.

When the long chain of closely hung red lanterns lit up all at once, the children clapped their hands in delight. Shinagawa emerged from the dark interior of the house to make sure all the lanterns were burning properly.

Saya suggested that for the raccoon dance Shinagawa should take the part of the great abbot.

"Oh, I'm really too tall for that," Shinagawa protested

with a laugh, but the children all shouted that Shina-gawa would make a good abbot.

"Well, all right," he finally said and allowed his wife to drape the black robe over him.

"We need three monks."

Saya called out, "Yuri-chan!"

Yuri-chan, who had been keeping close to Saya, tried to hide behind the others. After all, her father was Korean. She snuggled up to Saya and asked, "Do you really think I'd be allowed to go up on the stage?"

"Yuri-chan must be a monk!" Saya called out again emphatically. She threw her whole little personality behind her demand that Yuri-chan must appear on the stage together with two boys.

"Saya must be the head raccoon!" Yuri-chan and Mi-chan then called out together.

This suggestion was immediately supported by many of the other children, and Saya was promptly chosen for the part. Then four more girls were chosen. Saya said firmly, "But Bo has to go up onto the stage too!"

Bo squealed with delight and tried to scramble up onto the platform. Because it was a bit too high for him, one of the children lifted him up. On the stage Bo drummed with both hands on his stomach, chanting, *"Pong poko-pong no pong!"*

Then the front part of the platform was cleared. Down below in the lane the children who were not taking part on stage sat on the reed mats. Behind them, on pedestals of varying height, stood the stone Jizo figures with their red bibs. The red glow from the lanterns shone on the gray stone faces of the Jizos and restored the faraway Bodhisattva smile to even the oldest and most weather-beaten of them.

"It's not really right, you know, for that girl Yuri-chan

to be allowed onto the stage," one mother whispered to another. "After all, she's half Korean."

"I quite agree," the other mother whispered back. All those who had overheard these remarks nodded in agreement but allowed their smiles to remain on their faces.

Some of the children clapped their hands and started to sing, whereupon the rest joined in. The raccoon children came dancing onto the stage, drumming rhythmically on their thrust-out stomachs and performing comical contortions to the laughter of the children down below in the lane. Then came the monk children, dancing stiffly with crossed arms, their feet stamping out the rhythm.

Bo was too small to take part properly in everything, so he danced all by himself at the front of the stage as the raccoons and monks formed hopping, whirling circles, dancing apart and joining up again.

When Shinagawa appeared, tall and imposing in his black abbot's robe, the raccoons darted away in all directions. Bo hid his face in his hands and peeped out through his fingers as he looked around for Saya.

The first little monk stepped reverently up to the abbot. "Through my carelessness I have broken this precious vase," he declaimed, holding up the imaginary broken pieces with both hands.

"All that has form passes away," Shinagawa said in a deep voice.

The second little monk stepped forward and confessed that he had lost his purse.

"One loses that to which the heart is attached," said the abbot.

Yuri-chan stepped forward as the third little monk and announced that her beloved kitten had died.

"All that has life will someday pass away," said the abbot.

The dancing and singing resumed. All the raccoon children who had hidden inside the house emerged again from the darkness, writhing comically and drumming on their thrust-out stomachs, *Pong poko-pong no pong.*

They all danced around Shinagawa the abbot, who first stood quietly in the middle but then also started to dance—with stiff legs and slowly swinging arms. The children below brought up more and more Jizo figures and lifted them onto the edge of the platform so they could share in the merriment. The children on the stage moved the stone figures with the quiet, timeless faces into the center so they could dance around them.

At the front of the stage Bo stomped from one leg to the other, his shrill voice piping out above the rest:

> *Come, ye little children.*
> *Come! The ancient Jizos*
> *Are watching day and night.*
> *Pong poko-pong no pong!*

4

GENERAL MACARTHUR HAD LANDED IN TOKYO AT ATSUGI
Airfield. The newspapers carried a picture of him planting his big foot on Japanese soil. People besieged the
newsstands and looked at the picture in apprehensive
amazement.

So that was their new master. From now on, all power
lay with him. He was the conqueror. He was America.

It had been said that the enemy would never set foot
on the sacred soil of Japan. Now the American general
had planted his big foot on Japanese soil, and nothing
seemed to have changed. The Emperor's command had
been to bear the unbearable and to stop fighting. People
found it good that the Emperor had said this.

They had long since tired of the war and asked themselves why all that dying had been necessary. When the
papers reported that yet another person had committed
hara-kiri in front of the Imperial Palace in Tokyo, people
merely shook their heads pensively. Some respected the
person because his grief over Japan's defeat would not

allow him to go on living; others merely remarked, "Perhaps that satisfies his soul."

That was all they would say about it. Somehow or other the war seemed to demand blood even when it was over, as if this had become a habit. It was good to know that there were men crazy enough to offer themselves voluntarily as a sacrifice, but no one said this aloud.

People wondered what General MacArthur would do now. They were prepared to bend to his will like reeds in the wind. They had long accepted the fact that the dream of the great Japanese Empire was over, that a glorious Imperial Army had ceased to exist and had been replaced by nothing but vanquished Japanese soldiers, that more than a hundred Japanese cities now lay in rubble and ashes.

During the last few days, people had been hearing more and more about Hiroshima and Nagasaki. By this time they knew that it was a fearsome miracle-weapon that the Americans had employed there. No one seemed to remember how patronizingly the Americans had been referred to at the start of the war, how it had been said that, properly speaking, Americans could manufacture only tin cans, not real weapons, that at the first sight of Japanese soldiers they would run away in panic or immediately put up their hands.

The news photo showing General MacArthur descending from the aircraft, nonchalant, looking almost like a civilian, pipe in hand, emphasized more than a thousand words the finality of the American victory. People kept gazing in astonishment at the photograph. They had imagined that the great conqueror would step onto Japanese soil with full military honors, his chest laden with medals. They had expected a crisp demonstration of power and were almost shamed by the sight of this American general who carried no weapon and wasn't even surrounded by an escort of saluting soldiers bristling with weapons. The fact that he concealed his eyes behind sunglasses enhanced the uncanny impression. In Japan only the blind wore glasses that hid their eyes.

It was a time of waiting as before a typhoon. Everything lay in the semidarkness of uncertainty. How strong the impact of the typhoon would be and from which direction it would come, no one knew. In any event, everyone was prepared to submit to the force of the wind, as flexibly as reeds in a storm.

In many of the gardens, people dug holes at night where they buried old ceramic bowls and antique scrolls that they had wrapped in layers of oilpaper and packed in kiri-wood boxes. Anyone who owned valuable silk kimonos packed them with plenty of mothballs into large, zinc-lined chests and buried them in what had been the air-raid shelters below the tatami floors. They replaced the precious silk kimonos in their cupboards with plain cotton ones to fill up the drawers and not make it look as if something had been taken away and hidden.

"The honored victors," many would say, "maybe they will loot after all?"

"One never knows."

People wrapped their savings books, family seals, cash, and whatever securities they owned in plain cotton cloth and placed the bundles behind or inside the family altar.

In most of the houses in the silk weavers' quarter there were two family sanctuaries: a Buddhist altar of black lacquer ornamented in gilt or inlaid with genuine gold, and a simple little Shinto altar of plain wood.

The Buddhist house altars were in the living and dining rooms, usually standing on a low chest or in the space between two small cupboards. There every day the family would place a bowl of freshly made tea and one of freshly cooked rice for the souls who dwelled behind the altar's folding doors. Each soul had its name tablet inside the altars, fixed to little stands on each side of the Buddha, who sat enthroned against an aureole of golden flames. Often these massive, black soul-dwellings were equipped with drawers and secret compartments where valuables could be hidden so that they would come under the direct protection of the souls.

The little Shinto shrines had a different significance. There dwelled the gods who were said to bring blessings to the house and family, which was why whenever possible the little Shinto shrines were to be found in a northeastern room where the first rays of the morning sun would fall.

The people of the silk weavers' quarter felt a shy gratitude toward their two domestic shrines.

The Buddhist altar reminded them that death is never far away. At the same time it consoled them with the idea that, although death removes human beings physically, it grants the living the possibility of speaking in the language of memory to those they have once loved. Thus the Buddhist house altars were places of memory and of dialogue with the souls that, disembodied and all-knowing, remain connected with the living.

It was to the Shinto house shrines that people looked with that longing with which each person clings to life.

The gods of Shinto are not threatening, oppressive powers before whom humans stand in fear and trembling. They are joyful gods, sometimes capricious, full of whimsy; they love music, dancing, and sake. They may not always agree among themselves, but they know that time is too precious to be wasted in quarreling and fighting. Thus the gods of Shinto are the objects of people's cheerful veneration. They fill the realm of thought with hope and optimism, so it is good to offer them a place in the house that is to their liking. They are beings of nature. They love everything that is plain and unostentatious. For that reason their shrines are made entirely of natural wood.

The people in the silk weavers' quarter liked to imagine that the Shinto gods would transfer part of their vital force to them, for they, the immortals, had more than enough of it. Almost every house in the silk weavers' quarter had its little wooden shrine with branches of evergreen sakaki in white ceramic vases placed on either side of it. Milk-white ceramic bowls would be filled with sake and water, and salt would be set out, as well as a handful of raw rice that had been washed until all cloudiness was rinsed away. The intimacy people felt with their Shinto gods was genuine. But the nationalists, the creators of modern Japan, had declared Shinto a state religion and invested it with pomp and splendor. Before the war, the nationalists said that the trade restrictions imposed on Japan by the Western powers were an insult to the Japanese deities as well. Hence it was a divine mission for the entire Japanese nation to take up arms against the West. Every Japanese must be ready to die for the gods, for the Tenno, and for the nation.

Japanese soldiers were told, "In death you will be transformed into cherry blossoms, sea grass, and moss— to die for the nation is the supreme gift to the gods."

People had never quite understood why the Shinto gods should demand the death of human beings. They were gods of life, weren't they, oriented toward life?

The Guji, too, had said that. Even though his shrine was also a national shrine and hence under obligation to the state, he had not hesitated to point out publicly that any religion which allies itself to power—whether it be the power of the state or its own claim to power—forfeits its true authority. Religion, he had said, can truly serve the gods only so long as it remains a spiritual home for the people.

In the midst of the war, the news had spread like wildfire through the silk weavers' quarter that the Guji on the hill had been summoned to the headquarters of the secret state police.

"It looks bad," people had whispered to one another. A group of men and women had called on Shinagawa to ask him whether he knew any details or could help in any way. But even Shinagawa could do nothing. He told the group that the Guji, proud man that he was, had refused to go to the state police.

Not long after that, Nakamura the gardener was able to report that he had seen two men walking through the great torii, men who had looked to him as if they were from the secret state police. Their manner had been different from that of other people visiting the shrine on the hill, so he had secretly followed, which hadn't been difficult as dusk was already falling. In order to escape notice, Nakamura hadn't walked across the gravel of the forecourt but had groped his way through the dark forest. At this point in his story, everyone had nodded and praised his shrewdness. A person had to be particularly noiseless when the secret police was involved.

As Nakamura hid behind a tree at the edge of the forecourt, the two men had headed straight for the Guji's study. During the few moments when the sliding blackout doors were open, Nakamura had seen the Guji sitting at his desk. He fancied he had even heard his voice greeting the two men. But once the blackout doors were closed again, no further sound came from inside.

Nakamura had stood behind the tree for nearly an hour; after a while he had squatted down to give his legs a rest. At last the blackout doors had been slid open again, and he had watched the two men emerging backward. They were bowing deeply.

Hearing this ending, all those who had been listening to old Nakamura laughed in relief. They patted him on the back. "Well done, gardener!" they exclaimed.

Very early next morning, about the hour of sunrise, many people went to stand outside the shrine, even before the Guji appeared for morning prayers. They all bowed before the altar, their mood a shade more cheerful, their bows a shade deeper than usual. They thanked the gods for having protected the Guji from the clutches of the state police.

Once the Emperor had spoken on the radio, no one went to the parachute factories or worked in the war industry any more. The lanes of the silk weavers' quarter once again hummed with life. Men and women began fixing up their idle looms. They ordered iron clamps from the blacksmith with which they improvised repairs wherever supporting metal parts had been removed during the war.

Shortages were noticeable everywhere. Electric current frequently failed or was switched off. Even those weavers who could have started weaving right away were condemned to inactivity because there was no yarn. There wasn't even any raw silk available from which the weavers could have produced their own yarn with their old spinning machines. The few kilograms of raw silk distributed by the authorities to those weaver families whose names appeared on the official lists were spun in one day and woven in three. Although they were all trying to obtain more raw silk, the weavers knew it would be hard to find customers. No one knew what would happen to the value of money. The shops remained closed because there was nothing to sell.

People were worried by the knowledge that the harvest was bound to be a poor one. Although the rice was still unharvested on the farms, it was obvious that there wouldn't be nearly enough for the winter. Too little had been sown in the spring, and in June there had not been enough labor to plant the new shoots. Now people were beginning to grasp the full implications of the fact that losing the war also meant the loss of Manchuria and Korea. There would be no more food supplies from the Asian mainland, or from Taiwan either.

Meanwhile the first soldiers had returned home, but the majority were still overseas. People wondered whether their sons, fathers, and husbands were still alive.

Refugees in rags were roaming the streets of Kyoto. They came from Osaka or Kobe, where they had lost everything, or from still farther away. They carried all their possessions in bundles on their backs and asked their way to streets where they had relatives.

Others had swarmed back from the rural areas where they had been sent during the war. They carried bulging reed sacks or pulled handcarts behind them piled high with trunks, wooden chests, and sacks. The children running alongside in straw sandals were deeply tanned, although their scalps had a blue sheen. Because of lice, even the girls' heads had been shorn.

5

Most of the children looked forward to the first day of school. Going back to school would restore order. The children, too, had been affected by the general uncertainty and no longer enjoyed the freedom of those weeks of holidays. Besides, they were eager to learn how their schoolmates had fared. They all crowded onto the school playground to exchange as much news as possible before morning exercises began the first day.

Outwardly nothing had changed. The row of poplars bordering the playground still cast long, thin shadows onto the ocher-colored surface of the playground. In the school building the same windowpanes were still broken. On the playground, a few rungs of the big climbing ladder were still missing.

The Japanese flag waved as it always had from its pole. But when the music for morning exercises started up over the loudspeaker, the principal came out and spoke in a low voice to the teacher in charge. They both looked up at the flag and seemed undecided. The children standing in rows on the playground, waiting for the teacher's first command, also looked up at the flag, wondering what the problem was.

Finally the principal—an elderly, corpulent man—walked over to the flagpole and took down the flag. He folded it carefully, the teacher helping him.

"There won't be any drill today," Yuri-chan said to Saya.

The exercise music that came braying out of the loudspeaker was approaching the place on the record where, before the holidays, the needle had often become stuck. Sometimes it had also jumped a little and interfered with the sequence of the exercises. All the children were waiting eagerly for this place and were a little disappointed when only a harsh, crackling sound came from the loudspeaker without the needle jumping or getting stuck.

Saya watched the principal carefully smoothing the creases in the folded flag. Finally he laid the bundle of material over his arm and walked back to the school building.

As he passed Saya, she stepped forward and asked, "Why did you take down the flag?"

"Oh, it's you!" said the principal, with a little smile of embarrassment.

"Because Japan has lost the war?"

"Yes, that's right," he replied, "that's right."

Saya liked the principal. On one occasion he had come to her defense when she had clashed with her homeroom teacher. That had been in April, when Mrs. Nakarai had just taken over the class.

Mrs. Nakarai taught Japanese and calligraphy. She was young, in her mid-twenties, and striking on account of her very pale skin and her soft, almost Polynesian-looking features. Her eyes were large and black. Even when severe hairstyles were the rule, she tended to wear her hair rather loose. At a time when hardly any other woman used makeup, she brushed her cheeks with a fine layer of white powder, making herself look even paler and more refined.

Mrs. Nakarai's voice was mild. She spoke softly and with a marked Kyoto accent, drawing the syllables together into a melody and at the end of the sentence making them vibrate like a koto string. When, as was obligatory in all schools, she started the day's lessons by standing with the class in front of the Emperor's portrait that hung on the wall above the blackboard and repeating the oath of loyalty, it sounded as if she were reciting a romantic poem. She made her soft voice tremble reverentially. Even during normal lessons her voice always acquired a slightly awestruck note when she spoke of the Tenno, of the sacred Japanese nation, of the Shinto gods who in this war with America were holding victory in readiness for Japan.

Saya had been surprised that her new homeroom teacher could make such a statement, seeing that in April everyone was already saying quite openly that the American all-out attack on Okinawa had been a disaster for Japan and that, with the landing of American troops there, the first piece of native Japanese soil had fallen to the enemy. Even though the announcer's voice over the radio kept reiterating that the heroic Japanese soldiers would soon drive the Americans off Okinawa, faith in the Japanese victory was showing its first cracks.

It had always seemed that for Mrs. Nakarai the regular morning obeisance before the Tenno's portrait was almost the most important part of the lessons. She had insisted that all the girls stand stiffly at attention as they recited the oath of loyalty, their hands pressed to their sides and their eyes fixed straight ahead.

Despite her mildness, she had stiff punishments for

any girl who failed to keep to the letter of the rigid rules. Any girl whom she noticed looking less than solemn or making a forbidden movement was made to stand in front of the class and ordered, in that inexorably mild voice, to stand motionless for twenty minutes while bowing almost horizontally before the Tenno's portrait.

"Our soldiers at the front," she would say, "are punished even more severely when they fail to accord the Tenno the honor due to him."

Saya saw that Mrs. Nakarai was using the Tenno's portrait to exert her own unchallenged authority over the class. She did not hide her disdain for the teacher. She often made fun of her, imitating her morning ritual, but Mrs. Nakarai refused to react to any provocation. It was obvious that she allowed Saya to get her way more than the others in the class because Saya was the daughter of a Shinto priest. On one occasion she said ingratiatingly, "I am sure your father prays every day for the victory of the Japanese gods over the wicked enemy. It must be an uplifting feeling to be allowed to serve the Tenno in a function as high as that which he fills."

When Saya once yawned unmistakably during the morning ritual before the Tenno's portrait, Mrs. Nakarai merely shot her an irritated glance. Her eyes narrowed, but she said nothing to Saya. Instead, she picked on two other girls who had reacted to Saya's yawn with a loud giggle.

"What impertinence!" Mrs. Nakarai said to them and made them stand for twenty minutes in front of the class while bowing deeply to the Tenno's portrait.

"Things can't go on like this," said Saya in discussing the matter with her friends during the long recess, but no one could think of a solution.

Saya's friends included Yuri-chan, who didn't have an easy time in school. Saya protected her as best she could.

It seemed unfair that Yuri-chan should be constantly slighted because her father was Korean. Yuri-chan wasn't an especially good student, but she was a nice girl. She wanted to be just like all the other girls. She couldn't even speak proper Korean any more. She wanted to be a Japanese girl and was very hurt when other girls jeered at her for being a half-breed. The less able she was to hide her hurt feelings, the more scorn she brought down upon herself. She attached herself to Saya because she felt that Saya could protect her. On the other hand, her friendship with Saya also had its drawbacks.

Some of the girls in the class were too cowardly to take on Saya directly, especially Reiko. Reiko wasn't much better than Yuri-chan in terms of her schoolwork, but she was possessed of a burning ambition. She tried to create her own clique and to stir up her classmates against Saya. When she failed in that she aimed her spite at Yuri-chan, knowing very well that this was how she could get at Saya.

Mrs. Nakarai had continued to rule the class with her relentless gentleness. Only now and again did a silent anger against Saya flare up in the teacher's big black eyes, but it was an anger that she quickly covered up. She dealt particularly harshly with Saya's friends when Saya had been trying to provoke her. Out would come the teacher's notebook, and she would make some unfavorable notes. While she was writing in her notebook, her eyes would always narrow a little and a sensuous smile would play round her lips.

"You girls are at a flexible age," Mrs. Nakarai said once as she looked round the room. "I'll see to it that you learn to be docile. One day you will be grateful to me. Girls must show docility at an early age. Life will repay them for this with much love."

Reiko had raised her hand.

"We are grateful to you," she lisped. "Girls must be docile."

"That's very nice," said Mrs. Nakarai and with a complacent expression made a brief note in her book.

Later, at noon, when the big pot of hot soup was brought to the classroom and Saya took on her usual job of ladling it out, she mimicked Reiko's cloying lisp.

"Girls must be docile," she said with each dip of the ladle, "then they'll get good marks."

Doggedly virtuous, Reiko sat at her desk swallowing her soup in silence. Her revenge came later. She called Yuri-chan a stinking garlic-eater. She snatched up the gray cloth bag containing Yuri-chan's getas. "With a Korean half-breed like that, the garlic juice runs down her legs right into her sandals—phoo!—someone should plug up that dirty hole of hers!"

Triumphantly she held her loot aloft for all to see. Yuri-chan howled with rage. She wanted her getas back.

During the ensuing scuffle, one of the getas spun through the air and struck the windowpane.

When Mrs. Nakarai arrived she asked, "Who did that? Who has deprived Japan of a windowpane in these difficult times of war?"

"It was Yuri-chan's geta," Reiko promptly announced. "I was stupid enough to duck when Yuri-chan threw it at me." Reiko began to sob. "I'm responsible for the broken pane. I shouldn't have ducked."

Mrs. Nakarai was deeply touched. She walked over to Reiko and stroked her hair. "It's not your fault," she said in her gentle voice.

"But . . ." said Saya.

"Don't interfere," Mrs. Nakarai told her.

When Saya persisted in trying to describe what had really happened, Mrs. Nakarai repeated, a shade more

sharply, "Don't interfere. Do you think it right for someone to deprive Japan of a precious windowpane?"

"But Reiko called Yuri-chan a garlic-eater!"

"Be quiet," said Mrs. Nakarai. "That's no reason to
smash windowpanes."

"But that's not a bit how it was!"

"It so happens that some non-Japanese races often eat
a lot of garlic," Mrs. Nakarai stated, "so they must bear
the consequences."

Her words stunned the class. Reiko sobbed melodra-
matically. Yuri-chan had laid her head on her desk and
was weeping silently to herself.

Mrs. Nakarai ordered Yuri-chan not only to pick up
the broken glass from the floor but also to apologize to
Reiko, whereupon Saya shouted, "No, that's not fair!"

For the first time the mildness vanished completely
from Mrs. Nakarai's eyes. She gave Saya a long, wrath-
ful, censorious look. "You are the daughter of a Shinto
priest. Shinto, our Tenno, and the Greater Japanese Empire form a divine unity. How dare you try to defend a
Korean half-breed?"

"My father says," Saya retorted hotly, "that there are
good Koreans and bad Koreans, just as there are good
Japanese and bad Japanese."

"Silence!"

But there was no stopping Saya now.

"More than a thousand years ago Koreans not only
founded Kyoto but also gave Japan its Tenno!" she
shouted across the classroom.

"How dare you say that!" Mrs. Nakarai shouted back.
Her eyes held a look of outrage.

"I'll have to report that," she went on. "That has to be
reported to the secret police!"

She dashed out of the classroom.

The girls sat there as if paralyzed. Only Reiko lifted her head and grinned.

Saya ran over to Yuri-chan and leaned her head against her friend's shoulder.

"You shouldn't have said that," Yuri-chan whispered as she clung to Saya. "Now you'll be in big trouble."

"Don't worry," Saya laughed. "What my father says is right."

Shortly after that, the old janitor came to fetch Saya from the classroom.

Saya was reminded of this as she watched the principal walk slowly toward the school building with the folded flag over his arm. She liked him. He had taken her part against Mrs. Nakarai. Saya knew that he was on her side. He had nodded approvingly when Saya had been made to repeat in his presence, in a voice still ringing with emotion, that Kyoto really had been founded by Korean immigrants, who had also brought the art of silk weaving with them to Japan, and that the great Kanmu-Tenno, to whom the Heian shrine in Kyoto is dedicated, had also been half Korean.

Trying not to look too small, Saya had stood on tiptoe in front of the principal's high desk with its stacks of school records.

"Let her finish," the principal had told Mrs. Nakarai, who was sitting with narrowed eyes beside his desk and glaring murderously at Saya.

Saya had emerged from the principal's office convinced that she had defeated Mrs. Nakarai. In the corridor she looked at the mirror on the wall and made sure that the two bows in her hair were still in place. One was red and the other yellow. Both had slipped a bit. Saya straightened them in front of the mirror until they were exactly over her ears again.

"There'll be no drill this morning," said the gym teacher and sent the children into the school building.

Upstairs in the classroom, nothing had changed either. The desks still stood there in straight rows.

"Good morning, children," said Mrs. Nakarai in her melodious voice as she entered. "Why are you all standing around? Sit down, do!"

Hesitantly, the girls sat down.

So there was to be no standing at attention and no morning oath.

Mrs. Nakarai was wearing a white blouse with full sleeves and a smooth, pale blue skirt. That was something quite new. In town the women were still going about in their usual gray mompeis and peasantlike utility jackets.

Mrs. Nakarai moved the chair from her desk to the blackboard. She mounted it and took down the Tenno's portrait from the wall, placing it on the floor with its back to the class. Then she turned around.

"Girls, we're free," she said gently. "We are free people. Do you understand what that means?"

They all looked at their teacher in bewilderment, glancing from her to the Tenno's portrait propped with its face to the wall and back again to their teacher. Where the picture had been hanging, there was now a lighter square above the blackboard.

Saya was surprised that a picture that had appeared so dignified as long as it had hung above the blackboard should turn out to have such a shabby back. A few strips of brown gummed paper stuck across the back hung down loosely with their edges curling. The picture cord was knotted in two places.

"To be free means no longer to have to live for the

Tenno," said Mrs. Nakarai, "or for the Japanese nation. From now on, only the individual counts."

From the chalks lying on her desk she picked a yellow one and with bold, sweeping strokes wrote the characters for freedom on the blackboard.

While Mrs. Nakarai was writing, Saya suddenly burst out laughing.

"What's the matter?" asked Mrs. Nakarai as she spun round, obviously flustered. "What's the matter?"

Her voice had sharpened again. From the outset she had made it clear that she would tolerate no interruptions in class, by questions or by anything else.

"Raise your hand first, then ask," she had repeatedly emphasized. She would put off any questions not directly related to the subject until the end of the lesson.

Saya was still laughing as she pointed to the Emperor's portrait now on the floor. Mrs. Nakarai followed her gaze in irritation.

"Just look at the back of it!" Saya giggled. "A picture with so much authority, yet so shabby!"

The girls sitting toward the back who couldn't see the picture properly stood up, craning their necks and laughing too.

"So much authority yet so shabby . . . !" Saya said again.

Mrs. Nakarai joined in the laughter, although her own sounded somewhat forced, and glanced uncertainly at Saya. Then she quickly pushed the big wastebasket from under her desk so that it concealed the back of the portrait.

"Now, girls," she said with renewed confidence, in an attempt to restore order in the class without raising her voice too much. "Now, girls, the characters for 'freedom' consist, as you can see, of two ideograms which, when read singly, mean 'self' and 'relationship.' A person who relates everything he does to himself, not to the Tenno or to the nation, is free, spiritually free."

The heat of the day was already pressing in through the wide-open windows. Mrs. Nakarai carefully dabbed the perspiration from her neck with a little white cotton cloth.

She had brought along a pile of calligraphy sheets made of rice paper, the same rough, yellowish rice paper —wartime quality—on which the girls had practiced calligraphy twice a week before the summer holidays, usually writing patriotic phrases. The last of the specimens were still hanging on the back wall of the classroom. For the characters to which she gave the highest mark, Mrs. Nakarai had always folded a lotus blossom out of silver paper as she sat at her desk. While Mrs. Nakarai folded the silver paper and smoothed the creases with her small, plumpish hand, she would purse her lips, pushing them slightly forward so that, as Saya said, she looked like a parrot fish.

"Today I want you to practice the character for 'freedom,'" Mrs. Nakarai told the class as she distributed the calligraphy sheets.

While the girls were writing with their ink brushes, she walked slowly up and down the rows. When she came to Yuri-chan she stopped and bent down. Yuri-chan cringed and tried to cover her work with her hand. She was afraid Mrs. Nakarai would make yet another comment about her clumsy writing which revealed her half-Korean background.

But Mrs. Nakarai's voice radiated sweetness.

"Very good," she said, "very good!"

She asked Yuri-chan to hand her the calligraphy sheet and carried it up to her desk, where she took the silver lotus blossom and stuck it on the upper left corner of the paper.

"Here is an example of particularly beautiful calligraphy. Yuri-chan deserves the highest praise."

She held up the paper to show it to the class.

6

ALL LIFE MOVES IN WAVES. FOR EVERY LIFE THERE ARE PE-
riods of advancing and waiting, periods of retreating and
infolding. The important thing is to recognize the currents that carry a life forward or slow it down.

From time immemorial, mankind everywhere has been
trying to comprehend the nature of these currents, where
they come from and how to recognize them.

A vast amount of time has been spent describing the
interplay of nature with the forces innate in every human being.

Thought structures have been erected whose architec-
ture is claimed to comprise the whole secret of the cos-
mos. Zones and areas have been defined from which external forces that almost defy description are presumed
to rain down on human beings to bring them blessings or
disaster.

The known has been compared to the unknown. Labo-
rious and copious calculations have been undertaken as
to how the known can be used to predict the as-yet-
unknown.

Attempts have been made to lay hold on the future.

The *I-Ching* speaks in mysterious hexagrams of the correlation among five elementary forces, from which in turn five currents can be traced that mount in waves as a result of the polarity between yin and yang.

The origin of these forces remains unspecified, even though there are some names that point to planetary space. These names, the Guji had always said, are merely words to which no concrete reality may be ascribed. They are symbols for something that to this day no one has fully understood. Practical science denies the reality of these five forces because, misled by the planets' names, it has so far been looking in the wrong place for their origin.

The Guji held the view that these forces did not depend on the course of the planets but were determined instead by the interplay of the forces of the earth itself, combined with those of the sun and moon. They resulted from the rhythms of the earth, the fluctuation of day and night, the waxing and waning of the phases of the moon, the sequence of the seasons, and the even longer cycles perhaps related to the cycles of the sun. The movements of the planets represent no more than a clock face that can tell only one measurement of time. It would be wrong to confuse the clock with time itself, for time exists even when there are no clocks.

Over the centuries there had been a few men whose ability to deduce human destinies and the future from the hexagrams of the *I-Ching* was highly developed. In their statements they achieved a superb refinement as well as great accuracy. Often their careers were surrounded by an aura of mystery, for the knowledge to be derived from the *I-Ching* was regarded as esoteric. Those who had mastered a refined method guarded it closely or passed it on, if at all, to a single pupil who, however, seldom possessed the same gift as his master. Centuries might pass before the reemergence of someone whose mathematical gifts were so exceptional that he was able to unravel the secrets of the *I-Ching*.

In his three-volume work on the methodological principles of the *I-Ching*, the Guji had provided the first comprehensive picture of the matrix elements that go to make up the hexagrams. In the ten years since its publication he had assembled a mass of additional material.

The increasing accuracy with which he could make his pronouncements confirmed the correctness of his mathematical approach and proved to him that the method he had worked out could be further refined.

Sometimes even he was startled by the accuracy with which he could make his pronouncements. More and more details were revealed to him concerning the character of people, their inclinations, their weaknesses and strengths, their susceptiblities to certain diseases, and, finally, the probable cause and approximate time of their death.

The further the Guji advanced in his studies, the more clearly he realized that he was penetrating into the realm of the unknown. There were many details that appeared to have little to do with each other yet were connected through the correlations to be deduced from the wave pattern of each life. There appeared to be a higher principle at work.

Often he wondered whether what he saw and deduced wasn't mere coincidence after all. He subjected himself to repeated control experiments, checking wherever he could. But from the people who came to consult him he learned that everything he had told them was a precise depiction of reality.

The Guji realized that the stages of refinement he reached in his analyses emerged more and more automatically once the mathematical framework was in place and he was able to describe the interplay of the five elementary currents.

People were often thunderstruck when, almost casually, he disclosed their exact psychogram. He could tell them the very things they had tried hardest to conceal: secret desires that fed a constant fire within them and that were the true motivation behind their thoughts and actions. He could also tell them what they had been obliged until then to endure in silence: sufferings that they had suppressed to the point where they believed they had overcome them. Just as a doctor can look at an old scar and from it deduce the type of wound, so the Guji could see the wounds of the soul.

Those who consulted the Guji were continually surprised that he did not, by even so much as a hint or inflection of his voice, deliver any sort of moral rebuke. Even when he laid bare the hidden weaknesses or secret desires that were at variance with their outward respectability, he refrained from any moral judgment. Thus he took away their fear. He let them know that they need not feel ashamed if there were dark corners in the shadows of their souls. He told them that they would have to live with those dark corners. He offered no facile consolation but taught people to know themselves.

As his confidence in analyzing individual cases increased, the Guji soon discovered the existence of a higher wave pattern that also described world currents. This higher structure permitted pronouncements to be made about temporal currents, about the spiritual condition of the masses, and about the effects of this condition on politics and on the flow of events determining the course of the world.

From a higher wave pattern of this kind, the defeat of Japan in the war with America emerged with such clarity that the reverse—a Japanese victory over America—could be excluded with absolute certainty.

The Guji had possessed this insight ever since the day when that triumphal march music had risen from the city all the way up to the shrine on the hill. Down below, kettledrums and fanfares were celebrating the initial victory of Pearl Harbor with which Japan had launched its war against America; from up above, the Guji had seen that this victory would not be able to sustain its illusory glamor for much longer than six months, and that it would be followed by a long period of slow, inexorable decline.

After calmly and carefully rechecking his calculations, the Guji had decided to make every effort to speak to those responsible in Tokyo. He knew this to be a reckless decision that might cost him his life or at least his position as a Shinto priest.

The mood of the entire country was in favor of the war. Jubilation over the successful surprise attack on Pearl Harbor intoxicated so many people that those few who saw no reason for jubilation dared not display their shocked reaction in public. Everywhere people were saying that through this victory Japan had brought America halfway to its knees, that the Pacific-wide blitzkrieg demonstrated Japan's greatness to the world and had even surpassed Hitler's lightning successes in Europe. Fireworks against the night sky . . . torchlight and lantern processions in the city . . . with growing anxiety the Guji looked down from the hilltop shrine onto the city below.

More than once, warnings had reached his ears from the Imperial Ministry of the Interior. "Confidential information" was the term used, implying that it was the patriotic duty of a Shinto priest to concern himself with Japanese mythology rather than with a trashy book of

the Chinese like *I-Ching.* He had been warned to take into
account the fact that Japan was in a state of war with
China, that the imperial troops had many Chinese provinces firmly under their control and in other provinces
would continue their victorious reeducation of the Chinese people to be obedient subjects of the Emperor.

"Do you actually believe that Chinese book wisdom is
to be ranked higher than faith in Japan? Are the Japanese
gods not good enough for you?" one Shinto priest had
asked, making no bones about having been sent by the
Ministry of the Interior. "You might, for example, be deposed as Guji and expelled from the Shinto priesthood,"
he had said, sipping his tea with obvious enjoyment.
"You need only carry on as you are. And you know we
have ways of preventing you from sullying the purity of
our gods."

This conversation had taken place before the surprise
attack on Pearl Harbor. In Tokyo a group of militarists
had just come to power. They looked enviously at
Hitler's military successes, which were reported daily
over the radio. The Emperor supported those who
screamed the loudest for a test of strength.

The Guji knew he must be careful. He pondered day
after day. He considered the possibility of calling personally on the Emperor and pointing out the danger threatening Japan.

For hours he pored over the hexagrams that revealed to
him the Emperor's character traits. He searched the psychogram for some clue that might yield at least a hope of
a rational change of course. There was no such hope.
This Emperor was a man incapable of coming to any firm
decisions on his own. He lacked ideas. He relied on ad-
visers who used big words. He was susceptible to flattery. He enjoyed listening to someone unfolding great
plans before him. In his gullible simplicity he would then

trust such men and delude himself with the hope of
equaling in glory and military successes the Meiji Emperor under whose rule Japan had defeated Tsarist Rus-
sia.

Ever since the Meiji Emperor, following the example
of the German Emperor, had declared himself an absolute monarch and elevated Shinto to the position of state
religion, the religious content of Shinto had been split.
From being a uniform religion of the people, Shinto was
now divided into an official Shinto, the spiritual back-
bone of Japanese nationalism, and that old familiar, pop-
ular Shinto to which simple folk still adhered. The
deeper the involvement of nationalism with Shinto became, the further the two parts moved away from one
another.

It did not seem right to the Guji that the cheerful
Shinto deities to whom one would pray with a smile in
one's heart should now be endowed with the threatening
countenances of state deities. It did not seem right that
religion should now be so closely interwoven with
power, for, according to the wave pattern of time, power
must pass away. The Guji was deeply troubled. He decided to act and went to Tokyo to discuss the problem
with his old teacher at the university.

Harada received him in his study, where books covered three of the walls from floor to ceiling and a smell of
dust pervaded everything.

"You think too much," Harada said, "and you have
lost your sense of reality. Don't you read the encouraging decrees that come pouring out of the Imperial Palace
after every Japanese victory? We may well wonder when
the flood will dry up, but we must not ask this question."

"I cannot merely look on," said the Guji, "now that
week by week young soldiers are brought to me at the

shrine. I am supposed to give them courage and tell them
that the Shinto gods desire this war, that their death will
be a happy one . . . that is not Shinto."

Harada had risen and removed the iron kettle from the
electric hot plate. He made the tea and poured it.

"If the waves of time indicate war," he said slowly in
his creaky old voice, "then it's better to cling to a rock so
as not to be swept away by a great wave. There's not
much sense in spitting in the face of a typhoon and
shouting, 'Stop!' "

Nevertheless the Guji persisted in his idea that it must
be possible to secure a hearing for the voice of the
I-Ching.

"Basically, you know, the thing that plunges people so
deeply into the intoxication of war is simply the hope of
victory," he said. "If I take this hope away from them,
they will come to their senses."

As the Guji left, old Harada's parting words were "Be
careful how you handle your knowledge. No loss weighs
as heavily with people as the loss of the dreams that are
taken away from them."

After that conversation, the Guji had gone to the
shrine north of Tokyo where he had spent his novitiate.
He knew that not far away from it was one of the major
officer-training centers for the Japanese elite units. That
was his goal. That was where he intended to address the
officers.

The high priest of the shrine was amazed by his visit.

"Welcome," he said. "What brings you here?"

"I would like to address the officers."

The high priest praised his support of the national
cause.

"We Shinto priests," he said with much breath in his
voice, "can serve Japan by strengthening the national
spirit and beseeching our gods to bless our fighting men.

It is indeed the officers who are of particular significance in this great war. It is gratifying that you should have made the effort to come here from Kyoto to strengthen the fighting spirit of the officers and their spirit of sacrifice. How was your trip?"

"Fine, thank you," said the Guji. "When may I address the officers?"

"You *are* in a hurry!" The high priest promised to do what was necessary and also to supply seven additional Shinto priests as a ceremonial escort.

"I am sure the officers will be especially impressed," he said, "that a Guji from Kyoto, from the old imperial city, will be speaking to them. In Kyoto, as we know, the honorable national feelings enjoy a lofty tradition. An escort of seven priests is therefore appropriate."

The Guji spent the intervening days in silence. He avoided conversation with the high priest, whose belief in the role of Shinto as a state-supporting and war-promoting power he did not share. As it was, he was glad that the high priest had not asked whether he was still studying the *I-Ching*. Probably he assumed that the Guji's arrival was a sign of remorse, a sign that he had renounced the *I-Ching*.

When the morning finally arrived on which he could address the officers, the Guji put on the great ceremonial robes that he had brought with him from Kyoto, packed in an old suitcase. With the seven accompanying priests he was driven to the officers' training camp in a motorcade of three limousines supplied by the military authorities. It had snowed during the night. About a thousand men stood on the wide square onto which the misty winter sun cast its gentle light.

The Guji was aware of the effectiveness of his scarlet robes as he walked with his escort of seven brown-robed priests between the parted ranks of officers. As he passed by the men, he looked into their eyes. He knew that he could reach them with the words he intended to speak only if he did so with the full dignity of his office. He knew he would be able to speak only once. He did not think of what would happen after that. He did not want to think of that.

"Japan cannot win this war," he said into the microphone standing in front of him and was surprised at the resonance of his own voice as it was thrown back at him by the loudspeakers stationed round the square. From his raised platform he looked down on the thousand faces staring up at him.

"Japan cannot win," he said, "because the principal currents yielded by the wave pattern of time permit only a short-lived military success. This will be followed, I maintain, by an inexorable, protracted, and certain decline at the end of which darkness is waiting—a darkness such as this nation has never before experienced. Therefore the only hope for Japan and for all of us lies in a speedy termination . . ."

The Guji was surprised how smoothly his words flowed, how powerfully the loudspeakers carried them across the wide square. He was almost surprised how easy it was to say all this. From the shocked, widened eyes of the men who were staring up at him he could tell that they were taking in his words.

A hand fell on his shoulder and drew him slowly away from the microphone. He wanted to finish his last sentence, but the microphone no longer picked up his voice. He heard his voice cracking and fading away. He saw the men's bewildered, upturned faces, the wide square, the white snow, the surge of questions, the confusion.

He had allowed himself to be led away unresistingly. He had made no answer when he was questioned in a bare room that contained only a few chairs and an iron stove radiating heat from a corner. He had allowed himself to be stripped of the scarlet ceremonial robes and had put on the garments handed to him. A doctor wanted to know whether he had often suffered such attacks of mental disturbance.

After several hours a black limousine bearing a military pennant had driven up, and he had been politely requested to get in. In Tokyo he was escorted to the train. Not a word. Only grim faces. Two escorts who made sure that he duly arrived back in Kyoto.

Not until they had climbed the shrine hill with him and reached the graveled forecourt outside his front door did the escorts take their leave with short, stiff bows.

7

IN THE HOLLOWS OF THE GARDEN ROCKS THE AUTUMN AS-
ters were in bloom—cushions of mauve against the white
wall. The bronze asters growing a little higher up had not
yet opened, nor had the buds of the long-stemmed yellow chrysanthemums.

Every morning between nine and ten, the Guji's wife
would go into the front garden to tend and cut her flowers. Each room of her house had a corner for an ikebana.
The Guji's wife possessed many vases and shallow bowls
appropriate in shape and glazing for flowers of every
shape and color. She worked at her ikebana compositions
with great dedication, oblivious of time.

She knew the chrysanthemum buds would not open
until the flowers had stood in the vase for two days. In
those late blossoms the breath of winter was already per-
ceptible. Their colors were paler and provided an elegant
contrast to the richer hues of those flowers that had
opened outdoors under the warm October sun.

The special opulence of autumn flowers is nature's
gift, one last consolation to the hearts of men before the

arrival of winter, the Guji's wife would say, and she would often sit for a long time before her ikebana compositions, sunk in rapt contemplation.

She could not imagine a life without ikebana. Her love of flowers reached back into her childhood when she was growing up in Himari at her grandfather's. He was a proud samurai, rooted in the old traditions, inflexible, but at the same time of benevolent appearance. He loved everything that had proven itself through the ages. He was an aesthete who waxed ecstatic over the beauty of the No theater. Even his everyday gestures had become somewhat theatrical. When he opened his fan to waft some cool air in his face, he did so with the dignity of those figures from the classic No repertoire whose roles he himself sometimes performed on the stage as an amateur. When he walked through the house, he placed his feet in a precisely measured rhythm, as if on a stage. And even as a very old man he moved gracefully, almost floating, through the rooms.

He spent most of his time reciting ancient No texts and cultivating bonsai trees that he shaped with unflagging patience. The twigs that his aesthetic sense found superfluous were pruned away and the remaining branches forced with stiff iron wire so that they would grow into the shapes he desired. He uncovered the roots of the dwarf trees and pruned them exactly as he did the twigs. In this way he guided growth according to his will. He cultivated dwarf trees that resembled the old wild pines on the sun-scorched, stormy cliffs near Himari, or the cedars high on the slopes of Mount Fuji where the weight of winter snow twists the trunks and branches.

With the same relentless, benevolent patience her grandfather had also shaped the people who lived with him. He was incapable of putting himself in someone else's position, nor did he see any necessity for others to have their own wills, for his outlook was final, venerable, and immutable.

The grandfather had introduced his granddaughter to the strict rule of flower arranging. It was from him that she received her knowledge of the symbolism of flowers, of their colors and shapes. It was of him she thought when she combined various flowers, when she cut the stalks, removed superfluous leaves and buds, and finally arranged what was left in a bowl or vase to form a harmonious composition.

She would think back nostalgically to the way her grandfather's unerring glance had rejected this or that combination, the way he had pointed with his folded fan at aesthetically inadequate spots. How seldom he had been satisfied and how rarely he had uttered his sparing praise. She owed it to his strict training that she had become a master in flower arranging. It was true she had no diplomas, but all her friends confirmed that she had reached the highest level in the art of ikebana.

Whenever she was in doubt, she had only to think of her grandfather. Then he would stand before her with his kindly face. She would see him slowly moving his fan to cool his face and then making his irrevocable decision.

He was a man. He was a samurai. He despised indecisiveness and vacillation. He did not speak much, but his words carried weight. He would utter only what he had already decided in his mind. One look from him was enough to remove any doubt.

She had always regarded it as a boon to live with him. One had only to entrust oneself to his judgment, and everything acquired its meaning and its place.

With every ikebana the Guji's wife arranged she celebrated the memory of her years in Himari. She lived on these memories and, to keep them alive, placed a flower arrangement in every room every day. That made her feel that something remained of the old order where there had been aesthetic standards to which she could adhere.

Her sense of beauty was at the same time a sense of values. Her values were set and harked back to tradition. The deep gratitude she felt for her grandfather required her to reject everything that did not fit into the pattern set by him. She was very adroit at defending her sense of values.

The Guji's wife had embarked on marriage secure in her conviction that a Shinto priest felt committed to tradition. She had counted on a common ground of thought and judgment. She was disappointed when her husband hardly noticed the flower arrangements that she at first always placed on his desk. He had never acknowledged her mastery in ikebana. She took it as a personal affront when he said that he preferred flowers outdoors in nature to those in a bowl.

"Let them fade out there."

He failed to see that untamed growth is only the fermenting mash from which the aesthetically educated human spirit distills beauty.

He failed to see that a perfect ikebana captures the breath of truth.

When she was living in Himari and her grandfather was still alive, he had always told her that, because of the good education he had given her, she could be sure of finding the best husband any woman could wish for. So she felt betrayed when she noticed that her husband did not live up to her expectations. He was different from the way she wanted him to be. She did not understand him. She mistrusted him. She became very quickly aware that he was not prepared to adjust to her way of thinking. She in turn saw no reason to deviate by so much as a

hairsbreadth from her own path or to take a single step
into new territory.

When her grandfather died in Himari, she had inher-
ited a precious Kenzan tea bowl, white with a tinge of
mauve and an almost abstract, rust-colored floral design;
blades of grass with starry, pale yellow blossoms were
barely indicated. With this bowl she decided to put her
husband to the test. There was no mistaking Kenzan's
elements of style, yet it differed from other Kenzan
bowls to be seen in museums.

"Do you like it?"

All he said was "Kenzan," nothing more, nor was there
any vibration discernible in his voice. From this bowl he
drank the tea she had prepared for him with no sign of
the solemn emotion one is supposed to feel when drink-
ing tea from a Kenzan bowl.

The Guji's wife reproached her husband for having
consistently withheld from her, throughout their married
life, the profound experience of celebrating the tea ceremony together. Not once had he followed the strictly
prescribed gestures and rules that are required for the
ceremonial tea hour. Not once had she been able in his
presence to experience to the full the dignity of tea. Invariably she had been aware of his resistance.

It filled her with rage that her husband should reveal
by little gestures all the disdain he felt for the tea ceremony.

"Why do you do that?" she would snap at him. His
manner of replying never satisfied her. It even seemed to
her that he was emphasizing his display of contempt. He
could accept the precious bowl without making the ritual
bow. He would turn it around only once, although he
was fully aware that it had to be turned twice. He would
carelessly allow the tea to slosh about in the bowl and

would drink it without bowing a second time as the ritual demanded.

What pained the Guji's wife most was the fact that she knew perfectly well that her husband—if only he wanted to—was able to celebrate the tea ceremony to perfection. The tea-ceremony diploma that he possessed was carelessly left lying in a drawer instead of hanging framed on the wall.

"I don't care for this tomfoolery" was his only reply to her reproaches. The Guji's wife had a very accurate memory for words and for the tone of voice in which they were spoken. Every inflection was etched on her memory, especially when the words happened to injure her self-esteem. To call a tea ceremony "tomfoolery" was to her a slur on the entire Japanese culture. At the same time it was a slur on what she felt to be her own worth, a slur on the world in which she had grown up.

The Guji said, "Rikyu, who created the tea ceremony four hundred years ago, was a great despiser of ceremonies. He drank tea from a simple earthen bowl in order to ridicule the aristocratic customs of his time. He wanted to show that one can enjoy tea without ostentation and rigid forms, that it is in simplicity that the beauty of tea reveals itself. He would laugh if he could see what tomfoolery his original intention has been turned into."

"Tomfoolery is what you call the noblest achievement of Japanese culture!" cried the Guji's wife in exasperation. "That is an insult to the Japanese spirit."

"What you are expressing is that very rigidity that Rikyu despised," the Guji replied. "Culture can remain alive only if it is constantly questioned and hence constantly rejuvenated. Otherwise it becomes a stereotype of itself."

"Stereotype?"

"Yes, stereotype . . . the beautiful and the true are to

be perceived only out of one's own experience by casting
doubt on what is familiar."

"So that's the way you are!" replied the Guji's wife,
adding maliciously, "You cast doubt even on the gods."

"Not on the gods but on what people are making of
them."

Because the Guji's wife failed to understand how
much inner strength and courage was needed to cast
doubt on the familiar, she failed to understand what her
husband was saying. She failed to understand his motivation. His spiritual attitude was alien to her. She herself
saw things quite differently. She sought security in the
precise application of the rules she had learned from her
grandfather in Himari and had long since made an inte-
gral part of herself. She clung with uncritical admiration
to this grandfather who had shaped her childhood and
youth. He had formed her. He had taught her to understand the world as he understood it and had bestowed on
her the conviction that her education was perfect and
complete.

The Guji's wife knew no such thing as doubt. She saw
herself as immaculate. She often spoke of her heart being
as pure as fresh spring water that reflects the sky. She
never gave any thought to the reasons for and origins of
her existence. She was satisfied with herself. All she
wanted to do was faithfully to pass on the rules and
precepts she had learned.

For her *that* was the beautiful and the true. Anything
that did not fit her thought pattern she rejected. Consequently she felt personally attacked by her husband and
reacted with corresponding vehemence.

She despised him because he preferred to walk about
all day in the simplest of his priest's robes, because he
refused to change his robe when he went down into the
silk weavers' quarter, because down in the lanes he

would stop to listen to anyone without even making sure that people addressed him with the requisite forms of polite speech.

Even up at the shrine he allowed anyone who wanted to see him to enter freely. He ignored her advice to provide an anteroom where one of the shrine attendants could act as a buffer between him and the more tiresome of his visitors. Often important visitors had to wait simply because the Guji was talking to some artisan or other from the silk weavers' quarter.

"There are natural differences in rank that must be observed," she had told him. "Without such differences, culture will become mired in vulgarity."

"The dignity of the individual is the rank I go by," he had replied.

"But dignity is the very thing you lack."

For the Guji's wife, dignity was a matter of rank in the social hierarchy, of demeanor, of appropriate clothing, of appropriate speech. For the Guji, dignity was inherent in the personality of the individual. For him it was something not necessarily linked to social position. He, too, had his precise ideas as to the dignity of behavior and speech, but these were not—as his wife's were—linked to external forms.

For himself he rejected strict forms and rules that were to be followed merely because other people followed them. He created his own style, a style that displeased his wife.

"You could learn from me as I learned from my grandfather, if there were only a trace of modesty in your heart," said the Guji's wife. "My grandfather possessed dignity. He didn't have to read Chinese books to discover what is true and what is beautiful. He knew."

"Your grandfather was a living antique."

This was a remark for which the Guji's wife never

forgave her husband. She buried it deep within her, keeping it alive in her heart—for years, long after the wordy conflicts of the early years of their marriage were followed by quieter times.

Nothing really changed. She clung to her feeling for tradition. She clung to her concept of the dignity of culture as she understood it, of the importance of rules.

She tried to raise her children in such a way that they would adopt her values. She knew that in this she had an advantage. She had her children firmly in hand.

Once a month the Guji's wife met with her friends who, like her, all came from Himari and were now married and living in Kyoto. They were almost all the same age. There were not many, only eleven if all turned up. They had been meeting regularly for many years, taking turns in each other's homes. Most of them lived in houses large enough to be displayed. Those whose husbands did not have a good enough position or enough money to afford a presentable house preferred to invite their friends to a restaurant.

The Guji's wife seldom missed these meetings, even during the war years, although it wasn't always easy to choose the correct apparel. They all showed up in the same or at least very similar baggy trousers and without jewelry. The only way to show a little elegance was to take along the right handbag or to wear a good silk under-kimono beneath the coarse, peasantlike jacket.

Some of the women whose husbands were in the occupied territories overseas, in Manila, Hanoi, or Batavia, showed off the handsome gifts they had received from their husbands: a crocodile leather handbag or a photo album bound in snakeskin, or cloisonné boxes, French perfume and face powder, or Spanish dancing dolls, or Indonesian shadow-play figures. At home they could display Thai silks, genuine emeralds, and rubies from Burma.

Most of the women in her circle were married to men occupying good positions. Consequently none of those serving overseas were with the fighting troops but were all stationed with Japanese administrative authorities. The Guji's wife envied these friends. All she possessed was a handbag of braided silk, and she no longer had her diamond ring.

Still, she took part regularly in the meetings. She told her friends a great deal about Saya, passed around her most recent school report, brought along the calligraphy with which Saya had won first prize in the school competition. She talked about Ryo, who was coming along famously, and about Bo, her youngest. The other women also talked a lot about their children. The staff surgeon's wife, who was childless, openly admitted that she had longed for children. She would sit there with a sad smile when the other women bragged about theirs.

Only once had the Guji's wife been unable to attend one of these meetings. Right away the very thing happened that she had always dreaded. Someone in her circle—she never found out for sure who it was—reported gleefully and at length that the Guji had been seen on the streetcar, carrying an umbrella and a bundle. He had ridden as far as the Imperial Palace, where he got off. He had been alone, unaccompanied. The friends had thereupon discussed in detail the question of whether the Guji of a great national shrine didn't have enough shrine attendants at his disposal for at least one of them to accompany him to carry his umbrella and bundle. It was impossible, they said, to overlook a certain lack of dignity.

The luxuriant growth of autumn asters was an invitation to cut enough blooms to decorate every room in the house. But with a sigh the Guji's wife put aside her gardening scissors. It was now more than a week since the two maids had gone back to their village. They should have returned long ago. Perhaps they were ill or had been delayed on account of the overcrowded train that ran only once a day between Fukui and Kyoto. The Guji's wife would have accepted that as an excuse.

But day after day went by. The unwashed dishes piled up in the kitchen. The rattan basket in the room beyond the bathroom was overflowing with dirty laundry. The Guji's wife had long since laid out the various cloths needed for cleaning the house: the floor cloth for wiping the corridor and the entrance hall and the somewhat softer cloth for the tatami mats in the living and sleeping areas. There were altogether almost a dozen different cleaning cloths in the house, each with its special purpose. The cloth for the kimono closets and chests of drawers was different from the one for the worktable where the Guji's wife would sometimes sit down to sew. For the tokonoma niche there was a special duster that must never be used anywhere else.

Everything has its rank, the Guji's wife would say when it was a matter of keeping the cloths apart and choosing the bucket appropriate for each wiping job.

This order applied equally in the kitchen, ascribing to each object its specific use. The Guji's wife had always taken time to show the maids which pots and pans were provided for preparing fish, meat, clear soups and miso soups, for root vegetables and leaf vegetables. She knew she could never quite rely on the maids, when they were working alone in the kitchen, to keep the various utensils apart the way she had told them to. So she had to supervise them continually and, if necessary, reprimand them if they were about to steam a leaf vegetable in a saucepan meant for cooking root vegetables.

The same applied to the knives used in the kitchen. There were different knives for cutting meat and mushrooms, fish, seaweed, leaf and root vegetables. The knife holder in the kitchen cupboard contained many different knives with blades of varying widths and handles of varying shapes. If the Guji's wife caught a maid slicing mushrooms and bamboo shoots with the same knife, she would become very upset.

"You're from a village," she would scold her, "and you don't even know that mushrooms grow above ground whereas bamboo shoots are lifted while they are still *in* the ground."

When finally the postcard arrived with the news that the two maids would not be returning to Kyoto, the Guji's wife said, "What ingratitude! Those two girls were well treated here and learned such a lot from me."

Saya helped as best she could. In the morning before school she wiped the floor of the passageway and entrance hall. In the afternoon, when she came home from school at four-thirty, she went down to the silk weavers' quarter to shop for the family rations of vegetables, sweet potatoes, or rice. Often there was no rice. There had been no fish for weeks. As for meat or eggs, one could forget about those.

Saya's mother showed her how to work in the kitchen. She showed her that radishes that were to be cooked in miso sauce had to be sliced diagonally, whereas radishes to be cooked in soy sauce must be cut straight. She showed her how to cut grooves the whole length of a carrot with a small pointed knife.

"There must be five grooves," she said, "in order to obtain a five-petaled flower pattern when you come to slice the carrot. Look, I'll show you."

She carefully cut grooves along the whole length of a carrot and removed the five narrow strips. Then she handed the knife to Saya. "Now you may slice the carrot."

She arranged the carrot slices in circles and other patterns.

"That's the way it should be," she said. "Food tastes better when it is served attractively. Unfortunately there are people like your father who have no feeling for this."

Her mother spent a great deal of time in the kitchen in the preparation of each meal. First she would pick out from the cupboard the proper little bowls whose color and shape corresponded to the food she intended to prepare. She always spent a lot of thought on this, for, as she said, the color of the glaze must be in perfect harmony with the color of the food and must also correctly reflect the season. As she did this, her mother would keep reverting to the subject of the maids who had stayed away without giving notice.

"It doesn't really matter," Saya consoled her, "there's so little for us to eat."

Her mother nodded wordlessly. She looked at the little there was, at a loss how to prepare an evening meal out of it. A meal at which there were not at least five small bowls in front of each person seemed to her a pitiful affair.

"Actually there should be eight bowls," she would say, "eight carefully selected dishes harmonizing in color. In good families, eight individual bowls are served every day—every morning, noon, and evening. That's the way I learned it as a child. My grandfather never touched any food that wasn't beautifully served. He simply left it all untouched. Then one was aware as a woman that the man disapproved of the manner of preparation. It is the beauty of the food and the porcelain that counts."

"We have no more bowls," said Saya. Her mother gestured resignedly at the pile of unwashed dishes.

"We'll have to wash them," Saya said. But that meant new complications because the proper cloths for drying the bowls were lacking, and Saya's mother wouldn't agree to her using another dishcloth that could be used only for drying the bowls for the tea ceremony.

It was a few weeks before daily life without maids ran more or less smoothly.

Bo was his usual cheerful self. He played a lot by himself outside on the forecourt near the great stone stairway leading up to the shrine. There the emerald-green lizards sought the warm October sun, and Bo would often sit on the lowest step, waiting in silent patience for the emergence of the nimble, slender lizards whose fine-scaled skin shone with the gleam of damp moss. Sometimes he spoke to them, inviting them to play with him, but at the slightest movement of his hands they would dart away and vanish into the cracks between the stone steps.

When the brilliant emerald lizards refused to appear, Bo would watch the big forest ants as they moved in dense columns over the rough stone wall, marching around the foot of the big stone lantern and continuing on over the steps. Bo played trains with them. He built tunnels for them of dried, curling pine bark. He would watch the column of ants as it disappeared in one end of his bark tunnel and reappeared at the other end. He would place little twigs in the ants' path so that they had to cross them like bridges. Bo would laugh at his ants and sing *shu-shu-tu-tu*. He felt sad when they attacked a caterpillar.

He would continue to play outside even when Saya

had long since come home from school and was helping
her mother in the house. He was content if Saya came
running out once or twice to see his latest tunnel or
bridge. She would bring him the long, thin strips that her
mother had cut out of the carrots, or would pop one of
the grilled slices of sweet potato into his mouth. Supper
was often very late because their mother wasted so much
time on the aesthetic preparation of the food.

"Bo's hungry," Saya would tell her mother tentatively.
She knew her mother didn't like to be disturbed while
working in the kitchen.

"Don't rush me," she would often reply in a reproach-
ful voice. "It'll all be ready in a few minutes."

The "few minutes" frequently became half an hour or
a full hour because meanwhile something had burned
the pan or boiled over. Then Saya's mother would search
irritably for the cloth that was especially provided for
the top of the stove and wipe up what had boiled over or
transfer the top layer of the scorched food into an earth-
enware bowl. Then it was Saya's job quickly to scrape
out the remainder as well as the brownish black crust
sticking to the bottom of the pan so that her mother
could go on cooking, and by that time she would usually
have forgotten what else was standing over the flame.

 **8**

MRS. YASUMI, SO PEOPLE WERE SAYING, HAD EATEN NOTH-
ing for days. She sat in the twilight of her house, weaving continuously. Her door was always closed, but outside in the lane one could hear the regular clacking of her
loom.

Day after day one could hear the flying shuttle of her
loom striking the warp beam and the treadle activating
the hammer. The neighbors brought her grilled sweet
potatoes and hot miso soup, but Mrs. Yasumi touched
nothing. She sat at her loom weaving blue silk. Here and
there she would weave a few white cherry blossoms into
the fabric, singly at first, then more and more until a
dense white storm of blossoms crowded out the blue. As
she wove she sang in a monotonous high voice the poem
of the dying kamikaze pilots:

> *Like white cherry blossoms*
> *Borne by a gust of wind up to heaven,*
> *So will the souls of heroes*
> *Rise up to the clouds.*

She sang through lifeless lips, only her hands moving
swiftly and deftly. The broad blue band of silk with the
cherry blossom clouds flowed from her loom and spread
across the floor. When a sunbeam fell through the open
door, the cascading silken folds shimmered. No one was
allowed to touch the material.

"No!" Mrs. Yasumi cried out in a shrill voice. "Don't
touch! The wind is just carrying the souls up to heaven.
They haven't arrived yet."

She had to be fed like a child, the tea bowl raised to
her lips. She wanted only to go on weaving.

"Go away," she would say softly to those who had
brought her the food. Outside in the lane the neighbors
were saying, "It would be better if she could weep."

Often Mrs. Yasumi could be heard talking to the woven cherry blossoms. "She is talking to her dead son,"
the neighbors said.

Then the loom fell silent for a while. Mrs. Yasumi
stroked each cherry blossom one by one on the blue
background.

"Is this you?" she would ask. She sat with her head
cocked slightly to one side, as if listening to the blossoms' reply.

> *Like white cherry blossoms*
> *Borne by a gust of wind up to heaven,*
> *So will the souls of heroes*
> *Rise up to the clouds.*

Beyond the silk weavers' quarter, on Kita-oji, some
Americans had already been seen patrolling the long
wide avenue in jeeps. Usually they drove fast, but sometimes they slowed down, peering curiously, a little suspi-
ciously, into the narrow lanes. The children were the first
to overcome their shyness and wave to the Americans.

The Americans waved back and threw chewing gum from the moving jeep. They came back every day, and the children were already waiting for them.

It soon reached the point where the Americans stopped their vehicle and beckoned to the children. They gave them chocolate and still more chewing gum. After a few days the Americans actually got out of their jeeps and walked a few steps along Kita-oji. Then people saw how tall they were—immensely tall—and what long legs they all had. They walked with loose, easy strides, and their faces always wore broad smiles.

"They really do have green eyes," said Mi-chan, "but they're not monsters."

"No," said Tama-chan firmly, "they have blue eyes, that's what it says in my textbook."

"Mine had green eyes," Mi-chan insisted, "twinkly green eyes."

"You mean you dared go up that close?" the pawn-broker asked anxiously. "You shouldn't do that."

"But mine was so friendly, he laughed and gave all us kids some chewing gum."

"Just the same," muttered the pawnbroker, scratching his head. By this time he had stowed away his sharpened bamboo spears under the eaves. "Next spring," he had said, "I'll use them as bean poles."

Mi-chan broke the flat stick of gum into three equal pieces and gave a piece each to her foster father and Tama-chan.

"I'm not sure whether we should be eating this," said the pawnbroker. "After all, it does come from the enemy."

"There's no enemy any more," said Tama-chan.

The newspaper had reported that the Emperor had called on General MacArthur. A picture confirmed the truth of this report. The American general was shown

94 *Hisako Matsubara*

standing at ease in a plain, light-colored uniform, looking almost like a civilian, tieless but with a stern expression. His lips formed a narrow straight line. The Emperor was wearing a tailcoat, striped trousers, and a striped tie, but he was smiling as if he were not with an enemy but at some friendly gathering. Never had the Japanese people seen the Emperor smiling like that and in such a relaxed posture. Even his left leg was placed a few inches ahead of the other, contrary to accepted custom. One could actually sense that a new era had dawned.

"There's no enemy any more," Tama-chan repeated.

The pawnbroker was still testing the flavor of the chewing gum that he had carefully placed on his tongue.

"It's sweet," he remarked.

"You're supposed to chew it!" exclaimed Mi-chan.

"I no longer have as many teeth as you do," said the pawnbroker.

The first American headquarters had been established at the Kyoto Hotel, the Miyako Hotel, and in the Chamber of Commerce Building. The Americans were said to be looking for servants for their officers.

"There are jobs to be had with the Americans," Tama-chan mentioned tentatively to her father.

The pawnbroker pretended not to have heard. He chewed carefully on his stick of gum. His expression was not encouraging.

"Of course it won't be easy," Tama-chan went on, "to get a job like that. I'm sure a lot of girls will be applying. I would have to act quickly."

The pawnbroker spat out his gum. "That's utterly out of the question," he blustered. "Work for the hairy ones? Never! No decent Japanese girl would do that, and no decent Japanese father would permit his daughter to do so."

He tried to pick up the chewing gum that he had spat

out onto the tatami, but it was stuck. When he pulled at it, his fingers got stuck too.

"What kind of fiendish stuff is this?" he cursed. In his opinion the Americans were handing out chewing gum in order to drive the Japanese mad. "I was right, they *are* our enemies," he mumbled to himself.

Together Tama-chan, Mi-chan, and finally the pawn-broker himself tried to remove the chewing gum from the surface of the tatami. They tried with a piece of newspaper, with a damp cloth—nothing worked. The sticky mass was merely pressed deeper and deeper into the delicate woven surface of the tatami.

"The mat is ruined," the pawnbroker said sadly.

Tama-chan suggested trying benzine. That worked. Only a faint dark spot remained.

"You're not so dumb," her father told Tama-chan appreciatively and pointed at the bottle of benzine.

"One must never spit it out," Mi-chan said seriously. "The Americans always keep it in their mouths."

Tama-chan said, "I'm going to swallow mine now."

"Don't do that," the pawnbroker advised, "or it'll get stuck in your stomach!"

Finally they agreed to dig a hole in the garden and spit the chewing gum into it.

"May I at least find out whether I could get a job with the Americans?" Tama-chan asked tentatively.

"As long as my eyes remain black, I'll never allow you to do that," the pawnbroker blustered again.

Tama-chan knew her father well enough to realize that his words were not meant as harshly as they sounded.

"But we have to eat," she said in her quiet, firm voice. "We can't live on the pawnbroking business now."

"You can find work with Japanese," the pawnbroker grunted angrily.

"But where?"

"Anywhere."

"There's no work to be had."

The pawnbroker nodded to himself and rubbed his stump. "If only I still had both legs . . ." he said.

Tama-chan sensed that he was close to relenting.

"If you want to have beans growing up your bamboo poles next spring," she said gently, "we must see that we get through the winter in good shape."

"But do you *have* to work for the hairy ones," asked the pawnbroker, "the very people who have defeated us?"

"Just because they have defeated us it's a good idea to work for them," replied Tama-chan. "One can learn a lot from them."

That was a point the pawnbroker hadn't thought of. Pensively he closed his eyes and rubbed his stump. Tama-chan signaled to Mi-chan not to interrupt him now.

"Come to think of it, you're right," the pawnbroker finally said. "I mean, that business about learning. It would be a good thing to find out how the hairy ones live and what they think. Perhaps then one could also learn something about how they defeated us, with what kind of spirit."

He asked Tama-chan to hand him his bamboo pole with the leather strap. "I'll go and see Shinagawa and have a talk with him," he said. With new energy, he swung himself out through the door on his bamboo pole and hopped on one leg along the lane.

Shinagawa agreed that it was important to discover why the Americans had been able to conquer Japan.

"After all, we really did everything we could to win

the war, and yet the Americans were stronger than us," he said.

"It's a matter of the spirit," stated the pawnbroker. "The American spirit was stronger than the Japanese spirit. That's why we lost."

Some of the men from the neighboring houses joined them, wanting to hear what Shinagawa and the pawnbroker were discussing so earnestly.

Old Nakamura said, "Spirit . . . spirit . . . the Americans defeated us with bombs."

"They were terrifying," said one man who had taken part in the battle of Midway. "Their ships simply refused to sink."

"And yet we were always told that our battleship *Yamato* was unsinkable because she was built with an alloy of Japanese spirit and stainless steel."

"The *Yamato* went down on the way to Okinawa like a split coconut."

For a moment they were all silent.

"We had nothing left," said Nakamura, "simply nothing left."

"Only our spirit," said the pawnbroker.

"What can you do with spirit against bombs?"

"They say the Americans are all Christians," Mrs. Shinagawa twittered in her high, tinkling voice. "Maybe that explains it."

"Silence, woman," said Shinagawa. "The Germans are Christians and they lost the war. Even before we did."

Mrs. Shinagawa flitted back into the house and called from inside, "I'll bring out some tea."

Shinagawa crossed his long arms pensively on his chest and looked at the ground.

"Bombs . . . it's so easy to say 'bombs,' but what about all that's involved in building a bomb like the Hiroshima one? There's a lot of knowledge, technical skill, and intelligence behind it all. There's no denying that."

"If we had had a bomb like that . . ."

"Right, but we didn't."

For the past few weeks there had been no further mention of Hiroshima in the newspapers. The Americans were said to have placed the cloak of censorship over the event. As a result, rumors were circulating about the mysterious deaths that were still occurring in Hiroshima.

Many who knew people who had come out of Hiroshima alive passed on their eyewitness reports. It always started with the flash whose monstrous brilliance had extinguished light itself, and the thunderous explosion that with its monstrous roar had rendered the whole world mute.

Darkness and a stunned silence had spread while each person tried to stagger to his feet and escape from wherever he happened to be. Those who could no longer run still moved their arms and legs, trying at least to raise themselves.

But nothing remained of all that the warm morning sun had shone down upon only a few moments before. Everything was black, had vanished into a black dust, was destroyed. Only the flames that were beginning to lick their way up had any color.

From the dust that was like a fog, figures began to loom up, black, hairless, faceless.

They screamed with voices that were no longer human. Their screams drowned out the groans rising everywhere from the rubble, groans that seemed to rise from the very earth itself.

The hairless, faceless figures staggered haphazardly, aimlessly, toward one another, past one another, stepping over those who had been flung to the ground. They had staring, lidless eyes and held their arms away from their bodies. Shreds hung from their bodies. Shreds of clothing and skin. What was left of their clothing was black, the shreds of skin were black, the bodies were black. A gray, gruesome black mixed with the red of blood. Blood mixed with the dust and with the flames that were gradually flaring up from the rubble, blood mixed with the screams for water that were rising on all sides. The screams for water prevailed, drowned out the cries of those who had been buried, the whimpering of the dying.

Somehow the survivors had managed to escape that black world of death. There were no points of orientation. The hills at the edge of the city were invisible. The streets had melted and were strewn with rubble.

Some people said they had also experienced the black rain that fell, heavy and corrosive, like oil mixed with dust. They had simply staggered on, past the dying and the dead, over bridges and rubble-strewn roads, on and on until the sun became discernible again. At that point, so they said, they were surprised to find that there was still a sun.

The pawnbroker said, "My stupid daughter wants to work for the enemy. I don't know whether I should give my consent."

"They are no longer enemies," said Shinagawa.

"I know, I know," the pawnbroker conceded, "that's what my daughter says too."

"If one considers what our troops did in the occupied territories . . . ," someone said. "When I was in China as a soldier . . ."

"That's right, one never hears that the Americans are raping our women. And they don't seem to be looting either."

Old Nakamura nodded in agreement, "They don't have to."

"When I think of our soldiers in China . . ."

"They didn't really have to either, yet they did."

"They enjoyed looting and raping women. Maybe that's the difference."

"Maybe."

"So it really is a matter of spiritual attitude," Shinagawa summed up. "We should be ashamed of what our soldiers did in China."

The newspaper reported that the Americans had released all political prisoners from Japanese prisons, three thousand of them. News photos showed them streaming through the prison gates brandishing clenched fists. Instead, the Americans were now imprisoning Japanese war criminals, who marched with downcast expressions into captivity.

Mrs. Shinagawa brought out some tea and poured it. "May I? May I?" she said to each person in her high, tinkling voice. There were not enough bowls, and she had to flit back into the house.

"The sun's doing its best," said someone. "If only there were more to eat."

"The Americans have plenty of everything."

"I've heard that too."

The pawnbroker returned to the subject of Tama-chan and her desire to find a job with the Americans. "I don't know how to decide."

Shinagawa sucked air between his teeth and said, "What's stopping you?"

The others agreed. "There's no danger of her being raped."

"On the contrary, she's sure to get so much to eat that sometimes she'll be allowed to take part of it home."

"And she can tell us how the Americans live."

"I've already heard," said someone at the back, "that they don't take their shoes off indoors."

"What strange people!"

"The Americans eat a lot of meat."

"That must be why they're so tall."

"So you all seem to think that I should go ahead and allow my stupid daughter to work for the Americans," said the pawnbroker, seeking still further reassurance. When everybody nodded in agreement, he too looked satisfied.

"Then I'll go home now and tell her." Grasping his bamboo pole he hopped away.

9

"I'M GLAD YOU'RE BACK," SAID HER MOTHER WHEN SAYA
returned from school. "It's been a terrible day again."

Saya invariably found her mother sitting with droop-
ing shoulders at the dining room table. The door to the
kitchen was deliberately ajar so that Saya could see how
untidy the kitchen was. The dishes from the morning
and midday meals were still waiting to be washed. Saya's
mother was cradling her slim, pale face in both hands.

Every day it was the same. Every day her mother
looked miserable. Every day Saya tried to comfort her a
bit, tried to cheer her up. Saya became sad herself because she didn't succeed. She nestled up to her mother,
whispering tenderly in her ear. "But I'm here with you
now . . . I'll help you. . . ."

Every day Saya massaged her mother's shoulders and
back, drumming her little fists on the muscles that felt
knotted.

"My back's as stiff as a board, isn't it?" her mother
would say. "It hurts me to bend over."

Every day after school Saya would wash the day's

dishes in the kitchen, clean the pots, wipe the stove and the kitchen floor. She would talk about school and the interesting things that had happened there. Hoping to cheer her mother up, she depicted scenes from school, embroidered them a little and invented comic bits. She imitated Mrs. Nakarai and the other teachers, talked about her friends and about the others whom she liked less. She felt rewarded if her mother finally forgot to look miserable, if she smiled or even let herself suddenly be infected by Saya's ringing laughter.

At other times when Saya came home from school, her mother would be sitting at the table with moist eyes, as if she had been crying. On such days she would say, in an especially low, plaintive voice, "If you only knew, poor child, what your father is saying about you. . . ."

Saya never failed to be taken in by such dark hints. Invariably she believed what her mother said. Invariably her eyes widened in anger, and she would work herself into a childishly exaggerated indignation. She would throw her school satchel into the corner.

"What's he been saying this time?"

Her mother always took her time to answer. She would wipe her eyes and purse her lips as if what she had to say was unutterable.

"I can't tell you . . . I know you'd go straight to Father and blurt out your anger. You've never understood that by doing so you make everything much worse."

In the past Saya had indeed often run straight to her father with the idea of challenging him. For the next few days her mother would assume a stony expression and extend her icy silence to the entire household, even to Bo, who would look at her with puzzled, anxious eyes.

"I won't go to Father, I promise you," Saya would therefore say.

As it was, when Saya used to go to him in a rage her

father would never admit to having said anything derogatory about her. He had always merely looked at her in silence with a strangely sad smile.

"Little innocent," was all her father would ever answer, "poor little innocent."

Once he had added: "It's strange—usually you have no trouble seeing through people."

Actually Saya loved her father dearly. Although he was often unable to spend much time with her, he never gave her the feeling that he was unapproachable. The hours she could spend with him were therefore doubly precious. In his study he would show her the books he happened to be reading. He allowed her to rub the moistened ink stick on the ink stone when he wanted to do some calligraphy with his big, soft brush. He never became impatient when the grinding took a little longer than usual or the ink was not quite black enough. When he had finished his calligraphy he would read it out to her, explaining the characters and their meaning without ever sounding didactic.

Saya's father always tried to answer her questions. When he had no answer, he admitted as much with a smile.

He could be very amusing. He liked to laugh. He was a cheerful person. His laugh was never too loud, never sounded affected. It burst out from him naturally. If Saya had learned her own laugh from anybody, it was from him. At a very early age he had taught her to see the funny side of things. Through him she had learned to recognize or think up humorous situations.

Sometimes when Saya sat with him in his study or went for a walk with him in the forest surrounding the shrine, the two of them would invent funny scenes that they would act out to each other, savoring them to the full, until they both dissolved in laughter. Saya would collapse on the ground with laughter or clutch her father so hard that the seams of his priest's robe would tear.

"What kind of a father is that?" her mother would say afterward, when she had heard the laughter in the distance. "Such silly behavior is not compatible with the dignity of his office."

She tried to instill into Saya the feeling that her father's behavior in front of her bordered on the ridiculous.

"That is not setting a good example," she would say when she was alone with Saya. "A person who cannot set a good example, who in fact does not even want to try, should not become a Shinto priest."

In a strangely twofold way, Saya lived both with her father and with her mother, two lives that hardly impinged upon each other, although in time and space they were a part of each one of her days. At times she had managed to ignore the resulting conflict. At times she wished she could simply forget it or not worry about it, but that was possible only to a degree. Inexorably Saya was moving towards a decision. She could feel this happening and tried to evade it. She was afraid of a decision.

When Saya was with her father, he never asked what she had just been discussing with her mother, what she had been doing with her or for her, what incidents in school she had been telling her about.

On the other hand, when Saya returned from being with her father, her mother always wanted to know exactly how every minute of their time together had been spent. Saya usually told her mother everything, although sometimes she had intended to leave out all the fun that bound her so closely to her father. But her mother was a very skillful interrogator. She had always heard the laughter. Through her feigned interest she persuaded Saya to tell more than she wanted to. Over and over again, she let herself be carried away because then, for a short time, her mother's face would light up. She virtually hung on Saya's lips, would smile, nod in agreement, or tilt her head to one side with a speculative expression.

"But don't you feel yourself," she would finally say, "that all that carries no real weight? Fooling around is fine for a child, but you're growing up. Do you find that what your father has to offer you is enough?"

When she said such things, her mother always looked so sad that Saya felt drawn to her in childish sympathy. She believed this sadness to be genuine and did not know that her mother was merely pretending to be sad in order to bind Saya to her. She wanted Saya to blame her father for everything, wanted her to learn to despise him, learn to hate him—she wanted him to lose Saya's affection. She wanted to hurt him because he possessed an inner serenity and poise that she could not understand.

In a soft, flattering voice she would whisper to her daughter, "Now you know . . . I have told you a great secret. . . ."

Whenever her mother felt a dark suspicion emanating toward her from Saya, she would mitigate what she had just said. "He is the way he is. We must take him as he is, and perhaps even love him a little. We cannot change him, but I shall protect you with the heart of a loving mother. You must always believe that."

Then she would scurry off and come back with a little treat.

"Here, this is for you," she would say. "I saved it for you." And into Saya's mouth she would pop a candied chestnut, a mouthful of cake she had baked from sweet potato flour, or a dried persimmon.

"Nobody must know that I saved something for you. Your father is already grumbling because I spoil you. You know how he talks about you behind your back."

"You mustn't save anything for me." Something in Saya rebelled against this favoritism. "Why don't you give it to Bo?" she would say.

"Bo had a piece too," her mother would reassure her. "I gave an especially good piece to our little Bo, but of course you must get a slightly bigger piece because you're bigger and also because you do so much in the house."

The feeling that her mother was there, that she needed her and was waiting for her, made Saya hurry home from school every day. She never let her classmates delay her, not even her own special friends. When some of them begged her "Why don't you stay for a while and play?" she countered with "Walk home with me, then we can be together a bit longer."

When there were drama or choir rehearsals after school, Saya was tormented by a guilty conscience. She pictured her mother sitting exhausted at the dining room table, weeping softly to herself, her pale, narrow face cradled in her hands.

"Don't be angry with me," was the first thing Saya said when she was late coming home. On such days she would plunge with even greater energy into the work to be done in the house, she would massage her mother until her hands were numb, working herself up into forced gaiety to sweep her mother along. Then when the narrow, pale face finally relaxed and was lit up by a smile, Saya would be happy.

"But I'm never angry with you," her mother would say. "On the contrary, I'm glad you had a nice time in school . . . that's what I live for, after all."

"What makes you so sad anyway?" Saya would sometimes ask in the childish hope that there must surely be some way of relieving her mother of this persistent sadness. When she compared her with the mothers of her friends, she was baffled. She really couldn't imagine where her mother found any reason for her permanent unhappiness. She was much more beautiful than all the other mothers Saya knew. She owned many beautiful kimonos. She had three children, all of them healthy. No one lived in such a beautiful house, with a clear view over the city, surrounded by hundreds of trees and with plenty of room for flowerbeds. All Saya's school friends lived in much smaller houses, and their mothers, although just as responsible for the households, never had any maids.

None of Saya's friends had to help as much in the house. They all had more time to play. Food was scarce for all of them.

Some of her friends had confided to Saya that their parents often got into terrible arguments at home, that their fathers would sometimes come home drunk and proceed to beat their mothers. The fathers of some of her classmates would beat the mothers even without being drunk. Some of them, so she had heard, had women in the Gion or Pontocho quarter and were spending a lot of money there.

Because Saya was the best in her class, the mothers of other girls often said, "How happy your mother must be!"

"Oh yes, she's very happy," Saya would quickly answer. It hurt her to have to put on a radiant expression in order to be convincing.

"You are still too young to understand, Saya," her mother would say with downcast eyes. "You don't know the meaning of disappointment, and I hope you never will."

Another time her mother said, "When I was your age I was already learning ikebana and was allowed to help my grandfather with the tea ceremony."

Saya wanted to say that after all she did help her father prepare the ink for his calligraphy, and that she was already so advanced in calligraphy that she was even better than Mrs. Nakarai. But she swallowed her words. Whenever she said anything that in any way threw a favorable light on her father, it ended up with her mother in tears. Her face would collapse and suddenly look old. Everything would become so mixed up.

More than once her mother had said she would kill herself some day. There were times in school when Saya would be overcome by a leaden feeling of fear that her mother might be dead by the time she reached home. This fear would seep into her like the chill that heralds an attack of flu.

Saya would close her eyes and try to imagine what her mother was doing at that moment: whether she was sitting sad-eyed at the table, or wandering restlessly round the house dusting every surface, or watching Bo playing in the forecourt, or washing Ryo's dirty trousers or darning the holes in his socks. Her favorite mental picture of her mother was of her preparing tea or arranging flowers because then her face looked relaxed, beautiful in its regularity, and free of the shadows of sadness.

Sometimes, too, in her mind's eye Saya also saw her mother picking apart the seams of an exquisite, brightly colored silk kimono to make a new dress for her from the material. Her mother could sew exquisitely. From several old kimonos that she no longer wore because they were too colorful for her age she had already made Saya some lovely dresses.

But suppose she were to kill herself! Saya knew that in the kimono closet at home her mother kept a dagger. She had once shown Saya the needle-sharp weapon, the old, precious samurai dagger whose blade was engraved with a shadow pattern and which had been a family heirloom

for many generations. It represented the closeness of
death. Its blade was so sharp that with it, so her mother
said, a silk thread floating in the air could be sliced in
two. "I," her mother had gone on to say, however, "shall
use this dagger when I can no longer endure my life."

On one occasion, Saya's fear had become so overpowering that she ran out of class in the middle of a lesson
and dashed home. Images of blood passed before her
eyes. Breathless, she arrived at the top of the hill and
with a pounding heart crept softly into the house. A
bowl of freshly arranged flowers stood at the entrance,
but otherwise there was a deathly silence. Saya hardly
dared to breathe. She tiptoed to the partly open kitchen
door and looked in. There stood her mother, eating a
bowl of white rice with hasty movements of her hand
and outthrust lower lip.

"What are you doing here?" her mother snapped.

"I was scared . . . terribly scared . . . but you're
here. . . ."

Saya could not go on. The sight of her mother with the
rice bowl raised to her lower lip, shoveling the white rice
into her mouth with chopsticks, had taken her breath
away, more so even than running up all those steps.

"But you're here . . . ," she repeated.

"This is old rice," said her mother, noticing Saya's bewildered expression. "Two-day-old rice. It already tastes
quite stale."

Without hesitation her mother finished the rice in her
bowl. A few times her eyes scanned Saya's face suspi-
ciously. With unwonted asperity she sent her out of the
kitchen.

"What are you doing home from school at this hour?"
she asked after swallowing the last of the rice and enter-
ing the adjoining dining room. "Are you in trouble?" Her
voice was gentle again.

Saya couldn't answer. While standing in the kitchen, she thought she had distinctly smelled the aroma of freshly cooked rice. Two days ago there had been a little rice for supper, white rice, but there had been none left over. Bo had been given the last of it. Moreover, she had never seen her mother eating with such a greedy mouth. Her mother always insisted on good table manners and at the very most would let Ryo get away with a few bad habits.

"He's a boy," she would say. "He's allowed to do that." That her mother, too, could eat so greedily and hastily and while standing up—somehow it wasn't like her.

"What's to become of my three children when I'm no longer here?" she murmured, as if speaking only to herself.

"Don't say that," Saya burst out in a sudden upwelling of emotion. "You mustn't say such things!"

Her mother tried to smile, but the smile merely parted her lips. Because she was cupping her face in both hands, a few wrinkles showed up around her mouth that did not harmonize with the beauty of her face. Suddenly she stood up and went to her sewing room. Saya heard her open a drawer and close it again. Then her mother returned.

"This is for you," she said in a voice once again full of tenderness. "This is for you."

She held out a brilliant purple dress to Saya. "I have sewn all my love into it."

Saya could have shouted for joy. Such a lovely dress! She couldn't take her eyes off it. The bright purple with the pattern of yellow lilies made her forget everything that had happened, or rather, it was all swept away.

"I can wear it at the next school concert!"

Her mother held the dress against Saya. "You look sweet in it."

Saya beamed. Her mother stroked her hair.

"I'll make you some matching hair ribbons," she said, "but now—hurry back to school."

Saya ran down the stone stairway and along the lanes to school, where she sat down quietly at her desk. Once again the vision of her mother rose before her as she had stood in the kitchen hastily shoveling white rice into her mouth. Had that really been yesterday's rice? Had it really smelled stale? She still thought it had smelled fragrant, fresh. But then she became uncertain. She no longer knew what to think.

That afternoon when she came home from school, her mother was sitting at the dining room table, sad and silent.

"Tell me," Saya asked hesitantly, "did I come home sometime during the day?"

"Why do you ask?" replied her mother.

"You mean I didn't come home during the day?"

Her mother covered her face with both hands. "My back . . . ," she complained, "all that work . . ."

Saya massaged her back. "I must have dreamed it," she said as if to herself.

 10

THROUGHOUT ALL THE WAR YEARS, THINGS HAD BEEN VERY quiet around the Christian church on Kita-oji. Rarely did people go in or come out. With Japan's defeat, the situation changed. There were rumors that the Americans were going to introduce Christianity as the official state religion, with the result that the church on Kita-oji began to draw large crowds and the path to the church entrance had to be repaired. The uneven places were leveled with fine gravel. The gravel was wetted with a solution of lime and water and tamped down.

Looking back, it was seen to be an advantage that the broad firebreak which had been cut alongside the Hori-kawa during the last months of the war happened to join Kita-oji at the very spot where the Christian church was situated. The high pointed windows, and the neo-Gothic tower that looked as if it had been broken off at the top, suddenly seemed quite impressive, once the little wooden houses beside it had been torn down. By October, the unprepossessing exterior of both nave and tower had been transformed into a dazzling chalk white.

The first time Saya heard the Christian church bells ringing in the distance she didn't know where the sound came from. She thought perhaps the itinerant storyteller had returned. Before the war, he had regularly visited the silk weavers' quarter, but then, much to the regret of all the children, he had stopped coming. He, too, had had a clear, high bell that he would swing vigorously at the entrance to the lanes after parking his pedicab at a street corner.

He would clap his hands as more and more children gathered and bought his colored candies. The dozen little paper flags stuck into his headband would twinkle with every movement of his head. Finally he would pluck enticingly at the sheet covering the first picture story on the stand, rolling his eyes and looking at each child in turn with a fierce expression.

"Which one of you is afraid?" he would ask in a menacing voice. "Afraid of the horrible mountain spirits?"

Then all the girls would shriek and the boys shout, "Not me!"

"Just you wait and see," the storyteller would say, "how nice and scared you'll all be when I tell you the tale of brave Momotaro . . . here he is!"

Then, striking his shiny brass bell with his pointer, he would jerk the sheet away.

"Here is little Momotaro," the storyteller would whisper mysteriously, "still very tiny, born from a peach kernel, but already very clever. Just watch how fast he grows, soon he'll be stronger than even the most fearsome of all the mountain spirits."

The storyteller's singsong would rise to the highest pitch like the voice of a cicada, crack, then slip down into a deep rumble that the children would respond to with nervous little screams, for they all knew that the wicked mountain spirit was on his way and would stretch out his huge claws toward poor Momotaro.

"Just look how strong Momotaro is now because he has always chewed his food properly and swallowed it like a good boy. With every inch he's grown, his cleverness has grown too, for if that weren't so he'd have wet his pants with fear at the sight of the wicked mountain spirit."

The storyteller would dance around his picture stand, hide behind the frame, and emerge again as he looked around, turning himself into the mountain spirit who could multiply himself a hundred times by pulling out a hundred hairs and blowing them into the air. Then it would seem to the children as though the air were full of whirling mountain spirits, howling and screaming with terrible voices.

As soon as Saya heard the clear, distant sound of the bell, she hoisted Bo onto her back. "You've never ever seen the storyteller!" Clasping her hands under Bo's little bottom to support his weight, she ran down the stone steps as fast as her getas permitted.

Bo clung tightly to his sister. He wanted to hear the story of Momotaro right from the beginning.

"Faster!" he said in a childish voice of command, kicking his legs and pulling Saya's hair.

"You're hurting me," she said.

That made Bo stop kicking immediately.

"Bo no hurt," he piped apologetically.

Saya ran toward the sound of the bell. She was surprised not to find the storyteller down by the great torii or in one of the side lanes. Instead, no sooner had she entered the silk weavers' lanes down below than the clear tone could no longer be heard, although up on the hill it had sounded so close.

"I don't know where he is," she told Bo.

"There!" said Bo, thrusting his head as far forward over her shoulder as he could. "There!" He pointed down a lane where an old man was trying to put a bicycle chain back onto the sprocket wheel. His hands were all black and oily.

"No, that's not him."

"There!" said Bo, pointing in another direction.

Saya ran along the lanes, farther and farther away from the hill, toward the sound of the bell, a sound that seemed to become clearer and gayer the closer she came to the Hori-kawa firebreak. Bo was getting too heavy for her, so she set him down and put his getas onto his little feet. She had been carrying them by the straps all the way with two fingers. Her fingers were quite sore.

"Come along," she said, "that's where the sound of the bell is coming from."

Then they both stood beside the wide firebreak and looked across the white tower of the Christian church where the ringing came from.

"There!" said Bo, beaming. "Momotaro in there!"

They both took off their getas in order to scramble faster down the embankment to the dry streambed and up onto the other side. Then, crossing the open space, they cautiously approached the church and its entrance, where four enormous American cars were parked outside.

Bo was about to dash ahead impetuously, but Saya took him by the hand and led him past the parked cars. To her, the American cars seemed almost as big as the buses that had just started driving through the city again, with wood-gas burners that belched foul-smelling smoke. From the open church door a burst of music surged toward them that sounded like breaking waves. A stormy, mighty roar engulfed them. Never before had

Saya heard such overpowering music. She tightened her grasp on Bo's hand.

From long habit they both slipped out of their getas, and Saya quickly bent down to arrange the wooden sandals in such a way that she and Bo could slip into them again as soon as they came out. All the while she could feel Bo clinging to her hand with both of his. He was excited too. Barefoot and feverish with expectation, they walked through the lofty entrance. Bo's eyes shone when he saw the brightly lit interior where the music seemed to be pouring out of all four walls.

The ceiling looked quite different from that of a Buddhist temple. Instead of being made of massive gilded beams and black wood, it consisted of a high vault decorated with pink stucco and clusters of pale blue arches. The ceiling resembled a sky that was tied together at the top with a string.

The light falling through the stained-glass windows made Saya feel she was looking under water. Spots of light flickered before her eyes, and she wouldn't have been surprised if a shoal of red, blue, yellow, and purple coral fish had suddenly come swimming through the air.

She and Bo were still clutching each other by the hand. There they both stood, in their grubby bare feet and dingy, baggy gray trousers, Bo's with a bib held up by shoulder straps that crossed at the back. Instead of a blouse, Saya was wearing a smocklike jacket sewn by her mother from old kimono material—reddish brown with vertical white stripes and made with so much room to grow into that she had rolled up both sleeves, one higher than the other.

The music had stopped, but the resonance still seemed to hover under the ceiling.

Bo was looking with interest at the great figure standing high up in the chancel. It had outstretched arms and was dressed in a long flowing robe, almost like a Bodhisattva but with wavy hair the color of rice straw.

"There! That's Momotaro!" Bo burst out, pointing his chubby finger at the tall figure. "There! That's Momotaro!"

Many faces turned toward them, so that Saya smiled and bowed in confusion. There were many Americans in the church. They were smiling broadly. A tall white woman in a bright red dress leaned forward and said something. Saya interpreted her gesture to mean that she and Bo were to go to her. Rather hesitantly, Saya took a few steps forward, pulling Bo behind her. The woman in the red dress moved aside to make room for them on the bench. Saya lifted Bo onto the bench and sat down between him and the white woman. She would have liked to say "thank you" but didn't know the English words for that, so she merely gave an embarrassed little smile and said *"arigato."* Bo swung his legs.

It took a while for Saya to notice that there were also some Japanese sitting on the benches, but what struck her most were the Americans. She had never seen so many all at once and at such close quarters. They all had big noses. Sometimes one of the Americans would turn around and look across at Saya and Bo, and Saya would notice that he had blue eyes. But they didn't all have blue eyes, some of them had brown. They all looked very friendly.

The white woman in the red dress also smiled down at Saya from time to time. She exuded a delicate aroma of lilies of the valley. Saya looked carefully at the red dress to see whether the woman was wearing a bunch of lilies of the valley anywhere, but she couldn't see any.

Bo was still swinging his legs. He craned his neck to get a better view. Finally he stood up on the bench and looked around.

"Lots of big noses," he said to Saya. "All Momotaros . . . lots of Momotaros!"

Toward the front, a Japanese wearing a long black robe mounted a high pulpit. Above the black robe he wore a white bib. Bo studied him carefully and said after a while, "He has bib. He still dribbles. That's not Momotaro."

The Japanese man in the pulpit opened a fat book and read aloud from it. He spoke English. Saya had never heard a Japanese speaking English before.

Suddenly everyone in the church stood up, even the Americans. It looked as if they had risen at the command of the Japanese who was addressing them from the pulpit. Saya got up quickly too. They all said something in chorus. It sounded just like a Buddhist sutra, muffled, monotonous, sad.

The Japanese man led the chanting, speaking in a loud voice and moving his lips conspicuously. Now and again he let the tip of his tongue peep out from between his lips. Saya wondered whether it was necessary to do this when speaking English. She looked at the white woman in the red dress, who was also chanting but hardly moving her lips. Her lips were just as red as her dress. Her hair was brown and curly. From her ear lobe hung something that looked like mother-of-pearl. What impressed Saya most was the whiteness of her face, white as flour. She glanced quickly at the woman's hands, to see whether they were just as white. The woman had fingernails as red as lacquer. Were American women's fingernails naturally that red? wondered Saya.

At the end everyone said "amen."

The American woman noticed that Saya had been eyeing her. She smiled.

Then the engulfing, overwhelming music started up again, resounding from ceiling and walls. Saya could feel it penetrating her body and causing even the wooden bench she was sitting on to vibrate. She was sure the tall colored windowpanes would shatter.

Everyone opened a book and began to sing in chorus. Bo immediately chimed in with his high, childish voice. The words he sang were those of a children's song, but he followed the hymn tune exactly. The American woman held her book so that Saya could look at it too. Saya tried to move her lips a little, but no sound came out.

As soon as the hymn was over, Bo clapped his little hands loudly and was very proud when so many faces turned toward him. But slowly his pride changed to confusion because no one clapped with him, and he snuggled up to Saya, hiding his face under her striped jacket. However, after only a few seconds he peeked out again with one eye and asked Saya in a whisper whether there would be any more songs to sing. But apparently it was all over, for people were getting up and leaving the church.

The American woman in the red dress bent down to Bo and stroked his hair. She said something in English. Saya felt ashamed at not being able to answer. She said "thank you" in Japanese but wasn't sure whether this word expressed everything she felt. She would have liked to tell this American woman that she admired her white skin, that Bo would soon be three, and that actually she had intended to take him to the storyteller. Because she lacked the words to express all this to the beautiful white woman, she merely smiled.

The Japanese in the black robe, who had come down from the pulpit, approached them along the center aisle and asked Saya, "What's your name?"

He spoke normal Japanese. Saya admired him for being able to speak two languages.

"I'm Saya," she replied, "and this is my little brother Bo, who'll soon be three."

"And how old are you?"

"I'm ten."

Bo asked, "Why you have bib?"

"I'm the pastor here," said the Japanese, "and that's part of my priest's attire."

His voice sounded very gentle. He was wearing black-rimmed spectacles with round lenses that made his eyes almost invisible. His eyebrows began strangely high above the rims and slanted steeply downward. Where the side pieces of his spectacles were attached to the frame, his eyebrows were lower than the rims. This made his face look as if some onion juice had squirted into his eyes. From his forehead to the crown of his head the pastor was completely bald; all that was left of his hair was a black wreath growing around the back at ear level.

"Where do you live?" he asked Saya.

"On the hill."

Saya saw his face display a sudden interest.

"On the hill," he repeated. "Who is your father?"

"My father is the Guji."

"Oh," said the pastor slowly.

Bo had climbed down from the bench and run up to the front. He examined with keen interest the steep steps leading up to the pulpit and walked once around the table on its dais in the chancel where the fat book lay from which the pastor had read aloud. After Bo had carefully scrutinized the large figure with outstretched arms, he came hurrying back to Saya on his short legs.

"Over there—is that Momotaro?" he asked.

"That is Jesus," the pastor said gently.

Bo looked puzzled.

"The church is his house," said the pastor, "and we are his children."

"Me too?" asked Bo.

The pastor hesitated for a moment, then said, "All men are his children."

Saya listened in silence. She thought the pastor was very kind to spend so much time talking to Bo and herself.

"You can come here every Sunday," said the pastor, "and bring along your little brother."

"The bell sounds beautiful," said Saya, "but I don't understand English."

"We also hold services in Japanese."

"But I want to learn English," said Saya. It seemed to her that she had been thinking of this for a long time. Actually the wish had only just arisen in her, in this church, with this engulfing music, in this bright, colored light. The smile of the American woman in the red dress had also done its part. It must be something quite special to be able to speak another language besides Japanese.

The pastor told Saya that every evening from seven to nine English lessons were given in the church hall—by a real American—but that unfortunately the lessons cost money.

"Does one need ration cards too?" Saya asked, crestfallen. "Like for rice and fish?"

The pastor smiled, "No, of course not."

"Then I'll come!" Saya said confidently.

 **11**

THE LANES OF THE SILK WEAVERS' QUARTER WERE DARK. IN the few houses where lights were still burning, the paper windows and doors glowed softly yellow, showing up the delicate tracery of the latticework in sharp black lines. Saya hurried along the lanes on her getas, for the English lesson in the Christian church had lasted a little longer than usual. There had been a movie, and that had been followed by a discussion. Time had passed in a flash, and Saya had been quite unaware of how late it was getting. She hopped and skipped along, enjoying the sound of her getas on the tamped gravel and the way it spread in the silent lanes, accompanying her from one corner to the next through the darkness.

When she turned into the wide straight lane that led directly to the great torii, she could see from a distance that her father was waiting there with his lantern, as he did every evening, for her to come home.

"*Otosan* . . . ," she called, and ran even faster. The big round lantern floated in front of the amorphous black background.

"Otosan . . ."

Her father swung his lantern a little, the way he always did when he heard Saya calling from a distance.

"How do you do?" Saya said in English as soon as she reached him, somewhat out of breath.

Her father laughed and replied in the same tone of voice, "How do you do?"

"It finished a bit later this evening. Did you have to wait long?"

"Not too long," he said.

Saya gave a quick glance into the round opening of the lantern and saw that the candle had almost burned down.

"Much too long," she said. "Weren't you cold?"

"I've always got the lantern!" he joked.

The December air was dry and chilly. Her father was wearing his wide black cape of light wool. Saya buttoned up her jacket, which she had left open as she ran. Now that she had reached her father and was standing still, she felt the chill of the night. She shivered. She was hungry. She had eaten nothing before leaving for her English lesson because her mother was still busy grilling the sweet potatoes and assembling the correct little bowls for the supper table. Saya had time only to sip some hot tea before hurrying off. During the English lesson she hadn't thought of her hunger, but as soon as she started for home she remembered that, apart from the thin, sweet potato soup at noon in school, she had had nothing to eat all day.

"Come along," said her father, holding out his hand, but Saya suddenly hesitated. Until then it had been she who had run toward him, who had called "Otosan" from far away, and in her joy at seeing him standing there with his lantern she had forgotten all her mother's warnings. But the moment her father held out his hand to her she was once again assailed by that hesitation that made her shy. "Watch out," her mother had told her often enough. "I know he looks like a protective father, but you should hear him talk when you're not there."

Saya looked up at her father, whose face was illumined by the swaying lantern. He certainly didn't look as if he could spread all kinds of nasty rumors behind her back. He certainly didn't look as if he could lie, but her mother had warned her how clever he was at deceiving. "Watch out, he'll worm his way into your heart, but actually he loves only himself."

"Come along," her father repeated. "I'm sure you're hungry."

Ruefully Saya said, "Yes, I am."

She gave him her hand. The big round lantern cast its soft, faint light ahead as it hung from the flexible bamboo stick that her father held horizontally in front of him. The shrine's black seal imprinted on the belly of the lantern somehow imparted confidence. Her father's hand was cool. They walked through the high torii whose huge crossbeam cut a black slice out of the blue night sky. Fallen leaves rustled. With every step there were more leaves. The light from the lantern wavered over their brilliant red and yellow.

Then the topmost branches, already bare, of the great oak tree that stood at the bottom of the stairway stretched across the velvety blue sky, and the first steps of the steep stairway showed up in the light of the lantern. The roots of the oak had forced the steps apart and protruded here and there between them. Saya could see the black scar etched by summer lightning into the mighty trunk of the tree. It was as wide as her two hands placed side by side and ran from high up all the way down to the ground.

"Do you remember?" Saya asked her father, pointing to the black lightning scar. That summer, shortly after lightning had struck, they had come out together to look at the still steaming trail. Where it had disappeared into the ground stood the charred skeleton of a fern frond, and all around the tree trunk other fronds hung down limply, as if they had been boiled. Heavy raindrops were still dripping from all the treetops, but the sun had already broken through again, and the cicadas had immediately resumed their singing.

The candle in her father's lantern flickered and went out.

"Now we can't see a thing," Saya said, feeling a bit guilty because she had been so late, "but then we both know the way."

She felt the firm pressure of her father's fingers. Hand in hand they walked up the steps.

Above the little *Inari* altar that stood at the end of the second flight of steps in an alcove off the path, the trees revealed a segment of sky. A candle was burning there, cold and lonely, in one of the niches that had been carved out of the rocks. Its faint light fell on the red Inari shrine, showing up the contours of the two white fox figures that kept vigil before the altar. They are divine messengers, it is said, who carry the wishes of men to the gods. One is supposed to approach them at night by the light of a candle or early in the morning before sunrise in the light of the first hour. They have been sitting there since time immemorial, certainly for a thousand years.

In order to make their long journeys more attractive to the foxes, people would bring them Inari-sushi of the best quality, little cakes made of soy germ and rice. But these also attracted the cats, who stole from the altar steps the tidbits intended for the foxes. In the morning, on her way to school, Saya would often see a cat disappearing under a bush near the rock wall or behind one of the red wooden pillars supporting the roof of the Inari altar. Sometimes it would jump up onto the altar roof and hiss softly from above when Saya came, for she also liked Inari-sushi. As soon as the people who had brought them had left, Saya would sneak down to the Inari altar and make off with the fresh tidbits.

For a long time Saya kept quiet about the fact that she frequently raced the cat early in the morning to steal the Inari-sushi from the fox altar, but one day she confessed to her father. He gently tapped the tip of her nose with his finger. "Not to worry," he had said, "the foxes have seen many human generations come and go. They don't mind if a little girl occasionally makes off with their Inari-sushi—quicker than a wild cat."

"May I?" Saya now asked. She looked at her father, whose face was faintly illumined by the candlelight from the niche in the rock. Her father nodded with a smile and let go Saya's hand.

Saya stepped up to the two white foxes, whose noses were brightly painted, and pulled firmly three times on the rope woven of colored ribbons to which a little bronze bell was attached under the low roof of the Inari altar. The full tone of the bell spread out in the darkness, bounced against the rock wall, and was lost in the branches of the trees. Somewhere in the forest was a faint rustling. Saya folded her hands and whispered a few words to the two foxes.

"Yes," she finally said, and looked up expectantly. The foxes seemed to wink at her knowingly.

When she came back to her father, he pointed into the dark underbrush. "Look," he said.

Saya could see the cat's eyes glowing like amber.

"You'll have to hurry tomorrow morning," her father teased her. "Your rival is already lying in wait."

Her father's hand was warm now. Side by side they continued on up the dark steps. Saya was telling him about the English lesson and that she was still the only child among ten grown-ups.

"That American," she said, "you know, Mr. Everett, he talks to me as if I was already grown-up, and he listens when I say something."

"Well, you *are* a big girl."

"But no one's like Mr. Everett—I think that's very American."

In the few weeks of English lessons Saya had already learned a lot. Thanks to her quick grasp, and perhaps also because she was still a child, she found it all very easy. Mr. Everett said she had the best pronunciation, and he chose her more and more often when he wanted something read aloud to the class.

He was a very tall, thin man who always smelled of shaving lotion or some other scent that Saya associated with a big bar of pink or lemon-yellow soap.

What amazed her most was the quantity of black hair growing on his arms down to his wrists and even on the backs of his hands. When he wore his shirt open at the neck you could see that his chest was hairy too. But he did have a bald spot at the back of his head, exactly the size of a mandarin orange.

Saya wanted to ask him how old he was, because in Japan only old men became bald. But Mr. Everett didn't look that old, no more than maybe twenty or thirty. That was as close as she could get, since she had no basis for comparison. Not knowing whether it mightn't be impolite for her as a little girl to ask him his age, Saya postponed the question from one evening to the next.

"Do you think I should ask him?" she said to her father.

Her father thought she should simply look at it as a way of practicing English and that she should use the opportunity to ask Mr. Everett whether in America it was impolite for a little girl to ask a man how old he was.

"That sounds a bit complicated."

"I'll help you," her father said and suggested how she could put it in English.

"How come you know so much English?" Saya asked, full of admiration.

"Oh, I learned a little bit at one time and haven't forgotten it all."

"But your pronunciation is bad," Saya declared. She rolled *r*'s for him and showed him how to pronounce *l* and *th*. "Your pronunciation is terrible."

"I know," her father said, "but then my teacher was only a Japanese. So . . ."

"I'm so lucky," Saya said, nestling up against him. Her father paused on the step and returned Saya's affectionate pressure. "I'm so glad for you," he said. "Would you like to have my old English dictionary?"

In a buoyant mood they resumed their way up the long stairway, step by step, in the darkness. They knew the rhythm of the steps, every landing, every bend, and every tree that arched its branches across the sky. The stars danced between the bare branches. The fallen leaves rustled at every footstep.

Then they were at the top, and Saya remembered her mother. That put an end to her buoyant mood. She tore herself away from her father and ran ahead around the last few bends in the path.

Her mother was sitting disconsolately at the dining room table. "Everything has got cold again because you're so late."

"Don't be angry," said Saya, putting her arm around her mother's shoulder.

"What have you been doing all this time with Father?"

"Nothing—we came straight up here."

"Then why are you so late?"

"There was a movie . . . Mr. Everett showed us a movie, a movie about a family in America."

"I see," her mother said heavily. "And of course it never occurs to you that I'm sitting here waiting for you. You don't care that I have to work all day long just so you can have the pleasure of learning English."

"Please don't be sad," Saya implored her mother. "The movie was so interesting, I'll tell you all about it."

She sat down quickly at the table that was draped, as always in winter, with a thick, quilted cover. The cover kept in the heat that rose from the glowing charcoal on a bed of ashes in a hollow under the table. Saya put her feet against the protective grille and tucked the quilt around her legs to keep in the heat coming from below.

"Nice and warm," she said, rubbing her hands.

"I put more charcoal on especially for you," said her mother, holding her hand to the small of her back. "It's not so easy for me to crawl in there under the table."

"You shouldn't have done that," Saya said quickly. Her mother's pained expression gave her a sharp pang of guilt. Saya didn't want this feeling to gain the upper hand. She didn't want to see all the rest of the evening drowning in it, so she quickly took a deep breath and began her description. "This movie—you know—this movie was about an American father, an American mother, and two children—and a big car and a dog too."

"Now eat your supper first," interrupted her mother,

pushing three little bowls toward Saya. Saya forced herself to eat slowly. She would have liked to gobble it all down at once, but she saw that there wasn't much there. She chewed slowly and with concentration, just as her father always did. That takes away the hunger and opens up the food better, he had once told her. Since then Saya had made a point of eating as he did.

Her mother came in from the kitchen carrying one more small bowl, with a lid. "This is for you," she whispered. "I saved it for you."

It was a piece of sea bream, cooked with slices of ginger and sprinkled with chives. Saya almost cried out in delight. "Where did you get *that?*"

"Somebody brought it."

Saya sniffed the piece of fish. It smelled juicy and sweet. "Did Bo have some too?" she asked.

"Of course . . . ," said her mother, "but eat it up quickly, or your father may come and scold me."

"Why should he do that?"

"You've no idea how he is. This evening, when he saw that I was going to save a piece of fish for you, he said right away, 'Latecomers must eat leftovers.'"

Saya had suddenly lost all her appetite for the fish. Disconcerted, she put it back into the bowl.

"But he's glad I'm having English lessons."

"What an innocent child you are. You've no idea the arguments I've had with him over your English lessons. He's convinced it's not worth spending so much money on a girl."

"He never says anything like that to *me,*" Saya said, wavering between despondency and obstinacy. Her throat felt as if it were in a vise.

"We can't change him," her mother said consolingly. "I'm only telling you all this because I want to prevent your being taken in by your father."

Saya looked doubtfully at her mother. "But he's there every evening beside the torii, waiting for me," she blurted out. "He's always so glad to see me."

"Now eat up that piece of sea bream I saved for you from my own meager portion."

Saya tried to remember what had happened that first evening of her English lessons. She hadn't counted on her father coming to meet her, and then, at the sight of him coming down the steps in the darkness, she had felt a sudden surge of joy. She had run to her father and flung her arms around him. Saya could still hear her father's voice playfully saying in English "How do you do?"

"How do you do?" she had replied.

Saya's mother was studying her face.

"You don't quite believe me," she said. "That's your gratitude for all my worries and sufferings. I sacrifice myself for you, but you are an ungrateful child. You believe your father more than me. . . ."

"But I do believe you," Saya forced herself to say.

"Now do me a favor and eat up your piece of fish," said her mother in a husky, tear-soaked voice.

Obediently Saya started eating. All the flavor seemed to have vanished.

Meanwhile her mother removed the thin, parchment-like skin from an overripe persimmon. The orangy-red pulp oozed across the plate. She picked up a spoon after Saya had swallowed the last mouthful of sea bream. "Open your mouth," she said with a smile, holding out a spoonful of persimmon. "You don't understand the heart of a mother."

Saya still had some homework to do. She quickly washed up her little bowls in the kitchen and went for her satchel which that afternoon she had put down unopened in the corner by the front door because she had had to help her mother.

"I still have some homework to do for tomorrow," she told her mother apologetically.

It was almost eleven o'clock. Saya sat with her school books at the dining table, that being the only place in the house where she could at least keep her feet warm. Her mother brought her an evening cup of tea made from roasted barley.

"*Please* go to bed," Saya said to her.

Her mother sighed.

By this time Saya's nerves were all on edge because she had so much homework to do. There were still five tests to be written before the new year holidays. Saya was much too proud to allow her standards in school to drop because of the extra load of two hours of English lessons every evening. So she bent over her school books and covered her ears with her hands. Her mother was still wandering about, busying herself in the kitchen, noisily opening drawers and cupboard doors.

"*Please* go to bed now," Saya urged. "I still haven't finished my homework."

In spite of this, after a quarter of an hour her mother returned once more and tenderly placed a knitted cardigan around Saya's shoulders. "So you won't be cold," she said.

Saya stayed on until after midnight. By that time everything she wrote in her copybooks became blurred, but she persisted until she had finished it all. The light from the naked bulb over the table flickered intermittently, but Saya didn't know whether the flickering was in her eyes or whether it was a sign that the power was being cut off again in the city. As a precaution she had placed a candle and matches in readiness.

 **12**

THE FOOD SITUATION WAS BECOMING WORSE AND WORSE. Prices on the black market were rising from week to week. Although the allotted rice rations were being distributed they had become smaller and smaller, and people often had to wait many days for the rice dealer to hang the sign on his door announcing that some rice had arrived. Promptly a long line would form outside his shop, and those at the end of the line worried lest they might miss their chance again.

Even more unpredictable were the supplies of miso, cooking oil, and soy sauce, and what did become available was often of very poor quality. If a bottle of soy sauce was held up to the sky, the clouds could be seen through it. The vegetables that had been planted in the firebreak along the Hori-kawa had long since been picked, or else looted by thieves during the night. And more often than not the sweet potatoes that could be bought had gone bad in spots.

Those people who had gone to the trouble during recent weeks of drying sweet potatoes in the warm, late-autumn sunshine were fortunate. Everywhere in the silk weavers' quarter, long strings of thin sweet potato slices were to be seen hanging in windows and under eaves. On windless days, when the sun was shining, many people tried to dry the last of the slices on newspapers spread out on the roofs, but that attracted the sparrows. The result was much cursing and yelling. To drive away the sparrows, people hung up empty tin cans, and every puff of wind would produce a noisy clamor that the sparrows largely ignored.

The slices of dried sweet potato were ground into a powder of flourlike consistency. This was about the only way to eat them. In many of the houses there were metal grinders that could be screwed to the table and cranked by hand. If the slices were not dry enough to crumble, they would gum up the works, and the only thing to do was to take the machine apart. Even thoroughly dried slices had to be ground several times before becoming a proper flour, and it often took hours to grind enough for one meal. The women then shaped the flour into dumplings and boiled them in salted water.

By this time many soldiers had returned from overseas. They were to be seen everywhere in the streets, recognizable by the threadbare uniforms they still wore because most of them had nothing better to put on. Every soldier meant an extra mouth to feed. All in all, some six and a half million people—roughly half of them soldiers, the other half civilians—were expected to come flooding back to Japan from overseas. There were new arrivals every day.

Although everyone, men as well as women, spent most of each day trying to find something to eat or preparing what little they had managed to acquire, the newspapers at the kiosk sold like hot cakes. A great deal was written about democracy and liberty. The first Communist Party

convention in nineteen years had just been held. Those
present had demanded that the Emperor be deposed.
They had vowed to destroy the capitalist system. By the
establishment of a classless society, the principle of
equality and liberty for all was to become a reality.

There was talk of nationalizing the means of production.

"What does that mean?" people asked each other.
"Are our looms means of production too?"

There was talk of all property being expropriated,
property being against the principle of equality. Discussion in the silk weavers' quarter went back and forth as
to whether this also meant the possession of a house
with a tiny garden, or whether property in the Communist sense meant something else.

"After all, who does own three or four houses?" people asked each other. Small shopkeepers also heard the
word "expropriation" with misgiving, but others said
that the smashing of the capitalist system was a historical necessity since the capitalists and the militarists were
jointly responsible for the war.

"They must be eliminated," they said, "radically eliminated so that there'll never be another war."

The Americans also proclaimed, "Never another war."

This phrase united them all. Everyone was in favor of
there never being another war. In Tokyo, preparations
were under way for the trial of war criminals. Whether
the Emperor was to be prosecuted was not yet decided.
The Communists accused him of being chiefly to blame
for the war. The Americans said that heavy industry had
cooperated closely with the militarists and that this had
led to the war. On American orders, the Japanese indus-
trial concerns were broken up. Although this did not directly affect people in Kyoto, the word from Osaka,

Kobe, Nagoya, and Tokyo was that Mitsui, Mitsubishi, and Sumitomo no longer existed.

Tama-chan had found a job with the Americans, at the Kyoto Hotel, now occupied by the American military administration. She cleaned vegetables in the kitchen and washed the dishes. She reported that the Americans ate meat and eggs and drank milk every day. They also ate raw vegetables and spoiled milk.

"Pew!" cried Mi-chan. According to the pawnbroker, a person would soon get tapeworms from eating raw vegetables. As it was, most people were suffering from tapeworms anyway, which sapped their energy and increased their hunger pangs.

Almost every evening Tama-chan brought back some food that had been left over by the Americans.

"Don't let them catch you!" said the pawnbroker.

"I'm allowed to do that," said Tama-chan. "The Americans are very generous. They never finish their food."

No one checked up on the girls working in the kitchen of the Kyoto Hotel. In the evening they were allowed to fill their own square aluminum containers with leftovers and take them home. Some of the girls were even beginning to include unopened tins of corned beef and ham.

"They fetch a good price on the black market," they would say, but the others persuaded them not to try this for fear of ending the generosity of the Americans.

In the evening Tama-chan would heat up whatever leftovers she had brought home, after first cutting away the places that had been bitten into. Sometimes there was a whole chicken leg, or the leg of a huge chicken that the Americans, according to Tama-chan, called "turkey."

"With the Americans, everything is big," said the pawnbroker approvingly. He was long since reconciled

to the fact that his daughter was working for the enemies. He used the word "enemies" less and less often. He
was still mulling over the question of whether or not
spirit had been a decisive factor in the war.

"They've defeated us and are now generous toward
us," he said pensively while eating the remains of a turkey thigh. "They don't make us feel their power."

"They don't need to," said Tama-chan. "They really
are powerful."

"Powerful . . . powerful . . . We were powerful
too," he blustered. "There's nothing more powerful than
the Japanese spirit."

Tama-chan looked at him and slowly shook her head.
"Perhaps the generosity of the Americans is more powerful than the Japanese spirit."

"What d'you mean?" asked the pawnbroker.

"I don't know," replied Tama-chan. "It's just an idea
that occurred to me."

The first time Mi-chan took along a jar of peanut butter to school, all the girls—Saya, Mi-chan, Yuri-chan,
and the others of her clique—squatted in a circle around
the jar at the far end of the playground near the poplar
trees.

"It tastes good," Mi-chan announced. As the owner of
the jar, she decided that Saya should be the first to be
allowed to stick her finger into it. They all eagerly
watched Saya's face as she licked her finger.

"Tastes like *rakkasei*," she said.

"Well, it's the same thing."

"Oh, I see."

After that they all dipped in their fingers and confirmed that it tasted like rakkasei.

"But it's good," said Yuri-chan. Within a few minutes
the whole jar was empty. Yuri-chan, who had eaten the

most because she had always used two fingers at once to scoop out the peanut butter, complained of a stomach-ache.

"You had it coming to you," said Mi-chan.

In class, Mrs. Nakarai had a lot to say about freedom and about the time of blind obedience being past.

"The Tenno is all finished," she said in her gentle voice. "We are free. Now we can live our own lives."

She repeated many times that the characters for free-dom comprised the two concepts of self and relationship, which represented a great responsibility.

"Freedom is the strengthening of one's own will," she lectured the class, "the unfolding of one's own self. The future will be determined by freedom."

Most of the ten-year-old girls could make nothing of what she was saying, but they docilely bent their heads and wrote everything down. They could be sure that the next test would call for such phrases. Mrs. Nakarai was pleased when what she had said in class was repeated in tests verbatim. She praised those girls who did this. Al-though she constantly spoke about the unfolding of one's own self, what she really expected was blind obe-dience. She hadn't changed in the slightest, she had merely exchanged her old vocabulary for a new one. Her catchwords were no longer *Tenno, nation, divine Japan,* but *freedom, will* and *self-expression.* However, as soon as a spark of independence showed up anywhere in class, she inter-vened immediately.

"You are all much too immature," she would say. "So it's much too soon for you to have your own opinion."

To Saya she said, "Don't pride yourself on being the daughter of a Shinto priest. Shinto is all finished. Shinto has nothing more to say—nor do you. I'll make you eat humble pie yet."

Saya recalled the exalted words with which Mrs. Nakarai had once spoken of state Shinto.

Of late, Mrs. Nakarai had been wearing her hair shorter, loose, and lightly waved. There were obvious traces of the curling iron. Many of the hairs had split ends.

One day Reiko proudly told the class that she had won out over Saya in the contest for the leading role in the Christmas play at the Christian church.

"I've been chosen to play Mary," she proudly lisped. "Not Saya—*she's* only the daughter of a Shinto priest . . . but *I'm* a Christian by birth."

No one in the class—apart from Saya—knew at that point that Reiko was a Christian. She had never mentioned it before. Even Mrs. Nakarai was very surprised to hear it.

"You really are a Christian?" she asked with interest.

"Ever since I was born," Reiko bragged, then immediately remembered to assume her sanctimonious modesty. "That's why the pastor has chosen me to be Mary," she told Mrs. Nakarai, with a bashful drawing in of her shoulders. "Mary is the mother of Jesus, you know? And Jesus is revered by all Americans."

Saya chewed her lower lip. She had indeed cherished hopes of playing the part of Mary, now that she and Bo had already attended church on six Sundays and enthusiastically taken part in the preparations for the nativity play. Reiko had never been there, and Saya had no idea that Reiko's parents were Christians. The previous Sunday, Reiko had suddenly turned up with her mother, and after a brief discussion in a corner of the church the pastor had given her the part of Mary.

There was nothing to be done about it. The pastor said, "The part of Mary must be taken by a baptized girl."

"But Christ is only just being born," Saya had said, defending her hopes for the part. "His mother Mary can't possibly have been baptized a Christian!"

"That makes no difference," said the pastor. Behind the thick, round lenses in their black frames, his eyes once again looked as if he had been slicing onions. "I'm sorry, I really am."

Shortly after that, Saya again saw Reiko's mother talking to the pastor in the corner. He behaved very deferentially toward her. From this Saya realized that Reiko's parents must be important Christians.

Reiko never missed an opportunity to get in a dig at Saya. She did everything possible to inflict little meannesses on the other girls in Saya's clique. She left Yuri-chan largely in peace because Mrs. Nakarai had stopped making denigrating remarks about Koreans and other non-Japanese. Instead Reiko said to Mi-chan, "I've heard that your big sister is now working for the Americans. She must be a *panpan.*" Reiko tittered in her childish voice.

"What's a panpan?" Mi-chan asked innocently.

"Ugh, you don't know what a panpan is?"

"No."

"All right—when does your big sister come home in the evening?"

"Late."

"See? Just wait till she gets a big tummy. Sometime or other, all panpans get themselves big tummies from the Americans."

She tittered again and pointed at Mi-chan because Mi-chan didn't know that women who went with Americans were called panpans these days.

"Mi-chan's big sister is a panpan," she whispered around in the class.

Ever since finding out that Reiko was a Christian, Mrs. Nakarai had been favoring her even more in class, especially when democracy was being discussed. She would ask Reiko in a gentle voice, "Tell us something about democracy and Christian brotherly love."

Saya could imitate Reiko's affected way of speaking to perfection. Once even Mrs. Nakarai was fooled when she happened to be facing the blackboard and writing something on it.

"Very nice, very appropriate," said Mrs. Nakarai without turning around. "Go on, Reiko."

When the class burst out laughing, Mrs. Nakarai turned around angrily. It took a while for her to realize her mistake. Her white powdered face turned red. Her eyes narrowed to slits. Reiko wept affectingly with both hands in front of her face and shot furious glances at Saya from between her parted fingers.

The same day the news appeared in the paper that Shinto had now been separated from the state and had thus lost all the privileges of a state-affiliated religion, Mrs. Nakarai told Saya, "Well at last—now you can't throw your weight around any more!"

The news of the separation of Shinto and state triggered a profound uneasiness in Saya's mother. She was afraid her own reputation would now decline as well. She scuttled back and forth in the house, aimlessly, wordlessly, with such an angry expression that even cheerful little Bo crept away into a corner.

Saya's mother complained, "What a comedown . . . surely there should be something to invest the state with dignity . . . if the gods are no longer to protect the state officially, what is to become of Shinto?"

Saya's father said, "The separation will show what

Shinto really is—a religion, or window dressing for the state."

Slowly her mother raised her head. Drawing out her words, she said, *"I see, I see*—you speak of Shinto as window dressing, and at the same time you pretend to be a Guji? Shall I tell you what a true Guji is?" She raised her voice. "A Guji is a man of dignity, true dignity . . . who is proud to be a Japanese."

Saya's father stood there quietly, saying nothing. His expression seemed unmoved, almost smiling. It was a pained, pitying smile.

"Go ahead, smile if you like," Saya's mother snapped at him. "To speak of Shinto as window dressing for the state . . . my grandfather would never have let such words pass his lips. He was a samurai. He felt as a Japanese. He was a man of dignity."

"Dignity," her father repeated slowly. "What is that, anyway?"

"You see? He admits he doesn't know what dignity is," said her mother, turning to Saya, "but make fun of my grandfather, that he can . . . just listen to him when he says 'Himari' . . . he thinks he can look down his nose when he says 'Himari' . . . anyway, tell me"—she looked challengingly at her husband as she went on— "tell me whether a Guji who in his heart feels Japanese may even concern himself with Chinese stuff like *I-Ching?"*

Saya's father left the room without a word.

At the sound of his mother's raised voice Ryo had come to see what was going on. He was leaning against the doorpost. He was a quiet boy. He would often sit for hours in the fork of a big chestnut tree in the forest where he had built himself a platform of branches. He didn't make much effort in school. At home he never had to help because he was a boy.

He looked at his mother with uncomprehending but also indifferent eyes whenever she ran down their father. He showed no emotion. Saya sometimes thought that Ryo was stupid, but he was merely uninterested.

Saya wrapped a blanket round her mother to make sure her back wouldn't get cold. Somehow she felt repelled by her mother's constant reproach. Her father had said nothing bad. Why, then, did her mother reproach him so bitterly?

Ryo had gone away—whistling, as he always did when he was bored with listening. Probably he was already up there in his chestnut tree again.

Bo cowered silently in the corner, his face and his hunched-up position expressing forlornness. The sight of him gave Saya a shock.

"Bo's hungry," she said. "May I make supper?"

"Yes," replied her mother wearily. She had sat down at the empty dining table. She spoke of her continued failure to find a new maid in the city. It was true that a few girls had answered her advertisements in the newspaper and had even reported for work, but before they had properly understood which cloths were to be used for which kind of wiping they had stopped coming.

Saya glanced at the kitchen clock. The English lesson was due to begin in forty minutes. Even if she ran all the way down the steps and along the lanes in the silk weavers' quarter, she would have to leave in twenty minutes.

Bo had come into the kitchen and was watching Saya using a wooden spoon to turn over the strips of cabbage frying in oil.

"In a minute," she whispered to Bo.

Bo's eyes were large and hungry. With long chopsticks Saya picked out a soft piece of cabbage, blew on it, and put it into Bo's wide-open mouth.

"Times are bad now," said Saya's mother. "There's no sense of duty any more."

Actually it had long been her turn to invite her circle of friends to her home, but since she no longer had a maid she didn't know how to cope with all the work. Each ikebana she now arranged had to contain a branch, if possible a pine or cedar branch. Choosing the right branch out in the forest wasn't always easy. Cutting it with the gardening scissors required a lot of strength. She spent hours in front of her ikebana bowls, but a true December mood never materialized. Worrying about food and the impossibility of finding a reliable, conscientious maid prevented her from concentrating on the essence.

When her friends finally did come, they were full of praise for her ikebana composition. Apart from inferior tea, she could offer them nothing. Nevertheless, the afternoon with her friends left her with a pleasant feeling because they all had the same worries. None of them had raised the subject of Shinto and state. That suited her very well. They all talked about food and about how difficult it had become to find conscientious maids.

"They just don't want to work any more," one of them said.

"Of course, money isn't worth much."

"And there's too much talk about freedom. The Socialists—have you heard?—are demanding that working hours for domestics be regulated!"

"So are the Communists."

"It'll all end up in total lack of restraint."

"Nobody talks about how hard *we* worked when we were young."

"What's to become of Japan?"

"We must bring our children up properly."

All those who had children nodded with troubled expressions. Their children were their prize possessions. In such chaotic times, to keep them firmly in hand was a task requiring much thought.

"Housework is wearing me down," said one of the friends. "I'm worried about finding enough time for my children."

"They've recently been bringing such odd ideas home from school. What are we to do?"

"It's all due to that freedom."

In the past one had always spoken about loyalty to the state and gratitude toward one's parents. Now the state had fallen apart. In the newspapers there was even talk of the Emperor being prosecuted as a war criminal. It was certainly a fact that a new constitution was being worked on in Tokyo. Probably words such as freedom and democracy would be written into it whereas the much more important loyalty to the state and gratitude toward one's parents would no longer be mentioned.

"My son told me he wanted to become independent of me now. Isn't that sweet?"

"How old is he?"

"Only fourteen."

Everyone was amused that a fourteen-year-old boy would say such a thing, but the laughter was uneasy. Many felt that their claim to ownership of their children was in jeopardy.

"We must bring them up properly."

"It is like the art of flower arranging," interposed Saya's mother. "One needs a lot of patience and love . . . to be unselfish . . . for example, I am sending my daughter every evening to the English class . . . of course that's costing me a lot of inconvenience and money . . . but what will a loving mother not do for her child . . . ?"

They all nodded and glanced swiftly at her with a look

in which an element of envy combined with an element of doubt.

"I wonder why Mrs. Takano didn't come today?" asked Saya's mother as she refilled the tea bowls.

"Oh, Mrs. Takano . . . she's having problems with her husband."

"Really?"

"She recently found out that he's keeping a concubine."

"But where?"

"In the Pontocho quarter, of course. Obviously he can't afford a genuine Gion geisha."

Saya's mother shook her head in disapproval. "Dreadful, these men."

"Oh well, why waste tears? Sooner or later they all start doing it."

"We can be glad if our children are on our side," said the friend who had explained why Mrs. Takano hadn't come. "When you get right down to it, our children are the only ones we can rely on."

"True enough," said Saya's mother, and all those who had children agreed. Only the staff surgeon's wife, who was childless, sat silently at the table, sipping at her tea bowl.

 13

MANY PEOPLE CAME TO SEE SAYA'S FATHER. SOMETIMES SO many were gathered outside that some had to stand on the court in front of the house, waiting in the December sunshine for a chance to speak to him. But occasionally there was a lull, and then Saya would stick her head through the slightly open sliding door that led from the corridor into her father's study.

Am I disturbing you? her eyes would ask.

Invariably her father would be sitting in his simple white priest's robe at the long, narrow table that was his desk. Lying open in front of him would be one of his books on the *I-Ching,* and a sheet of paper on which he would be writing.

He would always look up and tell her to come in. She would quietly sit down on the floor cushion that lay on the other side of his desk on the tatami mats. In this way she could see his bookshelves, and look out onto the graveled forecourt through the narrow pane of glass in the shoji.

From time to time her father would hold his hands

over the charcoal that glowed in the blue-and-white porcelain hibachi and gave off a delicate, almost spicy odor
of smoke. A shallow wooden box beside the hibachi held
a supply of black pieces of charcoal and a pair of metal
tongs. Her father added a fresh piece to the glowing
charcoal on the bed of ashes in the hibachi. As he
touched the charcoal, the loose layer of ash dropped off
the pieces, and for a short while they shone strawberry-
red.

Saya loved to sit with her father, and he didn't mind
her being there. On the contrary, he seemed to be glad,
although he never expressed this in so many words. But
from his smile Saya could tell that he didn't feel her
presence to be a nuisance. So she sat quite still on the flat
cushion in front of his desk, the cushion on which hundreds of visitors had sat. She knew she had only to wait.
At some point or other, her father would wipe his pen on
the old, ink-stained rag and look at her with those deep-
set eyes that were always serious but never disapproving.
That was the signal that she might speak.

Ever since Saya had discovered an old Bible on his
bookshelf with many passages marked in red and blue
and with penciled notes in the margins, she had seized
every opportunity to question her father. By now she
had heard so much during the Christian Sunday services
and read so many of the words of Jesus that she very
much wanted to know what her father thought.

"I told the pastor that you own a Bible too."

"Hm," went her father.

"I told him that you'd already been reading it a lot.
Was that wrong of me?"

"Not wrong, but he may have been surprised."

Saya nodded and said, "He looked pleased with himself and smiled. I didn't like his smile one bit. He told

me, 'Your father needs the Bible, doesn't he? Shinto isn't enough for him.' "

"No religion is enough to answer all the questions of mankind. In that sense he is right to say that I need the Bible."

Her father stood up and, from the same section of his bookshelves where Saya had discovered the Bible, picked out two other heavy books and showed them to her. "Look, this one is the Koran, the sacred book of Islam, and this is the Talmud, the book of laws for the Jews, and that whole row of books up there, those are the Buddhist sutras and everything of Lao-tse's that has come down to us." He pointed upward.

"I must tell the pastor about that!" Saya cried, jumping up. "Then when we talk about you he won't smile so pityingly any more."

"His smile doesn't bother me, but ask him whether he owns the Talmud and the Koran and whether he has read them, and perhaps the writings of Confucius and Lao-tse too."

"I'll do that!" Saya said, full of eagerness. Ever since that business with Reiko she had been disappointed in the pastor. She had come down to earth. Until then, she had let herself be carried away by the beautiful music being played in the Christian church and by the colorful stories told by the pastor. She had begun to love the person of Jesus. She had absorbed his message of love. What she particularly liked was that even as a boy he had questioned the Pharisees in the temple, and that, when he was dissatisfied with their answers, he had not kept this to himself but had raised his voice in protest. Jesus, as Saya imagined him, must have been an intelligent, fearless boy. It was a pity that, apart from that scene with the Pharisees, the Bible contained so little about his youth.

The fact that Reiko of all people was to play the part of the mother of Jesus had made Saya lose almost all desire to participate in the Christmas play.

"What's the matter?" Mr. Everett had asked her. Saya was unwilling to speak out since he didn't know Reiko. He didn't know how mean Reiko was—and anyway, all the blame lay with the pastor, not with Mr. Everett.

"Are you upset that you're not going to be Mary?" Mr. Everett had surprised her by asking.

At that Saya could no longer hide her disappointment. "Yes," she admitted shamefacedly.

"I know what"—Mr. Everett had looked at her for a moment—"I know what . . . I have an idea. . . ."

Saya was thrilled. For Mr. Everett to trust her to recite the Christmas story on the stage—in English—was a spur to her ambition and her passion for work.

Mr. Everett had copied out the text on his typewriter and spent a whole Sunday afternoon rehearsing pronunciation and emphasis with Saya, explaining all the words that were new to her. Soon she knew the entire text by heart.

"You've underlined in red and blue all over the place," Saya said as she opened first the Talmud and then the Koran, "not only in the Bible."

"The Bible is a good book, but not the only one."

"The pastor says the Bible contains everything. He called it the Book of Books."

Her father replaced the Talmud and the Koran on their shelf. It was his habit never to leave anything lying on his desk that he did not immediately need. He never felt at ease with disorder.

"Isn't that true?" asked Saya since her father didn't reply at once.

"Each person would like whatever he believes to be the absolute truth. But truth is so vast and has so many faces—it cannot be fitted into a single book."

Saya's father spoke to her not as to a child but as to someone who was already grown-up. That flattered Saya's childish pride, and she tried very hard to look as if she understood. She wanted to justify her father's confidence in her. She wanted to prove that she was capable of carrying on a conversation with him. She considered what she might ask him next and wanted it to sound a bit grown-up. "What do you think about Jesus anyway? Do you approve of him?"

"He was a magnificent human being."

"The pastor says he was the son of God and at the same time a real human being. So he is God and man. But he was born of Mary. Mary is a woman, a real woman. The Christian God doesn't have a goddess, he has a human wife. It is all very complicated."

Her father smiled at the fervor with which Saya told him this. She leaned forward on her cushion, so excited that she could hardly sit still, her eyes shining because the story of Jesus seemed to her like a glorious, colorful fairy tale.

"Mary gave birth to Jesus," Saya went on. "Jesus is the son of God, but Mary's husband is called Joseph. He just stands around and doesn't do anything, really."

Her father said that all ancient religions developed a confusing, diverse image of their deities. It wasn't only in Japanese Shinto that the mythological images were so colorful and full of surprising figures. The same was true of the early Hindus, the Greeks, and the ancient peoples of the Near East.

"Now I remember," Saya broke in. "Joseph was a carpenter—that was his trade."

"I see you haven't missed much!" Her father smiled.

"But the Christians have only one God," Saya said thoughtfully, "one all-powerful, all-knowing God. He is tall and has a flowing beard. The Christian God knows everything that people think and do. He had a son by Mary, an only son. And then there's also the Holy Ghost. I've no idea what *it* looks like. Even the pastor says he doesn't know what the Holy Ghost looks like."

"Is that so important?" asked her father.

"No, but the Christians have angels too, lots of angels. They look like Bodhisattvas, except that they also have wings. One of the angels came to Mary and told her she was pregnant. Mary was very surprised."

Now and again an affectionate, slightly amused smile flitted across her father's face. He looked at Saya with his calm, clear eyes.

"What makes the Bible important," he said, "is the words of Jesus. They represent a great challenge."

"Jesus spoke a lot about love," said Saya.

Her father looked through the narrow pane of glass in the shoji, out onto the forecourt where the afternoon sun drew a sharp line separating the dark, shadowy area of the pine trees from the bright white of the gravel surface.

" 'I am the way, the truth, and the life,' " he slowly quoted from the Bible. "With those words Jesus excludes every other possibility and claims for himself the sole right to be the way, the truth, and the life. I have always regretted that he said that."

"What else should he have said?"

"He could have said, 'I am a way, a truth, and a life.' That would have been more truthful and more human."

"But Jesus is the son of God," Saya protested. "He knows better."

"The Christians call him the son of God, for the Moslems he is a prophet, for the Jews he is an ordinary human being. So what is he really?"

"The pastor says there can be no doubt whatever that Jesus is God's own son. All one has to do is believe firmly in that."

"Because the Bible says so." Her father smiled back.

"How come Shinto doesn't have any sacred books?" Saya said impulsively as she scanned her father's bookshelves. "All other religions seem to have their scriptures."

"The written word gives rise to quarreling," said her father. "Written words can easily be turned into instruments of murder if exclusivity is ascribed to them. He who really loves men offers them the comfort not of sacred words but only of sacred feelings."

"But Jesus did love men!" said Saya. "Surely that's true?"

"Doubtless he meant well," her father reassured her. "But he was a man from the desert. His people lived at the edge of the desert. I'm sure you've learned in school that Palestine lies within the great desert belt of the earth. This fact has formed the thinking of the people who live there. Because they felt nature to be so hostile, they laid down clear, unambiguous rules for everything affecting their lives. At the edge of the desert the best way to survive is to stand firmly together—both in faith and in deed."

Her father pointed out the strange fact that the idea of a single, all-powerful, personified God arose among those very people who were exposed to the hard, relentless life at the edge of the desert.

"I have never seen the desert with my own eyes," said her father, "but I can well imagine that in the narrow strip between life and death, between survival and dying of thirst, there is little room for tolerance. In those early times when such dogmatic religions arose, the foundation was laid for this 'either/or' thinking, a way of think-

ing that in the course of history has managed to assert
itself to such an extraordinary degree.''

Saya was all ears. She wished her father would go on
talking to her like that for a long time. It felt so good to
be with him and listening to him. It was a rare occasion
for her father to lose all sense of time while talking to
her. When Saya saw a woman walking across the graveled forecourt outside, she was afraid that the uninter-
rupted time with her father was at an end, but fortunately the woman went on up to the shrine.

In countries where the climate is mild, her father continued, where there is ample rainfall, where the sun is
welcomed, where it is green everywhere, where there are
many sources of nourishment, people have always
tended to see the divine in multiple forms. They envis-
aged many gods, helpful or destructive ones, good or
troublesome, benevolent or dangerous, but never a single, all-powerful, personified god ruling over all.

The first to bring them such a god, her father explained, were the Jews, followed by the Christians and
Moslems—Jehovah, God, or Allah, three variations of an
outsize notion of a god. With their claim to possession of
the one and only truth, the Christians and the Moslems
had tried to stifle all other concepts of the divine
throughout the world. Other gods being unacceptable to
them, they declared them to be false. They treated as
enemies those people who did not submit themselves to
their dogmatic notion of God.

"But Jesus did say, 'Love your enemies,'" Saya ob-
jected in some bewilderment.

"Yes, he did," said her father, "according to the Bible,
but the words 'He that is not with me is against me'—
weren't they also spoken by Jesus?"

Saya nodded.

"Very well then," her father went on. "How does one love one's enemies?"

Saya chewed her lower lip. She looked into her father's eyes and felt that he didn't mean to drive her into a corner with his question. His eyes held the challenge to go on thinking, to persevere, not to give up. Saya had no intention of giving up. She asked herself who her enemies might be. Reiko? Mrs. Nakarai? Some of those boys who tried to pounce on her in the playground and beat her up? She wasn't going to let them beat her up. The pastor said that as a Christian one must always turn the other cheek. Saya couldn't see that. But that was what Jesus was supposed to have commanded.

"I don't know," Saya said bleakly. "I don't know how one loves one's enemies."

"I don't know either," replied her father, who had been watching Saya's perplexity in quiet amusement. "I know only that there will always be enmity among men —envy, suspicion, hatred, just as there will always be friendship, love, and understanding. Those are the fluctuations of nature. It's good to know, however, that enmity can sometimes be transformed into friendship."

Saya had found her self-confidence again. She sat up straight and looked at her father with a mixture of admiration and childish pride. "The pastor said, Jesus is love, and one simply must believe in that."

"Not everyone finds it easy to believe in love."

"The pastor said that too," Saya agreed eagerly. "That's why such people must be converted."

Her father saw someone coming across the graveled forecourt. A tinge of regret showed in his face. He rubbed his hands together in the warm air rising from the glowing charcoal in the hibachi.

"Converted," he mused, "if necessary by force . . . millions of people, many millions, have died for that."

"But . . . ," said Saya, looking questioningly at her father. From outside came a stranger's voice. "Excuse me —may I come in?"

"Wait a minute please!" her father called back. Then he turned again to Saya.

"But . . . ," she said, "one doesn't die from being converted. Surely being converted is something beautiful."

"Not if one is converted by force," her father gravely replied. "The Christians have often used force. The trail of their conversion campaigns throughout history is a trail of blood. Many millions of human beings were killed in those campaigns. In the name of God."

"I don't believe that," Saya burst out. "Jesus brought only love, God's love, and said that all men are brothers. Sisters, too."

Her father stood up and took a big book out of the lowest bookshelf. When he opened it, Saya saw that it was an atlas containing many colored maps. Her father leafed through it for a while, then opened up a map covering two pages and turned the atlas round so that Saya could look at the map.

He showed her from where Christianity had spread, from Palestine to Rome, from there to Byzantium, to France and Spain, to Portugal, England, and the other European countries. With his thin hand he traced the areas which over the centuries had been converted to Christianity from Rome—the heart of Europe, England and Ireland, Eastern Europe, Scandinavia.

Pointing to the dates, he showed Saya how Christianity had then jumped across to America, first to Mexico and Peru, simultaneously to the Philippines and Africa, and how it had spread across all of North America and the rest of the world.

Saya followed his hand with interest as it moved

across the map of the world. "There are so many Christians," she said, impressed. "Is that bad?"

"Not bad"—her father smiled—"but all the peoples that are Christian today at one time possessed a different faith. Whether good or bad, their divinities were as different as the plants and animals in every country in the world, as diverse as the mountains and rivers, as variable as the wind. When Christianity arrived, it declared all other gods to be false gods with an exclusivity such as can only flourish at the edge of the desert."

Saya nodded to show she had understood. "But if it's true that there is only one all-powerful God," she said, "then he must be greater than all other gods."

"If he is that great," said her father, "people will come to him on their own. Then there is no need to force them."

He fell silent, and Saya sensed that she must neither say nor ask anything more now. When her father carefully closed the big atlas and leaned back to return it to its shelf, Saya jumped up to help him. In his playful way her father tapped the end of her nose with his finger. Then Saya slipped out of the room, quietly sliding the door shut behind her. She heard her father call out to his visitor, "Come in, please!"

"What have you been talking about with Father?" asked her mother. "You were with him for such a long time. Tell me about it."

But Saya told her nothing.

"I have to learn my part," she said and hid herself away in her bedroom with the English text that Mr. Everett had typed out for her. In order to keep warm, she pulled her quilt up over her shoulders and head.

"Long, long ago in a place called Nazareth . . ."

She pushed her tongue way out between her teeth to make the English *th* sound right.

After a little while, her mother came into Saya's bedroom bringing a hot-water bottle. She pushed it under Saya's knees and covered her legs. "I've already ironed your dress for this evening," she whispered.

"Thank you, Mother."

"I've also checked Bo's little sheep suit again, to make sure the white woolen threads will all stay in place. It would be most embarrassing if they were to start falling out on the stage."

"You're so kind," said Saya with faint qualms. She wanted her mother to go away, but her mother sat down on her heels beside her. "I think we should take along a present for Mr. Everett. You can never go wrong with that." Her mother put a lot of concern into her voice.

Saya pulled her quilt more tightly over her head.

"I've already wrapped up the present. Do you think I should wear the dark blue kimono with the snowflake pattern or the ebony-black one with the ice flowers? Both are suitable for this time of year, but I don't know what Christians wear when they go to church."

"It really doesn't matter."

"It does matter." Her mother's voice sounded hurt. "What are you thinking of? If I accompany you as your mother, it is very important which kimono I wear. People must see what kind of a mother you have."

"I have to practice my lines!" Saya shouted at her mother.

"How dare you speak to me like that!" her mother retorted.

"I have to practice my lines," Saya repeated in a somewhat milder tone, but her defiance and impatience still showed through.

"Aha!" said her mother. "You think it's all right to be

rude to me . . . each time you come back from being
with your father, you're rude to me. You'll be punished
all right, sometime or other . . . don't forget that I gave
birth to you, that you owe your life to me, that you must
be grateful to me for that . . . grateful all your life."

She turned and, with quick steps that scuffed across
the tatami mats, left the room.

Grateful . . . grateful . . . went round and round in
Saya's head, always harping on gratitude and love.

Love and gratitude.

With a shock she remembered that in church the pastor had said over and over again that men owed their life
to God. He said men must be grateful to God for that.
God was love. He who truly understood the love of God
could not fail to be grateful. But he who did not accept
the love of God would surely be punished sometime or
other. That was what the pastor said. Every Sunday.
Gratitude or punishment. Promises of love, and threats.

Just like Mother, Saya thought.

The pastor said that not to accept God's love was a sin.

Saya didn't know what sin was.

A person who commits a grave sin goes to hell.

The Buddhists also have a hell. There, people are tor-
tured who have acquired guilt during their lives. In that
hell there are horned minions who toss naked people
into the fire with their long three-pronged forks. The
pictures of hell that Saya had seen showed burning,
screaming people and grinning monsters.

She wondered whether according to the Christians
people would also have to burn in hell.

The Nazis had burned people. Saya had seen pictures
in the newspaper. The Nazis had shoved people into
great ovens and burned them.

Father had said that the Jews and the Christians both
believed in one all-powerful God.

Would that be the same God, then, or were they two different gods?

The pastor had once said that the God of the Jews was quite different from the God of the New Testament.

Yet in the case of Jesus, there could be no doubt that God was his father. But then that must have been the God of the Jews, thought Saya, for Jesus was a Jew, and besides, when he was born there was no such thing yet as a New Testament. So his father can only have been the Jewish God who conceived him with Mary. Mary was Jewish.

Saya wondered whether Mary had really been as beautiful as the pictures in the Christian church showed her to be.

What distinguished the Christian God from the Jewish God? If almighty Jehovah was the father of Jesus, there could be no difference between the God of the Jews and the God of the Christians.

Even so, the Nazis had burned the Jews.

It occurred to Saya that maybe she should stop going to the Christian church. Perhaps the Christians are dangerous people, she thought. But her father had said there was no reason she shouldn't continue to go to church. She should listen attentively and think things out for herself.

The Nazis weren't Christians, the pastor had claimed. Mr. Everett had said that many Jews had fled from the Nazis to America.

In Kobe there were also several thousand Jews who had fled from the German Nazis, although Germany and Japan had been allies in the war. Saya had seen pictures of the Jews who lived in Kobe throughout the war. They all looked like Americans. But the Nazis also looked like Americans.

Saya could make no sense of her thoughts.

Maybe the Jews had sinned and that was why they had been burned?

Saya didn't know what sin was. A person who sins goes to hell. In hell, people are burned. That was what the Buddhists said too. Maybe the Nazis were minions of hell.

But then who decides who goes to hell and who doesn't? Who—apart from God—knows which people have sinned? So is it God who sends people to hell? Did he also know that the Nazis were burning the Jews?

Why didn't Jesus save them?

Wasn't he a Jew too?

When he was alive, there were no Christians yet. People had first to be converted.

How does one go about converting people?

The pastor had said that every Christian who truly believes in Jesus must undertake to convert at least one unbeliever to Christianity every year. There were so many people in Japan, he had said, who had never heard anything about Jesus. One must go out to them and tell them about the love of God. Then they would ask to be baptized.

One a year.

God is watching, the pastor had said, and Jesus will be happy too.

Saya imagined that it must be wonderful to be a Jew because Jesus was a Jew. Jesus sits at the right hand of God on the heavenly throne and watches over all mankind. But the Nazis burned the Jews.

So what religion do the Nazis belong to?

In school Saya had learned that all of Europe and America was Christian and that everyone there was baptized right after he was born. Just like Reiko. Reiko was also a baptized Christian. Saya didn't like that at all.

She wondered whether the visitor was still with Father

and whether she should go and see him again. But she also knew that she couldn't go to see her father without her mother knowing it. Her mother was sure to be sitting in the dining room again. She was always watching. Her eyes missed nothing.

"Long, long ago in a place called Nazareth . . . ," Saya began again from the beginning. Actually she no longer needed to repeat her lines. She knew them quite well enough. She never suffered from stage fright, even when she stood in front of all the students and had to say something as their spokesman. She never lost her breath or felt her legs tremble. On the contrary, the more people there were, the more at ease Saya felt. She loved a large audience.

Saya looked at the places on the two typewritten sheets where in red and blue pencil she had marked emphases and pauses between sentences. Some of the sentences she had—like her father—underlined in red and blue with a ruler.

The church hall was full. It was well heated. From every lamp hung silver and gold paper stars and shiny baubles. On the stage, behind the closed curtain, the lights of the nativity scene were already burning. There was also a big Christmas tree hung with cotton wool and tinsel. Saya wondered whether fir trees grew in the desert.

The pastor was flushed with excitement. He rushed about on the stage, disappeared behind the backdrop, reemerged, looked through the peephole into the hall, and warned all the children not to make too much noise.

Bo and five other small children were supposed to be little sheep.

Bo came toddling over to Saya. A few wisps of rice straw from under the Christmas tree were already hang-

ing from the white woolen threads that his mother had
sewn by the hundred onto his white pajamas.

"I want to go washroom," he whispered to Saya. She
quickly told Mr. Everett not to start yet and was about to
hurry off to the washroom with Bo. At that moment
three of the other sheep-children decided they also had
to go, and they all ran after Saya and Bo. When they had
at last returned to their places on stage, the pastor wiped
the sweat from his forehead.

"You're on now," he whispered to Saya and pushed
her through the gap in the curtain.

The hall lay in darkness. Voices died away. Although
the bright spotlight dazzled Saya a bit, she immediately
saw Mi-chan, Yuri-chan, and the others of her clique all
sitting in the front row, where she had reserved places
for them.

"Long, long ago in a place called Nazareth. . . ."

Gradually Saya's eyes became accustomed to the dazzling beam of the spotlight. She found it lots of fun to
stand at the front edge of the stage, look down into the
hall, and stick her tongue way out between her teeth at
each *th*. At the very back of the hall she recognized Mr.
Everett. When she spoke the next sentence her eyes remained fixed on him. *"The stars were brightly shining. . . ."*

Mr. Everett raised his hand slightly, to indicate that he
was satisfied.

Then came the organ music. Just as she had been told,
Saya stepped a little to one side. The curtains parted.

Bo raised his head impatiently. As soon as the curtain
was open wide enough for him to see Saya, he shouted,
"Here I am! Here I am!"

Many of the audience laughed.

Saya caught sight of her mother. She saw her slim,
lovely face, and the thought passed through her mind

that she shouldn't have yelled at her earlier. Her mother looked so lonely in these alien surroundings.

Maybe it was a sin for me to have yelled at her, Saya thought, maybe yelling at people is a sin.

The organ music wiped out almost all thought, but even through the organ music Saya could hear her mother's weary, moaning voice saying that ingratitude would be punished. Saya didn't mean to be ungrateful. In fact she was very grateful—for the pretty dress that her mother had made specially for her appearance on the Christmas stage. She must have had to work very fast, for she hadn't had much time. In gratitude Saya had tidied up the kitchen and given the floors an extra good cleaning throughout the house.

Reiko was kneeling at the crib with a pious expression and folded hands. The boy playing the part of Joseph stood beside her and was also looking into the crib.

From her place at the side of the stage Saya, as soon as the organ music stopped, went on with her Christmas story.

The three wise men from the Orient arrived. Two of them were enveloped in flowing, colorful cloaks. One wore a turban with a big jewel on it. The second walked beneath a parasol held over him by a little boy with a blackened face. The third was wearing a loose white burnous and a golden circlet around his forehead.

Reiko was still kneeling with a pious expression and folded hands. Saya suddenly felt glad she didn't have to play that boring role, even though Reiko's ankle-length, hooded dress of pale blue velvet really looked very pretty.

After the performance, many Americans came up to Saya and spoke to her in terribly fast English.

Saya hardly understood a word but kept on saying, "Oh, thank you . . . Oh, *thank* you."

Mr. Everett was laughing.

As a little sheep Bo had only been allowed to sit quite still under the Christmas tree. Now he hopped about like a rabbit on the empty stage, loudly bleating baa . . . baa . . . baa. . . .

Standing beside her daughter, Saya's mother bowed to each person who spoke to them, inclining her head and smiling.

The beautiful white lady, the one whom she had seen on her first visit to the church, also came up to Saya. This time instead of the bright red dress she wore a dark gray one. She said, "You simply must come and see me."

Opening her big leather handbag, she took out a visiting card on which her address was printed in English and Japanese.

 14

NEW YEAR'S DAY WAS COLD AND SUNNY. A STRONG WIND
was blowing. That was good for the boys who were flying their kites, for which they made use of the broad,
open Hori-kawa firebreak. The big kites, which they had
built and painted themselves, floated high up in the air,
swaying in the gusts of wind or performing spiral capers.
When they hit a wind pocket, their long, multicolored
tail-ribbons would suddenly hang down limp, and almost at once the kites would begin to tumble. That was a
signal for all the boys to start shouting and try to run
against the wind so as to tighten their kite strings again.
Some of the strings would become entangled, and the
result would be a crash.

Many of the kites were painted with big faces, solemn
or comical, of mountain spirits or Kabuki actors. Others
looked like giant butterflies or long-tailed birds of paradise or flying fish. Each boy was intent on having his kite
fly the highest. Their fingers stiff with cold, they paid out
the thin, strong strings made of parachute silk wound

onto little wooden boards that they held in front of them.

"Mine is highest up in the wind!" some would shout.

"No, mine is . . . look at it!" others called out.

It was hard to judge the actual height. Only when Shinagawa, standing among the children with a thick woolen scarf around his neck and acting as a kind of referee, announced his opinion did the arguing subside for a few minutes. They all accepted it when Shinagawa said that the yellow bird of paradise had soared higher than the flying fish or the samurai face.

"Now yours has fallen down," the rivals of the owner of the bird of paradise would soon announce, looking inquiringly at Shinagawa to see whether he would not recognize *their* kites to be the highest.

"Every kite should rise very high at least once and take a sweeping look into the new year," said Shinagawa. "That brings good luck."

He had managed to rustle up a two-wheeled field kitchen from old army stocks and had pushed it to the edge of the Hori-kawa firebreak. The air had long since escaped from its rubber tires. Nakamura the gardener stoked the fire under the big caldron of thin gruel in which a few slices of white radish were floating.

All those who wanted some hot soup were welcome. Flourishing a wooden ladle, old Nakamura doled out the soup into tin mugs, which were also from army stocks. The mugs were piled up on the edge of the field kitchen. From time to time a gust of wind would rock the pile.

Shinagawa turned to face the sun and tucked his hands under his arms to warm them. The sky was so blue and bright that it made one's eyes water if one looked up too long at the kites. If it hadn't been for the cold wind one could have been outdoors without a coat.

"The wind is from the northwest, from Siberia," said

old Nakamura. The last of his sons was reported missing in Manchuria. Since the end of the war he had heard nothing from him and for a long time had feared that he was dead. Nevertheless, he was reluctant to consult the Guji about his son's fate, although his wife had urged him many times to do so. Finally one December evening —when he was sweeping up the autumn leaves on the forecourt outside the shrine—he had screwed up his courage and gone to see the Guji in his study.

Shinagawa patted old Nakamura on the shoulder. "I advised you often enough. You should have gone to see the Guji much sooner."

"That's what my stupid wife kept on telling me too." Nakamura stirred the gruel with his ladle.

"She's got more sense than you have," Shinagawa said, laughing, "and above all, more faith."

"It wasn't a matter of faith," said Nakamura. "I was simply afraid that my third son, too . . . surely that fear is natural enough, isn't it?"

"Yes, of course, we all know fear in one way or another," answered Shinagawa.

"And after all I had already lost the two older boys." Old Nakamura wiped his eyes with his sleeve. On seeing that Shinagawa had noticed his gesture, he quickly added by way of apology, "The sun is so dazzling, it makes my eyes smart."

"True," said Shinagawa, "the sky is especially bright today. Only kids can look up all the time without their eyes watering. We with our old eyes . . ." He squinted up at the kites swaying in the wind.

"Is mine flying highest now?" called three or four boys who were following his speculative gaze.

"That one there," Shinagawa decided after a thorough look around. He pointed to the silhouette of a bat kite.

"That's mine!" the owner cried out proudly. "Now I

want my mug of hot soup as a reward." He handed his
string to another boy and came over to Nakamura. "But
with a slice of radish, please."

"Supposing the Guji had had to tell me that my youngest boy wouldn't be returning either . . . then what?"

"Yes, then what?"

"After all, three sons for the fatherland that has lost
the war anyway."

Shinagawa patted old Nakamura's arm encouragingly.
"But your youngest *is* coming back. If the Guji has said
so, it's true. Even though it may take a long time."

"At cherry blossom time, the Guji told me. That's not
far off."

"So much the better," said Shinagawa. "Then you'll
have someone to help you again, and meanwhile I'll start
looking around for a wife for your youngest. I'm sure
we'll find a good wife for him."

Old Nakamura thanked Shinagawa. "Do you remember," he said, "how my three boys used to fly their kites?
From the bridge, that was, over by the Kamo River.
There was always an especially strong wind blowing
over there at New Year's."

"Yes, it was cold on the bridge." Shinagawa nodded.
"It's a fine thing to have children. Too bad my wife and I
. . ."

"Adopt some," advised Nakamura, "adopt some."

"My wife and I have already discussed that, and we've
also kept our ears open in case any of our relatives want
to give up a child. In Fukuoka—I had a cousin there, she
and her husband were both killed in an air raid, but their
kids are still there."

"Now that's a good idea," Nakamura observed. "Then
you'd know where the child came from, and after all—
Fukuoka isn't Hiroshima, is it?"

"No, no, one oughtn't to adopt a child from Hiroshima

or Nagasaki," agreed Shinagawa. "There's so much talk about things that make you wonder."

"But the newspapers—they never say a word about it."

"That's only because the Americans won't permit it. It's precisely that silence imposed from above that makes one wonder. Apparently those two big bombs have a long-term harmful effect. There's a curse on the people of Hiroshima and Nagasaki, if you ask me."

"Yes, so one hears—although outwardly they look quite healthy, they suddenly lie down and die."

"Eerie, the whole thing is quite eerie," said Shinagawa. "No one wants to have anything to do with them. Understandable, I suppose."

While they were talking, the soup had to be doled out.

"Yes," said Nakamura, "of course it is. What a piece of luck that your cousin lived in Fukuoka and not in Hiroshima or Nagasaki."

"That's what I think too." Shinagawa nodded as he unbuttoned his coat to soak up more of the sunshine. "My wife keeps nagging me to adopt those two kids as soon as possible. That'll brighten up the house and provide for our old age."

"How old are the children?"

"Fourteen and twelve . . . two boys."

"Ha!" Nakamura laughed. "I can already see our area warden Shinagawa and his two sons flying their kites next New Year's Day!"

Ryo was one of the boys who were flying their kites. His was a cuttlefish with eight long legs that fluttered in the wind. Saya had helped him cut out the eight legs, and their father had taken his fattest ink brush to paint on the black suction cups, which were clearly visible. The eye of the cuttlefish consisted of a piece of rice paper

dipped in red dye and pasted over a large round hole.
The sun coming through the thin red rice paper made it
shine brightly.

"Ryo's kite is flying well," said Shinagawa. "I
wouldn't be surprised if it was soon the highest."

Ryo grinned, somewhat embarrassed but obviously
enjoying the praise. He tugged at his string to increase
the slant of the kite against the wind so it would rise
higher. Then, while running a few steps backward with
his eyes turned up to the sky, he fell. Before he could
scramble to his feet, his string became entangled with
another one, and both kites tumbled to the ground. One
leg of Ryo's cuttlefish got torn off by a telephone wire.

"Never mind!" Saya called out to him as she and Mi-
chan were passing by on stilts. "It'll still fly even with
seven legs."

Mi-chan said, "Come on, let's have a bowl of soup."

When Ryo saw Saya hurrying on, he pouted sulkily.
He had expected her to jump down from her stilts and
hurry over to him to pick up his kite from the ground.

"Never mind," echoed Shinagawa, who was standing
close by. But Ryo was no longer listening. Furious at
Saya's failure to help him, he stamped on his kite and
grimly trampled it into the ground.

"You didn't have to do that," said old Nakamura.
Shinagawa paused in his ladling and also seemed about
to say something, but after a moment's thought he
merely said to Ryo, "Come and have a bowl of soup."

Obediently Ryo went over to him.

"D'you want to play shuttlecock with us?" Saya called
out to him.

"Oh, goody!" said Mi-chan, but Ryo was still fuming.

"That's a woman's game," he retorted. "I'm not playing."

"D'you want to have my stilts?"

"They're too low for me."

"I'll set them higher for you," said Saya, but Ryo had already turned away in a huff. Saya watched him flounce off. She felt an urge to call out something after him.

"Fathead" was on the tip of her tongue, but she quickly swallowed the word because it would have turned all the boys within hearing against her. A girl must never say anything like that to a boy, not even to her own brother. A girl must always be nice to all boys. A girl must be prepared to give in, to smile, to give way. A girl must always apologize. She must put up with boys' moods—that is the proper way for a girl to behave.

A girl must never show that she knows better. She must never laugh when boys make fools of themselves. She must never walk ahead through a door, never talk out of turn, never look cheeky.

All that was taken for granted—in school, on the way to and from school, and anywhere else where it was unavoidable for girls to come in contact with boys. Invariably public opinion was on the side of the boys.

"She made a rude face" was frequently the only explanation given by boys when they had once again beaten up a girl so badly that grown-ups had to intervene. Such an explanation was enough for the victim to appear in everyone's eyes—even those of the grown-ups—as the troublemaker. Although the grown-ups didn't say that any boy had the right to beat up any girl who made a rude face at him, it actually amounted to the same thing.

"Why don't you behave more like a girl?" the grown-ups always said. "Then the boys will leave you alone. A girl who gets beaten is never quite blameless."

Usually the boys picked on girls who were good students. They're cheeky, the boys said, we don't like their noses. They held their fists under the noses of such girls.

"Well?" they would say. "How about it?" Then the

girls would have instantly to stammer out a thousand apologies, admit they'd made a rude face, promise not to do it again. The safest thing was to burst into tears right away. Then the boys would feel they had won.

Normally the boys weren't violent. It was probably quite rare for them to start out with the intention of beating up a girl. They were merely annoyed, felt insulted by a girl's thoughtless remark or gesture, so they wouldn't leave her in peace until they had taught her a lesson, or until the girl had promised not to do it again.

Ryo was no different from the other boys. At home he suffered from the fact that he couldn't keep up with Saya, although he was a boy and she was only a girl. Sometimes, without warning, he would hit out at her. Only the slight turning down of the corners of his mouth betrayed that his pent-up sense of grievance was so strong that there was no other way to get rid of it.

"Thanks a lot for the soup!" Saya called out to old Nakamura, then mounted her bamboo stilts again. Side by side with Mi-chan, she stalked back into the lanes where many other children were also parading around on their New Year's stilts. The boys had set their pegs very high and made fun of the girls, who were more cautious and preferred to stay closer to the ground. "Just like girls!" they laughed as they tried to push them over.

"Should we put our pegs a bit higher too?" asked Mi-chan.

"I'd rather not," said Saya. In spite of her woolen gloves and the hot soup, her fingers were stiff with cold. "I'm getting off now."

Next they watched Mrs. Shinagawa playing shuttlecock with her neighbors. Tama-chan was playing too. The black wooden balls with their five colored feathers flew high up into the air and, twisting and turning, came down again but quite slowly, so one could see the play of colors in the sunshine. The wind was so strong that the women often had to run after the shuttlecocks. They would miss them and as a penalty a black line or circle would be drawn on their faces with charcoal.

Saya and Mi-chan quickly asked for a piece of charcoal and vied with each other in blackening Mrs. Shinagawa's and Tama-chan's faces. The more they laughed, the more they missed their shuttlecocks. Soon there was no more room for new black lines.

"Now I'm as black as a charcoal burner who's just cleaned out his kiln!" twittered Mrs. Shinagawa.

When Saya and Mi-chan played shuttlecock too, it was their faces that got blackened. Mi-chan was given cat's whiskers, Saya black spectacles and a clown's mouth.

"I must show this to Bo!" Saya said suddenly and ran off toward home.

"I'm coming with you!" Mi-chan called out as she hurried after her. Saya didn't know how to tell Mi-chan that it wasn't a good idea for her to come up with her to the house. Her mother didn't like Saya bringing anyone home. Saya's friends were not to her taste.

"Are there no better girls in your class?" she would ask. Saya always replied that none of the girls in her clique was a bad student and that she loved them all as her friends.

"Don't be cheeky," her mother would snap back at her. "When are you going to understand that the daughter of a pawnbroker is not suitable company for you?"

Halfway up the steps Saya stopped. "Mi-chan," she said, "please don't come any farther."

"Why ever not? It's New Year's Day today."

"I know, but I still have a few things to do for my mother," Saya quickly lied. She saw disappointment

spread over Mi-chan's jolly little bewhiskered face. She
tried to smile, and Saya smiled too.

"See you tomorrow, then," she said.

"See you tomorrow."

After Mi-chan had disappeared around the bend in the
stairway, Saya sat down on the cold stone steps and cried
a little. She couldn't understand why her mother kept
finding fault with her friends. Because Mi-chan was only
the pawnbroker's daughter, her mother said she wasn't
good enough. She had been against Yuri-chan from the
very beginning. "A half-Korean girl like that," she
would say.

Just like Mrs. Nakarai, Saya suddenly thought, and
was shocked at the idea, for of all the teachers she had
had so far Mrs. Nakarai was the one she liked least.
Something in Saya rebelled against equating her mother
with Mrs. Nakarai, but the more she tried to get rid of
the nagging thought the more it tunneled its way into
her. Like a woodworm ticking away at night in a beam
and keeping one awake.

Mrs. Nakarai, too, had nothing but flattery for the
daughter of Mr. Iida, the magistrate, for the daughter of
Mr. Yamada, the branch bank manager, for the daughter
of the owner of the biggest textile business on Kita-oji.
. . . Lately she had also been making a particular pet of
Reiko, and would emphasize in class that Reiko's father
was an important Christian and had very good connections with the Americans.

Saya covered her ears, for she seemed to be hearing
Mrs. Nakarai's gentle voice, as well as her mother's
somewhat husky one, advising her to cultivate her
friendship with Hana-chan, the daughter of the clinic
director.

"At least *one* girl among your friends with whom you

can afford to be seen," she heard her mother say. "At least *one* girl from a good family. Now *that's* someone you should invite! Such an association will be much more profitable—you must also think of the future. . . ."

Saya was as fond of Hana-chan as a friend as she was of all the others in her clique—not because her father was the director of the clinic but because Hana-chan was good fun, could sing nicely, and was loyal—all reasons that to her mother meant nothing.

When Saya looked at her hands, she noticed that they were smeared with black from charcoal and tears. In wiping away her tears she had ruined the comical black design on her face that she had wanted to show Bo. Now Bo wouldn't be able to laugh at the black spectacles drawn around her eyes.

Sadly she got to her feet and walked on up the steps. But before she reached the top she was laughing again, for she didn't want anyone to see she had been sad. She turned her face to the wind and laughed out loud.

The air was crystal clear. The eastern hills rising on the other side of the valley, beyond the city, seemed to have moved much closer. They had turned a dull, wintry green with tinges of brown and iron gray where the rocks were bare.

Through the leafless branches Saya could see the houses in the silk weavers' quarter below.

She looked down into a few of the lanes, but they weren't the ones where the women were playing shuttlecock. A few figures were walking along there, and Saya thought one of them might be Mi-chan making her sad way home.

Down below she could see the kites being flown by the boys along the Hori-kawa firebreak, mere tiny dots of color. From up here they seemed not nearly as high in the air.

In the distance, far beyond the old Imperial Palace, beyond the Kamo River, almost at the foot of the eastern hills, was the district where, three days after Christmas, she had gone to see the white woman who had given her the visiting card.

Saya was proud that, as a big sister, she had taken Bo on the streetcar all by herself, hugging to her chest the bulky present that her mother had wrapped. Bo had hung on to the bottom of her jacket, trotting half beside her, half behind her.

On the streetcar, which was very full, Saya managed to find a narrow space for Bo to sit. When the conductor came she had to put the parcel on Bo's lap in order to get out her purse.

The conductor had asked them where they were going.

"To Mrs. Graham's," Saya said confidently. "My little brother and I have been invited. He's already three years old."

Bo hid behind the parcel and squinted with one eye round the edge. "No one can see me," he crowed happily and ducked his head back again.

"*I* can see you!" said the conductor and ruffled Bo's hair.

Perhaps Bo will still laugh when he sees my clown face with all the black smudges, Saya thought. Perhaps I look even funnier to him now.

She turned round and ran up the last few steps to the house.

15

EARLY IN THE NEW YEAR, SNOW FELL. THE SUPPLY OF FOOD
went from bad to worse. Hungry and cold, people hud-
dled even closer together. Sometimes Saya slept under
the same quilt with Bo, to keep warm.

At school, which was not heated, the children's hands
became stiff with cold. The teachers came to class all
muffled up and kept warm by walking up and down.
Several times during each lesson they made the boys and
girls do exercises between the rows of benches. Everyone
enjoyed that.

The windowpanes, especially the broken ones, had
long since been pasted over with cardboard and newspaper, but the cold penetrated just the same. Some of the
children had half-frozen hands, with open chilblains between their fingers.

The only really well-heated room in the school was
the one in which the school doctor examined the children. Because every day there were so many waiting to
see him, they had to stand in line half undressed. Almost
all of them had darned underpants. The girls felt

ashamed when they had unpatched holes in their pant-
ies. Almost every day the school doctor sent some children home and barred them from further attendance at
school because he had found them to be suffering from
open tuberculosis. Then, with the doctor's certificate, the
parents would be issued special food ration cards, but in
the food shops they were often told that there was nothing to buy.

Families with children were issued extra ration cards
for shoes. With the snow that had fallen, this was particularly important. Of course, the shoes they could buy
were only running shoes with rubber soles. When the
snow melted, Saya's feet always got wet immediately.

On the black market there was plenty of rice, fish,
meat, and the best soy sauce. There were shoes too, real
leather ones, and cigarettes, sake, and genuine American
whiskey. Women could buy rayon blouses, sheer stockings, lipsticks, and scented soap. One had to have good
connections, or a lot of money, preferably both.

It was said that the Koreans controlled the black market. They knew where to obtain articles that were in
demand and fetched good prices. They also had contacts
with the Americans, since the Koreans were regarded as
a liberated people. The Americans claimed to have liberated Korea from Japanese militarism and imperialism. So
it was in line with the official policy of the American
military authorities to facilitate a new start for the ap-
proximately two and a half million Koreans living in Japan at the end of the war.

There was no denying that, on the streets where the
black market flourished, a lot of Korean was to be heard.
Usually the merchandise was quite openly displayed, for
the Japanese police took no action against Korean black
marketeers. That may have been why the black market

was controlled by Koreans. Many Koreans were armed.
That was another good reason.

Yuri-chan's father stayed out of the black market. He
was a baker and was allowed to bake for the Americans.
For this he was supplied with good flour, sugar, even
vanilla powder and chocolate icing. Every day Yuri-chan
brought two doughnuts to school and gave one to Saya.
Saya would break the ring in two, eat one half, and take
the other home for Bo.

Mi-chan often brought along a slice of white toast
bread for Saya, the kind Saya had had at Mrs. Graham's,
with a slice of ham. When she chewed the ham, Saya
would close her eyes to concentrate fully on the flavor.
Unconsciously she was imitating her father, who almost
always, when he was eating, closed his eyes and chewed
slowly, almost reverently.

Saya felt more and more drawn to her father. Her
mother seemed to sense this and did everything to hold
on to her. She unpicked another old kimono of a bright
color no longer suitable for her age and made it into a
dress for Saya.

"With every stitch I've sewn my motherly love into
it," she said as Saya tried it on. "You do look nice in it.
What a pity you have a father who has no sense of
beauty."

Her mother's remark almost took away Saya's pleasure
in the new dress, but when she saw herself in the mirror
she was quite overwhelmed. The full skirt fell in wide
folds.

"Turn around," said her mother.

With her hands on her hips, Saya turned in a swift
circle, making the skirt fly up as high as that of the
American girl she had met at Mrs. Graham's. The girl
was called Linda and wore a pink dress. She was so free
and easy in her behavior that Saya was really worried

that Donald, the boy who was also there, would hit her. But Donald, who was thirteen, didn't hit Linda, although she ran through the door ahead of him, snatched a piece of cake from his plate, and even beat him at Monopoly. Saya would never have dared win if a Japanese boy had been present. That would surely have led to trouble.

But Donald didn't look at all put out, nor did he seem to have to make any special effort to endure Linda's cheek. He didn't seem to find her cheeky at all, and obviously Linda found nothing wrong with that. Saya was flabbergasted that a girl could behave so freely toward a boy.

Later, when she was back at home, she told her father, "Someday I want to go to America. The boys are much nicer there than here."

Saya spun around once more in a circle to make her new bell skirt fly up. She saw that her mother was smiling. She would go on spinning until she collapsed with giddiness if that would keep the smile on her mother's face.

"Do you like your new dress?" asked her mother.

"It's the loveliest you've ever made for me."

"I made it exactly the way you described the one worn by the American girl."

"I know. You're so clever with your hands."

Her mother looked at her hands. "So much work," she said, as if to herself.

"You need some warm stockings," she added. From a drawer she pulled out a pair of thick woolen stockings. "I knitted these from the yarn of an old moth-eaten cardigan. You can't begin to imagine how much work it was to knot all those ends of wool and knit the stockings for you . . . just so you can have warm feet."

These days her father often seemed quite remote. There were times when he was more or less inaccessible.

He spent many hours in his study, even when no one came to ask him anything. He read through his notes, consulted his *I-Ching* books, calculated, compared matrix tables, and from time to time penciled remarks in the margins of the closely printed pages.

He didn't seem to feel the cold. Sometimes the glowing charcoal fire would go out, but her father would go on sitting there, with only a black, lightweight outer kimono over his white cotton kimono, the simplest of priestly robes.

After all state support had been cut off, the attendants employed by the shrine had been forced to change their vocation. One had returned to his native town, where his family owned a large tea plantation. For two of them, her father had been able to find jobs as teachers of Japanese and history at city high schools. The fourth was trying to return to university.

The only one left was white-haired old Tanaka, who had been at the shrine for years and knew every nook and cranny. He looked after the necessary administrative work to relieve Saya's father.

After every new snowfall, old Nakamura turned up to sweep the steps leading to the shrine's forecourt. Sweeping the long flight was too much work for him alone, so Nakamura usually brought his wife or his daughter-in-law along. Sometimes Shinagawa would help too, or send someone to help.

The Guji had grown thinner. His shoulders looked frail. As a result of so much sitting at his desk, they had become a little stooped. Often when he stood up, he stretched. He would stand in the doorway and lean his head way back, moving it from side to side until the tendons made a snapping sound over the joints. His head seemed almost too big for his thin, fragile neck. His eyes were very deep-set and often wore a look of complete remoteness, as if he was thinking of something that existed at a great distance in time and space.

He needed that remoteness in order to sustain his strange faculty—one that he didn't quite understand himself—that enabled him to see through the pattern of those fields of forces for which he had written his mathematical theory.

The Guji knew that, in addition to his faculty for pure deductive analysis, he also possessed the gift of recognizing correlations for which his theory provided no compelling linkages. When he placed himself in a state of total emptiness he was able, by means of his hexagrams, to find answers to questions the details of whose contents he did not even need to know.

He himself felt that, each time he set up his matrix of hexagrams, he need only apply his mathematical method of ordered linkages. Then the answer would come almost spontaneously. But he was also fully aware that somewhere in this process there was always a crucial moment at which, by his choice of the matrix elements, the answer was anticipated.

However, what took place within him at that particular moment, and why he invariably chose the right matrix elements with almost frightening accuracy, remained inexplicable even to him. He had given up thinking about it, sensing that any introspective probing for a plausible explanation would only be harmful to himself. It impaired his ability to concentrate, to attain that degree of inner emptiness that was the prerequisite for inward vision. So he no longer spent much time wondering why he possessed this gift. He accepted it as a fact.

The Guji never asked the name of anybody who came to see him. Names did not interest him. If someone did not volunteer his name or hand him a visiting card, he would not ask him.

From their accents he knew that many of his visitors came from beyond the city, some of them from far away.

He could tell from the questions that he was being consulted by doctors, senior civil servants, judges, and politicians. Artists came to him, owners of large or small businesses, as well as men occupying leading positions in industry. There were bankers as well as university professors, restaurant and hotel owners, proprietresses of tea houses, and many a glittering geisha, even the abbots from important Buddhist temples as well as Shinto priests from other shrines. One way or another, they had all heard of him. Often they arrived with initial skepticism. This skepticism quickly evaporated. Most of those who had come once returned again and again.

The Guji never allowed himself to become involved in a long discussion and would cut short any such attempt. He did not want people to tell him half their life story.

"I don't need to know that," he would say to anyone who seemed inclined to be long-winded. "I don't need your help to tell me the kind of person you are and what your life looks like."

At that they would fall silent before his clear, firm gaze. They bowed to his will.

"Your question?" he would resume. "In one sentence, please."

Somehow the atmosphere surrounding the Guji did not encourage visitors to consult him about trivialities. It was as if people felt that his time was precious, as if they knew they should not come to him without a compelling reason.

The questions people put to him concerned very personal affairs, problems directly related to themselves, to their families or their occupation.

Often it was a deep-seated fear or an unexpressed despair that led people to the Guji, anxiety about a child, about a wife, a husband, about parents or relatives—urgent questions, crucial to those affected.

The issue might well be a decision determining the course of someone's life. Often it was a matter of money, of success or rivalry in a career, and of finding out the best route to an aspired goal.

Many who had come more than once and had known the Guji for years talked to him as if to an intimate old friend who knew all their worries, who had seen their children grow up, had had a hand in their business success, and was familiar with the fortunes and misfortunes that had accompanied their lives.

There may have been some who, while still mounting the steps or crossing the forecourt, wondered how best to conduct themselves in order to make a good impression on the Guji. But as soon as such people stood before him, and the Guji, with a brief gesture, had waved them to a seat on the other side of his desk, their bolstered self-confidence would melt away. His presence reduced them to what they really were, in the good sense as well as the bad.

When the Guji looked at them with his calm, clear eyes, there was no room left for pretense. His calmness, his poise, the impossibility of impressing him, drew everyone under his spell.

Only his wife was opposed to him.

She would not accept him the way he was. She would not submit to his calm greatness. She rebelled against him because he would not share her own values. She wanted him to be like her grandfather in Himari, to whom she clung with increasing idolization the further her own youth receded into the past. Her image of her grandfather had long since undergone a transfiguration: It had turned into a monument.

Her husband's way of dressing displeased her. His way of talking did not impress her. She found his gaiety ridiculous. His material frugality was something for which she had no appreciation.

With grim self-discipline she played the role of the good wife in front of other people. She beamed as if she were very happy with her husband. She pretended that in spirit she was very close to him. She camouflaged her fury by hiding it behind the refined behavior she had so perfectly mastered. She adjusted flexibly to every situation. Outside the home, she smiled. In the presence of others, she invariably addressed her husband with a look of tender adoration.

All the harsher were the looks she threw his way when there was nobody to see them, when she could level accusations at him without the risk of betraying herself.

 16

THE EARLY MORNING LIGHT WAS STILL LEADEN GRAY WHEN
Saya and her father arrived at the railway station. It had
taken them over an hour to get there on the streetcar.
Now they were standing in the dense crowd pushing its
way toward the five or six open ticket windows. Saya
was carrying a rucksack, the red one with white patch
pockets that she had been given for school outings when
she had first entered school. Her father's rucksack was
the one from his student days when he had often gone
hiking in the Japanese Alps and carried his sleeping bag
with him.

The station hall was lit by only a few naked bulbs high
up in the ceiling. It smelled of dust, sweat, urine. Saya
clutched her father's sleeve. He was wearing his shabby
gray suit and underneath, as a protection against the chill
morning air, a knitted gray waistcoat. From time to time,
the throng of people in the hall surged in one direction,
carrying everyone along. Then it would stop and veer in
another direction.

Saya could see only a constantly shifting segment of

the high gray ceiling. Time after time a naked bulb would enter her field of vision, hurting her eyes. Close to her face she saw gray-green army cloth, wide leather belts, sagging rucksacks, and most of all strange hands. Dirt was embedded in the creases of the skin, and the nails had black edges.

To get through the barrier and onto the platform took another half hour. It was already daylight. Saya looked at the clock hanging over the platform; it said six forty-five. As the train drew in, men with coarse faces pummeled their way through to the front from behind, uttering threatening grunts. Women were screaming and imploring.

Saya's father managed to lift Saya into the train through a window. She landed on a wooden box. Her father was borne along with the crowd through the door as far as the center aisle, from where he could see Saya.

"Otosan!" Saya called out, reaching up both arms as she stood on the wooden box. "Otosan!"

Her father waved back.

People were standing so closely packed that most of them didn't need to hold on when the train rattled over switches and bad sections of the rails. Many of the men wore threadbare army coats. The women had hung their old, padded, splinter-proof jackets round their shoulders, for it was cold and drafty. Some of the train windows were smashed or couldn't be properly closed.

The window beside Saya was also gradually sliding farther down with the joggling of the train, letting in a cold blast of air. The two men occupying the window seats would yank it up, but they would hardly manage to sit down again when the window would start to slip down with a rattle of the train.

In the first tunnel, acrid smoke from the locomotive poured into the carriages, and in the darkness voices were to be heard cursing and shouting, "Shut those windows, can't you?"

Almost all the passengers were carrying rucksacks or carrier bags, which were mostly filled to capacity. Their owners had hung them on their chests and, for fear of knife-wielders, encircled them with both arms. Most likely they contained silk kimonos or valuable old scrolls that the owners were hoping to barter with the farmers for rice, eggs, or vegetables.

Most of the passengers stared unseeingly ahead. Heads swayed with the rhythm of the train. From her wooden box, Saya had a good view of almost everything. She studied the faces.

They were weary faces. When someone caught Saya's eye, a hesitant smile would appear that didn't stay for long. It would soon fade away in the exhausting back and forth of the swaying motion of the train.

Saya saw that she was the only child in the whole carriage. She could see only one boy, but he was already almost a man.

Saya was struck by how tall her father was, much taller than all those round him. He kept his eyes closed. His face didn't look tired, just relaxed. Saya could see him in profile. His forehead was very high. His head seemed large. The tendons in his neck stood out when his head swayed with the rhythm of the train. Somehow he seemed to sense that Saya was looking at him. He glanced up and smiled. She waved her hand.

Lying in the luggage net above her was a little man wearing laced ankle boots and puttees. He lay partly on, partly under some sacks and had pushed a wicker basket under his head. He looked down with a satisfied expression on the people crammed in below him. His army trousers were patched, and his bootlaces were knotted in several places.

"Hold on tight!" he called down to Saya as the window beside her suddenly slid all the way down. He had a high falsetto voice.

The train plunged into the next tunnel, and it seemed as if the roaring tunnel walls were trying to reach in through the open window. The air was nothing but smoke, and many people were coughing in the darkness. The two men in the window seats made a united effort to yank up the window again, and Saya had to lean well away from it to avoid being poked by their elbows. As soon as the window was closed, everything suddenly became quiet again, and the coughing and cursing could be heard more clearly.

"Like the antechamber to hell," said the man with the falsetto voice up in the luggage net. "May Buddha have mercy on us!" He loudly intoned the first line of the Nam Amida Butsu. Just then the tunnel came to an end, and Saya noticed that a woman seated on her right had joined in the recitation. Several other people were also silently moving their lips.

The next tunnel darkness wiped away the scene and swallowed up the voices. Again many were coughing. Saya also found it hard to breathe. When the train emerged into the light again, all the faces looked even grayer. A grimy film lay over everything, making eyes smart.

"So this is what the divine Japanese race has been reduced to," came the falsetto voice of the man in the luggage net—loud enough for everyone in the carriage to hear. "The rulers of Asia and the Pacific are revealing their sardine nature. That's all we are—dirty, hungry sardines!"

"Shut up!" someone shouted, but the little man with the falsetto voice stuck his wrinkled face over the edge of the luggage net. "Yes!" he shouted, even louder. "And

there are also some sea cucumbers among us, and some
carrion-eating moray eels, and a few sharks—may Buddha have mercy on us!"

"Shut up!" yelled a man very close to Saya, his face
contorted with rage.

The man in the luggage net started reciting his Nam
Amida Butsu again, in a monotonous, singsong voice,
but this time alone. No one joined in the sutra. Every
face was stony. At the next tunnel, when the walls
seemed to roar in again, his singsong abruptly broke off.
When the train emerged into daylight, the man's nose
was bleeding and his lips were bruised. The other man,
the one who had shouted "Shut up!" with an angry, contorted face, was now looking complacently out of the
window.

"Why, you're bleeding!" Saya said to the man in the
luggage net.

"Buddha isn't always merciful," he replied, trying to
smile, but his blood-smeared face turned his smile into a
grimace. He took a big towel from the wicker basket he
was propped against and pressed it to his nose and
mouth.

"After all, we're all Japanese," a stalwart voice resounded through the embarrassed silence. "We are proud
of our nation and always will be, no matter what kind of
a mess we're in right now."

The speaker had risen and was standing on his seat,
casting a challenging look round. His military haircut
was so short that his scalp showed through. No one
looked up at him in agreement. He eyed the crowd encouragingly. When his glance fell on the man with the
falsetto voice, he loudly declared, "We are Japanese. We
will always be Japanese. If we stand united, just stand
firmly united, we will overcome our present difficulties.
We will pull ourselves out of this mess."

A woman sitting beside him with a basket on her lap raised her face to him.

"My husband was killed in the war," she said, "and I have six children. Do you know of any good place where I can get some rice?"

The man with the military haircut climbed down from the bench, somewhat awkwardly so as to gain time. With one hand he wiped the place on the bench where he had been standing. Finally he sat down, ramrod straight, and said something to the woman beside him. Saya saw from her face that the answer wasn't a good one.

Later, as she was walking along the path through the winding valley, holding her father's hand, Saya asked, "If everybody had enough to eat, that would be nice, wouldn't it?"

The path wound along the slope, at the level of the first woods above the valley floor where terraced rice fields could be glimpsed through the trees. The bare soil was black. The leaves blown down by the autumn wind from the wooded slopes onto the fields had already rotted and darkened to the same color as the earth. The bulrushes growing beside the stream thrust up a few late brown spikes, but their leaves were already dry and bent. Their feathery white seeds were floating into the wind.

Saya's father walked steadily up the rising path.

"Yes, that would be nice," he said.

"Then people would stop quarreling and punching each other all the time. The man in the luggage net was really bleeding badly. Did you see him?"

"I heard his voice," her father replied, "when he was reciting the sutra."

"Someone punched him in the tunnel. All these things happen just because people are hungry."

Her father walked on silently, striding along the old familiar path. Saya had to make an effort to keep up with him. Holding his hand, she hopped along beside him, her empty red rucksack on her back. Her father's rucksack was empty too. He had unstrapped it and was carrying it in his hand, for the sun shone hot on his back.

"Even when people aren't hungry, they quarrel and punch each other," he said.

"But then they have no reason to—or do they?" asked Saya.

"Reasons can always be found," her father replied. "It's just that in times of hunger they show up more blatantly."

"But in the movie," said Saya, "Mr. Everett showed us a movie . . . everyone was happy and kind. Americans all have enough to eat, that's why they're always happy and kind to each other."

"I don't know America," said her father, "but I'm sure there are just as many people there as in Japan who quarrel, are envious, and even punch each other. Wherever people live together there is bound to be friction. That's unavoidable. Those at the top bear down on those at the bottom. Those at the bottom would like to get to the top. Among those on the same level are often the people who are the most envious. Wherever people live together there is envy, ruthlessness, stupidity, and arrogance, for which no religion or medicine can offer any cure."

"That's not true!" Saya protested, giving another little skip beside him. "All Americans are friendly and kind because they're Christians. The pastor assured us of that!"

Her father halted and looked at Saya with an indulgent smile.

"You're laughing at me," pouted Saya. "Don't laugh at me."

"It just seems to me that the pastor is overstating his case a bit, or that he doesn't know human nature. The Christians want the kingdom of God to spread over the earth. That is wonderful. But how? By everyone being kind and modest, renouncing their own wishes, thinking not of themselves but of others, never putting themselves first? In any society there are very few who can do that, and also always a few who do it without the need for any religious justification. No religion in the world has yet succeeded in keeping human nature in a permanent state of peace. On the contrary. Human beings are not peaceful—neither here, nor in America, nor anywhere else."

"But the pastor knows America," Saya retorted. "Before the war he spent a whole year there."

"Nevertheless," said her father, "human nature is much the same everywhere, and if there *is* any society in this world that outwardly displays only a good and noble face, only kindness and only helpfulness, it is merely a thin varnish."

"What's a varnish?" asked Saya.

"A layer of lacquer that you can scratch off."

As she walked beside her father up the gently rising path, Saya was thinking of all the Americans she had met so far: Mr. Everett, Mrs. Graham, Linda, Donald. All were peaceful. All were kind. All were helpful. All were Christians. So there *must* be some connection. Maybe the pastor was right after all when he said that the Americans were better human beings than the Japanese?

Because they know Jesus.

He who knows Jesus becomes a better person. But Reiko . . . ?

"But you know Jesus too!" Saya suddenly said to her father, almost stopping dead in her amazement. "You've read the Bible a lot. So you must surely be a better person."

"Who says I'm a better person?"

"The pastor . . . the pastor says that all those who read the Bible are better people."

"It is strange," her father said reflectively, "how some people presume to sort out others, to give them marks. Surely that should be left to higher beings, to God or the gods. All we human beings can do is remain in awe of those higher beings."

Her father had stopped. He looked along the path ahead of him, then down at Saya and smiled. Without a word he walked on, his shoulders, as always, slightly stooped. Saya gently patted his back.

"No round shoulders!" she said in the same voice her father used when sometimes he admonished her as she sat hunched over her homework and he patted her affectionately on the back. "No round shoulders!"

"You're right." Her father smiled, straightening up, but after a hundred yards he had already forgotten again.

She calculated how often her father must have walked this long path through the valley. For eight years, so he had told her, day after day, he had gone along this path from his home in the village at the end of the valley to the school in the city. Eight solid years, down in the morning, up in the evening, six days a week . . . eight solid years . . . that was eight times three hundred days . . . that was two thousand four hundred times down and two thousand four hundred times up. Saya had let go of her father's hand and dropped back a few steps. Her calculations finished, she ran to catch up with her father.

"You walked along this path at least four thousand eight hundred times when you were a boy," she proudly announced. "I've just worked it out!" She felt the warm pressure of her father's hand and fell into step with him again. She tried to imagine how the forest might have looked when her father had walked this path to school day after day, and how the maple forests on the slopes of the valley must have turned fiery red in the autumn.

"Are there cherry blossoms here too?" she asked.

"Not many," said her father, "but when they bloom in the spring it's a lovely sight."

He looked up at the wooded slopes with their many different shades of brown, the scattered green of the pine trees, the still darker green of the undergrowth of azalea bushes.

As they came through the bamboo forest, the wind rustled like water bubbling over pebbles in the leaves that interlaced into a shimmering roof overhead.

Saya remembered this bit of the path. In the heat of summer, when she had last walked along here with her father—in the second year of the war, when she had just turned seven—the bamboo forest had seemed strangely cool under the dense roof of its billion whispering leaves. It was as if the smooth bamboo trunks cooled down the air of the valley as it wafted through the forest.

Now, in winter, the bamboo leaves were a dull green, so that the blue of the sky, where it shone through, seemed even darker and more intense than out on the open path.

Her father slowed down. He, too, was looking into the bamboo forest. Here and there stood some dead shafts. Where the sunlight struck them, they shone like gold.

"Do you remember?" he asked her.

Saya nodded.

"Perhaps that's the origin of the old fairy tale that somewhere in the mountains there grows a bamboo that has one whole section of its shaft filled with gold. The brightness of the gold casts its radiance far afield. The people who find such a bamboo will—according to the fairy tale—live happily ever after."

"Because they will never have any more worries," said Saya, "and most of all they will never be hungry."

"You're hungry, aren't you?" said her father, putting his arm round her shoulders.

"Yes," she said in a small voice.

"Only another half hour," he encouraged her, "and we'll be there."

Last time, in summer, the path had seemed much shorter. On the valley floor the sky had been reflected in the flooded rice fields. In some of the fields, the green rice shoots had already been planted, in others the surface of the water was still smooth. There were many dragonflies in the air. When the path finally left the narrow end of the valley and crossed the highest point, a strange, rhythmic drumbeat had sounded from a distance.

Her father had walked on with springy steps as Saya skipped along full of curiosity and anticipation. The path led through the maple forest, but the dense undergrowth still obscured the view. Then suddenly the whole valley with its low-roofed farmhouses, its terraced rice fields and the wooded slopes of the surrounding mountains, lay spread before them.

Close by, in the first rice field, at the edge of the forest, Saya had seen a long row of women, bent over, planting rice. Behind them men with drums were wading in the water. One of them was playing a bamboo flute. Another would sing, and the women would answer in chorus. With every drumbeat they planted rice shoots in the flooded field.

The women as well as the men wore flat, broad-brimmed hats of rice straw, wider than their shoulders, and short cotton kimonos of various colors. Their long sleeves were tied back with bright red ribbons. Each time the women bent down, their yellow straw hats nodded at each other in the water. When the drummers threw their tasseled drumsticks high in the air, their reflections looked like darting, bright-hued carp.

The song the leader was singing in the strange rhythm, adapted to the movements of the rice planters, invoked the blessings of the rain and the sun. It sounded nostalgic and measured, as if from the distant past.

When her father raised his voice singing the same tune, the lead singer had looked up in surprise. He had beamed with delight and waved with both arms. The women, too, had stopped their work to come and greet her father. There had been no time for Saya to bow to each and every one.

On that last visit Saya had stayed three weeks in the village. One evening as she lay in bed under the white mosquito net, her grandmother had told her that this hidden valley had once served the Daimyo of Imamura as a final refuge. His castle down by the sea had been destroyed by fire. Most of his samurai had fallen in battle. Only he, his wife, his children, and twelve of his samurai—some of them with their families—had managed to escape. They knew that the enemy Daimyo would pursue them into every last corner in order to kill them.

"In those days," her grandmother had told her under the mosquito net, "the Ainus still lived here. They ruled over the forests and slept on bearskins in caves. They led our ancestors into this valley. Chestnuts grew here then and wild persimmons. Our ancestors found mugwort, cinnamon, chamomile, and ginseng. In the damp valley bottom they picked cranberries and edible mushrooms, ginger and lotus pods. In the meadows there were wild millet and barley."

Outside, that summer night, thousands of glowworms

had danced in the darkness. They had settled on the mosquito net, flashing their light signals. From every corner of the house and garden came the chirp of cicadas, and from some corner of the ceiling the soft, high call of the gekkos.

"Were there already glowworms here in the valley in those days?" Saya had asked. "And just as many gekkos as now?"

"I'm sure there were."

Her grandmother had also told Saya about her father's boyhood. He had ridden horses bareback. Wild raccoons had come to him and eaten out of his hand. He had known all the medicinal herbs in the valley and on the mountainsides better than anyone else. Whenever anyone fell sick in the village, he had been called in.

As she talked on, her grandmother's voice had grown softer and softer. Saya could still remember the song with which her grandmother had gently sung her to sleep.

Just as he had in that summer three years ago, her father now hastened his step as the path descended through the leafless maple forest to the valley below. Through the branches and the undergrowth Saya could make out the farmhouses huddling against the slope, and the big farm where her father had grown up. The massive, reed-thatched roof was the color of the wintry earth.

Someone was crossing the yard, a small figure dressed in black. Her father walked faster and grasped Saya's hand. Then he almost ran, with Saya skipping gaily along beside him.

 **17**

THROUGH TALKS ON THE RADIO AND ARTICLES IN THE NEWS-papers, the Americans let it be known that they regarded the Japanese Christians as the spiritual elite of the country. They said the Japanese would be better off without Shinto. Shinto was a threat to peace. The time was ripe for a new start.

No other religion, they said, could measure up to Christianity.

No other religion was as universal.

No other religion had such high ethical values.

Under no other religion were men as equal before God as under Christianity.

No God other than the Christian one truly loved men.

In no other religion were men so greatly imbued with justice and so just themselves.

No other religion required man to love his neighbor.

The Japanese were not forced to become Christians, yet a general feeling of uneasiness spread through the country. A certain pressure came from above, from the honorable victors. The Americans were admired for having won the war, but it was not clear what their victory had to do with Christianity. Nor did the people in the silk weavers' quarter understand why Shinto, as they knew it, was supposed to have fostered the war.

"That's the funniest thing I've read in a long time," said Shinagawa's neighbor Ito, who had just returned from the Philippines where he had spent six months in an American prisoner-of-war camp. He folded up the newspaper that contained the long article on the war-mongering nature of Shinto. It had been written by a university professor of philosophy.

"A queer bird," said Ito. "Maybe the Americans gave him ten cans of corned beef for it."

"Ah yes, everyone's hungry . . . one can understand that."

"If I were given ten cans of corned beef," twittered Mrs. Shinagawa, "I'd also persuade my husband to write an article like that."

She went around replenishing bowls of green tea or bringing more charcoal so that all the visitors to Shinagawa's house could warm their hands.

"A good idea." Ito laughed.

"Nonsense," protested Shinagawa. "I'm no good at writing."

"That's why we hardly ever have any corned beef," said Mrs. Shinagawa. "If it weren't for Tama-chan . . ."

All the neighbors in the lane were proud that Tama-chan was working for the Americans. She was now employed by an officer's family and came home only once a week. Tama-chan's father, the one-legged pawnbroker, distributed the food she brought home, according to what he called a fair system.

Shinagawa received at least something every week, on

two occasions even a can of corned beef, since as area warden he was the most respected person in the lane.

Mrs. Yasumi, who had long ago run out of silk for her weaving, also received something every week. Day in, day out, she did nothing but sit in her cramped little weaving room and speak with vacant eyes to her dead son, the kamikaze pilot. She never left her house any more and would certainly have starved to death if the neighbors hadn't regularly brought her some food.

All the others in the lane were also remembered, but not every week. Although Tama-chan always brought home two cloth bundles of leftovers, of course this wasn't enough for the whole lane. The pawnbroker kept strict account of the recipients and how much he had given them—not because of the return gifts he received just as regularly (a few pieces of charcoal, half a cake of laundry soap, a few new straps for getas, a little bottle of lamp oil), but for the sake of good neighborliness and because, as he said, nothing tasted good when the neighbors were starving.

On his single leg and with the aid of his long bamboo spear, whose sharp point he had long since sawed off, the pawnbroker hopped along the lane, the gifts of food dangling from his shoulder strap. Sometimes he sent Mi-chan and had her distribute the gifts of food. "That will bring a blessing to the child," he said, and everyone agreed.

"Is it true that the Americans walk around in their houses with their shoes on?" the pawnbroker was asked.

"Surely that would make the house dirty in no time!"

"I've been told there are machines that suck up the dirt and make a lot of noise," said the pawnbroker.

"Wouldn't it be much more sensible to take off one's shoes? Then one wouldn't carry any dirt into the house."

"The Americans are afraid their feet smell bad. That's why they keep on their leather shoes."

"But surely that must ruin the tatami mats?"

"My daughter told me that in American homes there are no tatami mats. They lay thick woven fabrics on the floor."

"Cotton?" asked a weaver.

"I don't know," said the pawnbroker. "Tama-chan claims it's wool."

"But that's so expensive!"

"The Americans are rich."

"Even so . . . wool on the floor . . ."

"The houses the Americans live in are always very hot."

"Yes, so I've heard, they heat their houses so much that the beams and wooden posts start to crack."

"Then they paste paper over everything and paint it."

"They paint everything anyway, even the tokonoma niches."

"With oil paint?"

"Yes, in bright colors."

"But that's terrible."

"They have no feeling for the beauty of natural wood," said one of the group who was a carpenter, "no feeling for a beautiful wood grain."

"The Americans think oil paint is beautiful."

"Maybe the Americans aren't so dumb," said someone. "If you cover wood with oil paint, you can use cheaper wood, even plywood. Then the color and grain of the wood don't matter."

"But then who wants to live surrounded by cheap wood?"

"Well, if it's been painted over . . ."

"All the same . . . ," Mrs. Shinagawa twittered, "it's certainly not my taste."

"If the honored Americans have different tastes from ours, we should respect that," said Shinagawa. They all shared his opinion.

Because so many of them were sitting in one room, and charcoal was glowing in all six hibachis, it had become quite warm. By this time, too, the sun was shining on the shoji, lighting them up. Shinagawa suggested opening the shoji on the sunny side.

"What can we do jointly to get out of the worst of our difficulties?" asked Shinagawa, this being the real reason why he had summoned all the neighbors from his district to his house.

No one had any answer, so Mrs. Shinagawa bridged the gap by refilling the tea bowls.

"Perhaps our carpenter can make some furniture for the Americans from cheap wood," someone suggested.

"That's a good idea," said Shinagawa, "but then he'd need some oil paint."

The carpenter nodded. "I do have some poor-quality wood, but I'd hate to use it to make furniture for the honored victors."

"Even if the wood is painted over?"

"Even then . . ."

"Just the same, it's worth a try."

"I'll think about it," said the carpenter.

Then the question of how they could get hold of some oil paint was debated.

"Maybe we can produce it ourselves," someone said.

"Yes, but how?"

The silk weavers who were present dismissed the idea of using silk dyes to produce paint. The dyes for silk fabrics were of much too low a strength; besides, they were far too expensive.

"But the Americans, so I've been told," said Mrs. Shinagawa in her swift, soft way of speaking, "love shiny silks. One could start weaving shiny silks for them, with dragons and other Chinese designs."

"A typical woman's brain wave," Shinagawa grunted with a disdainful look so as not to show that he was pleased with his wife's bright idea.

"Not so stupid at all," said old Nakamura, who had quickly grasped Shinagawa's true feelings.

The weavers were reluctant to agree because in their eyes shiny silk was not good silk.

"We'll ruin our reputation as silk weavers," they pointed out, but Shinagawa replied that a good reputation wasn't enough to fill their stomachs.

"Why don't we make dolls?" one of the women weavers suggested. "I've been told that the honored victors pay a good price for well-made dolls, in dollars, too."

The proposal met with unanimous and unqualified approval, for it turned out that in the manufacture of dolls a good division of labor would be possible. The weavers were to supply the silks. Other women were to sew the dolls' faces and hands. The basket maker was to shape the bodies by bending stiff wires. The carpenter was to supply the black-lacquered bases. The shoji maker promised to glue the miniature dolls' fans and umbrellas. The pawnbroker was given the job of finding out through Tama-chan how best to approach the honored victors so they could be shown the dolls as soon as they were ready.

When everything had been decided upon, a sense of satisfaction spread through the group.

"For all we know, this may turn into a regular industry," observed Nakamura.

"We should walk up to the shrine," said Shinagawa, "and pray for success."

"I still have a piece of American cheese," said the pawnbroker. "We could take that up with us."

"Ugh!" said one of the women weavers. "Milk gone rotten. . . ."

"No, cheese," the pawnbroker contradicted.

"One shouldn't offer anything to the gods that one wouldn't like to eat oneself."

"By now I like cheese just as much as . . ." The pawnbroker was searching for a suitable comparison.

". . . ants and grasshoppers!" Ito laughed.

"Shut up," said the pawnbroker, in some annoyance.

"Stop arguing, please," decided Shinagawa. "If the pawnbroker likes cheese, then cheese is a suitable gift for the gods."

"Who knows whether our gods haven't long since acquired a taste for cheese," twittered Mrs. Shinagawa, "in times of hunger like this?"

"Can anyone tell me," asked one of the weaver women, "do our gods also suffer from hunger—just like us?"

Nobody dared to give a straightforward answer, but the general opinion was that of course the gods were linked with men—for better or worse, that they shared the burden of human destiny, that, although they would never die of hunger, they still knew what hunger was, and therefore it was necessary to go periodically to the shrine and report to the gods in prayer on the state of one's own hunger, on one's own hopes and fears.

That was why those who lived in the silk weavers' quarter would so often walk up the hill to the shrine, where, silent or murmuring their prayers, they would stand for a few minutes before the altar. The quiet up there, the simplicity of the shrine, its lack of ornamentation, the sense of being cradled in nature, all had a soothing and reassuring effect.

"Yes," said Shinagawa in a loud voice, "we should go up to the shrine and pray for success."

"We still have a fine white radish at home, one from the black market," said Ito. "I'll take that along for the gods."

"But is it still fresh?" asked old Nakamura.

"Crisp to the core."

"I bet you've taken a bite of it already, haven't you?" Ito laughed, revealing his magnificent, close-set teeth.

"What splendid teeth," said a weaver woman.

"I rub them every morning with salt," Ito said proudly. "That keeps them white and healthy."

"Nonsense, they're simply the teeth of a thirty-year-old," said old Nakamura. "When you're sixty like me, all that splendor will be gone."

"When I was in North China," said another man who, like Ito, had just recently returned from a prisoner-of-war camp, "I saw many men of fifty, sixty, and even seventy who still had good teeth."

"Because the people there don't eat fish," twittered Mrs. Shinagawa.

"That's right, and because they chew hard stuff—raw carrots and barley bread."

"The Chinese eat pork."

"So do the Americans."

"Then we should try it too."

"Where can you find pork?"

"Tama-chan has already brought some home twice. The Americans call it 'ham.' "

"But that sounds so Chinese."

"Well, it's supposed to be hundred percent American."

"What fantastic people they are, these Americans . . . they have everything they need."

"And we have nothing."

"If we become Christians, maybe we'll be better off."

"I don't know," said Ito. "In the Philippines, in the prison camp, the Americans showed us movies of Germany. They're practically all Christians there, yet they're starving now."

"But those are the Nazis."

"The Americans say that religion is something political. That's why they want us all to become Christians."

"Nonsense," said Ito.

"But Christianity preaches brotherly love."

"Why is it, then, that the Germans, although they're Christians, were the first to start the war?"

"But that was the Nazis."

"Aren't the Nazis Christians?"

"One can't be quite sure of that."

"They are said to have killed Christian priests as well."

"Only a few—they were mainly after the Jews."

"Well then—the Jews were Germans, or weren't they?"

"One can't be quite sure of that either . . . in any case, the Jews weren't Christians."

"But isn't a Christian church open to everyone? After all, everyone's free to go in and out of our church on Kita-oji."

"I went there once."

"So did I."

"I've never been there."

"It's worth going. It's always nice and warm inside."

"The Guji's daughter, young Saya, also goes there regularly."

"She's already learned to speak English there," said the pawnbroker. "Mi-chan is always showing me how quickly that young Saya moves her lips in English without biting off her tongue."

"What about Tama-chan? She must have also learned English from the Americans by this time," someone asked the pawnbroker.

"Yes," he answered proudly. "The American family is very satisfied with her."

"It is really very commendable of the Guji to send his daughter to the Christian church," someone said.

"But then he's been to university. He sees the world differently from the way we do."

"But not only because he's been to university," Shinagawa interjected, raising his voice, "not only because he's been to university."

"Can anyone tell me the difference between a Christian and a Jew?"

No one knew the answer to that. Everyone looked at Ito because he had said that among the Americans he had met while he was a prisoner of war in the Philippines there had also been two Jews.

"But what is the difference between a German Jew who was just a Jew, a German Jew who was also a Christian, and a Jew who is an American?"

"They say there are also English, French, and Russian Jews."

"Well, of course, there are Buddhists in many countries too."

"Stop it!" shouted Mrs. Shinagawa, clapping her hands over her ears. "You're driving me crazy with all that complicated stuff. After all, we can go just as easily to a Buddhist temple as up to the Shinto shrine. Nobody cares."

"The Christians do care."

"But *I* don't care! If it would mean us all getting more to eat, we'd go to the Christian church too."

"The Christians do care. They make a great distinction."

"But surely religion must be a personal matter. There are times in life when you just simply want to stand before the shrine, and other times when you're drawn to a Buddhist temple."

"Or you simply have no religious needs at all."

"Yes, that can happen too."

"When you grow old, religious thoughts come back to you."

"That's only natural."

"Well, as far as I'm concerned," said Ito, "although I'm not old, I'm still going to take our white radish up the hill to the shrine. I believe in the gods because they brought me safely home from the war."

"I'm coming with you," said old Nakamura, who had sat there the whole time hardly saying a word. "The gods still have to bring our Saburo back to us."

His wife wiped her eyes. "It must be cold this time of year in Manchuria," she said softly.

"I'll say it is!" exclaimed the man who had returned from North China. "It's so cold there in winter that your nostrils freeze up."

"I'll go up to the shrine too," said Mrs. Nakamura, with anxious eyes from which she couldn't wipe away the tears quickly enough. "My poor Saburo—I do hope his nostrils don't freeze up."

"That was really the biggest mistake of all," said Ito, "that we Japanese should have latched onto the Germans in the war."

"That is no doubt true," Shinagawa agreed in his loud voice, raising his large hand in emphasis. "That is why the Americans say that those of our people who collaborated with the Germans are guilty of crimes against humanity."

"One shouldn't be in cahoots with a government like that," said Ito. "Our Emperor should have known that."

"Indeed he should!"

"Anyway it was a mistake to get involved in this war."

"Of course it was a mistake. There's simply no way of winning against the Americans."

"But not because they're Christians. . . ."

"Ha! Christianity has nothing whatever to do with that. The Americans simply have more brains, and they had more ammunition in their guns."

"And all those planes . . . Japan never had that many."

"And then those fearful flash bombs of Hiroshima and Nagasaki . . ."

"Yes, the Americans were simply superior to us."

"Perhaps it has something to do with that democracy the Americans have. We read and hear so much about it these days."

"Yes, perhaps democracy is important."

"Then we should also get ourselves a democracy."

Everyone looked at Shinagawa as if he had said something very clever. The faces expressed bewilderment.

"But how?" asked one of the weavers.

Shinagawa scratched himself pensively behind the ear and audibly sucked in the air between the gaps in his teeth.

"The Americans want to democratize us, don't they?" he finally said. "Now if we were to get ahead of them . . . that would be a good thing."

"Why would that be a good thing?"

"I don't know . . . it's just a feeling I have. I don't like reading in the paper every day that we should discard Shinto, that the Shinto gods are worthless, and that we should all become Christians."

Everyone felt that they shared Shinagawa's feeling but that they couldn't express it any better than he could.

"But isn't Christianity necessary to our democratization?" the carpenter joined in hesitantly. "That's what I heard on the radio," he added.

"Nonsense," said Ito.

"Religion is a private matter," twittered Mrs. Shinagawa.

"If we could forestall the Americans and democratize ourselves without Christianity," Shinagawa mused, "what a good thing that would be. . . ." He scratched himself again behind the ear and gave his wife a sidelong glance to see how she was responding to his words.

"It would be worth a try," said Ito. "Then we would take the wind out of the Christian sails of those Americans."

"What is democracy anyway?" asked Mrs. Shinagawa in her rapid, bubbling manner while she looked into the teapot to see how much water was left in it.

"Stupid woman," replied Shinagawa in a tone of rough tenderness. "Democracy is democracy."

"Yes, but . . ."

"Democracy is . . . well, it's . . . the way the Americans live . . . enough to eat . . . strong, rich, self-confident."

"And what has all that to do with Christianity?" persisted Mrs. Shinagawa.

"Maybe Christianity makes people self-confident, but the question is whether one can't become self-confident without Christianity."

Everyone nodded, much impressed. Mrs. Shinagawa went on twittering that she considered self-confidence to be a very personal attribute that was certainly not limited to Christians.

"That's precisely why I believe," agreed Shinagawa, "that we can democratize ourselves without Christianity."

"That begins with free elections!" someone called out.

"We women will also have a vote then," said a weaver woman.

"I know I'll always vote differently from my husband," Mrs. Shinagawa decided.

"You stupid woman," blustered her husband. "Do you think I'll tell you how I'm going to vote?"

"Do you imagine I wouldn't find out?"

Everyone laughed. As the mood relaxed, Ito spoke up, "Well, about that radish . . . we mustn't forget to take the radish up the hill."

"And the cheese too," said the pawnbroker.

Shinagawa gave the signal to start. Ito sent his wife home to get the radish and, joined by Shinagawa, the two old Nakamuras, the carpenter, and many others from the neighborhood, strode off toward the hill. Mrs. Shinagawa didn't want to go along because, she said, she first had to tidy up, but Shinagawa proclaimed in a loud voice, "Woman, you're coming with us."

 **18**

AT FIRST RYO'S ILLNESS LOOKED LIKE AN ORDINARY COLD. He had a temperature and couldn't go to school. He didn't want to eat anything, only drink. It obviously hurt him to swallow since he grimaced with pain each time he had to do so. The doctor diagnosed a moderately severe throat infection and recommended hot flour poultices followed by aspirin and a warm, dry cloth wrapped round his neck.

But Ryo's fever rose, and he became quite apathetic. His illness had begun a couple of weeks before the school spring vacation and persisted well into the last week. He missed all the written tests that had to be taken before the end of the school year.

When Ryo's fever continued to rise and the doctor found that he had acute pneumonia, the mother spent the whole day and night at his bedside. Because Ryo had developed a rasping cough, she moistened the air in his room with steam. His father steeped a bag of herbs in the kettle. His mother constantly renewed the damp, hot packs around his chest. His father came often to his bedside and looked very worried.

Because of the danger of infection, Saya and Bo weren't allowed to come close to Ryo. As it was, the year-end tests took up all Saya's time. She made use of every free minute to prepare for her exams. She didn't even leave much time for Bo—except in the evening when he had to be put to bed. Bo always waited until Saya came home from her English lesson. Until then he refused to go to sleep.

"Tell me a story," he would beg Saya each night as he lay under his thickly padded quilt, looking up at her with expectant eyes.

Saya would pull a quilt up around her back and shoulders while she knelt beside Bo on the other unrolled sleeping mattress.

"Tell me," he would beg, "tell me."

Because the electricity was cut off every night after nine o'clock, everything was in darkness. There were only oil lamps. One of them stood on the floor in the corner of the room. From time to time the flame would flicker, which meant it was time to adjust the wick.

As always when Saya told Bo the fairy tale of the cranes at dusk, she would first take a deep breath and nod her head very significantly three times. That's the way Bo wanted it.

"Well then," Saya would begin, "high up in the blue evening sky the white cranes flew over mountains, fields, lakes, and ocean. With a steady, rhythmic beat, they flew through the cool, clear air on their great wide wings. They flew so high that the sun caught the underside of their wings. Now and again they would look down from high up in the sky onto the land that was sinking away beneath them into a thousand evening shadows. Far, far below, in a little village in the mountains, stood a boy looking up at the cranes. The little boy could hear the distant call of the cranes—traaa—traaa—traaa . . .''

". . . traaa . . . traaa . . . traaa . . . ," said Bo.

"The cranes replied from way up high—shraaa—shraaa—shraaa . . ."

". . . shraaa . . . shraaa . . . shraaa . . . ," Bo repeated.

"The little boy ran along the village road so that the chickens cackled and scattered, the village cockerel crowed in alarm, the cat mewed, the dog barked, the water buffalo mooed, and the horse whinnied."

"And then . . . ?" Bo would ask with shining eyes.

"The little boy spread out his arms and flapped them like wings, for he wanted to join the cranes and fly to the land where time never ends. 'But you can't fly!' cackled the chickens, crowed the cockerel, cooed the doves, chirped the sparrows, and twittered the titmice. 'But you can't fly!' came the mocking shouts of the other village boys who happened to be building a trap with bamboo sticks, silk threads, and sharp-edged iron. They wanted to catch the raccoon."

"Poor raccoon . . . ," said Bo.

"That's what the little boy thought too," replied Saya, continuing with her story. "So he quickly crept into his warm little bed and drew the quilt up to the tip of his nose."

Bo drew his quilt up to the tip of his nose. "Like this?" he asked Saya.

"Yes, just like that, for the little boy wanted to fall asleep as quick as a wink so that next morning he would wake up earlier than all the other village boys and lose no time in setting the raccoon free again."

One night, in the subdued light of the oil lamp, Bo's wide-open eyes looked feverish. When the flame flickered, restless shadows flitted about the room. As always,

Bo wanted Saya to tell him his bedtime story in exactly the same sequence. He wanted to hear it again and again, although he had long since come to know it by heart. The whole sequence of events was depicted in advance on his little face. He knew when to expect the places where he could utter squeaks of fear, or the other places where he had to clap his pudgy hands in glee. Sometimes he became so excited that he would start kicking his legs under the quilt. His quilt would then slowly work its way down, and Saya would bend forward to pull it up again.

"So when the little boy in the little village in the mountains had fallen asleep under his warm quilt," Saya went on, "he heard the gekko calling—gok . . . gok . . . gok . . . , the cricket chirping—chinchiro-rin . . . chinchiro-rin . . . chinchiro-rin . . . , the wind blowing through the branches outside—srrr . . . srrr . . . srrr. . . . He heard the soft tread of the moon as she parted the clouds and drew them shut again—hyuu . . . hyuu . . . hyuu. . . . He heard the sparkling of the stars—pikka . . . pikka . . . pikka . . . , and when the little boy listened very, very carefully the voices of the cranes also reached his ear as he slept—traaa . . . traaa . . . traaa. . . . He could understand what they were saying to each other.

" 'The wind has grown harsh.'

" 'My wings are weary.'

" 'A storm is brewing.'

" 'Down there is a sleeping village.'

"That was the voice of the great white crane leading the flight of cranes. He knew all the mountains, valleys, rivers, lakes, and the ocean. He knew all the winds. He knew the rain, the lightning, and the thunder. He was the oldest of all the cranes, the wisest and the most cautious. He had already fought off the deadly teeth of the

marten in the reeds. He had already done battle in the air
with the falcon that had tried to pierce his shining white
plumage with its sharp talons. He was so skillful that in
flight he could even elude the hunter's arrow as it sped
toward him with a whir.

"The little boy heard the great white crane saying to
the other cranes high up in the evening sky, 'Let us land
down there near the village in the mountains and wait
for the storm to pass.'"

At this point Saya had to break off her story, for now
it was Bo's turn. He would cry excitedly, "Look out, look
out, look out, a trap!"

"Yes," said Saya, "'A trap has been set with a sharp
iron,' the little boy called out in his dream. He saw the
cranes circling high up in the air, in ever-narrowing circles, heard the rush of their wings drowning out the
wind, heard them deliberating in the air whether it was
safe to land here. . . ."

"No!" cried Bo. "A trap . . . !"

"The little boy saw that it was already quite dark outside. Only the moon gave some light through a window
in the clouds, but the storm was already there, sweeping
across the sky. The little boy saw the cranes beating their
great white wings in the storm and landing. 'Look out!'
he wanted to call, but he could already hear the iron trap
snap shut. He ran as fast as he could to the rice field
where the poor trapped crane—the youngest in the flight
—was thrashing his wings. The great white crane and all
the other cranes raised their pointed beaks in fear. 'The
wicked humans have done this!'

"'I have come to help you,' cried the little boy. 'Don't
be afraid.'

"'We'll peck out your eyes,' all the cranes threatened,
but the great white crane counseled them, 'Don't harm

him . . . shraaa . . . shraaa . . . shraaa . . . he is a good boy.'

"The little boy carefully freed the trapped crane and saw blood on the bird's slender, fragile leg. Quickly he ran home and brought back herbs, salves, and a piece of fine cotton cloth he used to bind up the wound."

Bo looked exhausted. His face was burning. Saya placed her hand on his forehead and was shocked to feel how hot it was.

"You have a fever," she said.

"Go on with story," Bo begged her.

"The storm had passed," Saya continued, looking down anxiously at Bo. "The night-blue sky was once again calm and clear. The moon illuminated the plumage of the cranes so that it shone like snow and the rice field was flooded with golden light.

" 'You are a good boy,' said the great white crane. 'You may now make a wish.'

" 'I would like to fly with you,' said the little boy.

" 'Climb up on my back . . . climb up . . . climb up . . . ,' said the great white crane, bending down so that the little boy could climb on his back. Then he spread his powerful wings and ran a few steps across the golden rice field until he had gathered enough wind and silver moonlight under his wings. Then he took off, and all the other cranes flew after him.

" 'Sleep well . . . sleep well . . . sleep well . . . ,' he said to the little boy on his back, 'so that I can carry you far away—to the place where time never ends.' "

Saya saw that Bo had fallen asleep. She pulled his quilt a little higher and lightly touched his face. It felt very hot.

She wanted to go back to her homework. All was silent in the house. Her father and mother were both asleep. During each of the past few nights they had taken turns watching over Ryo, who by now was hardly coughing any more. Saya could have both oil lamps, which gave her a good light for her homework. The electricity was still cut off.

The next day was to see the last of the tests. To be given by Mrs. Nakarai of all people. Once again Saya leafed through all her notes and homework of the last two months. She must get an A. She must prove to Mrs. Nakarai that she wasn't going to give in to her. "You're too cheeky," she could hear Mrs. Nakarai's gentle voice that disguised so much lust for power, "but I'll make you eat humble pie yet."

Saya refused to eat humble pie. The girls, with only one dissenting vote, had reelected her as their class spokesman.

Two more years of elementary school, thought Saya, then high school. English lessons don't start until then. By that time I'll be able to read and write English quite well.

Mr. Everett seemed to enjoy having Saya in his evening class. He was patient with her when she tried to say something in English and was stuck for the right words. Since Mr. Everett spoke no Japanese, Saya had no choice but to find the English words.

Mr. Everett would wrinkle his brow, roll his eyes, stroke his chin, put his head on one side, shrug his shoulders, make encouraging movements with his hand, try out various words, until the block was overcome.

"Very good, Saya, very good," he would say, and then repeat the sentence.

Saya said the sentence after him. What she had once repeated, she never forgot.

"You must learn to think in English," Mr. Everett kept telling her. "You are young, you can do that."

"Someday, when I can speak English really well," said Saya, "I'd like to go to America."

Mr. Everett said that would no doubt be possible, and she might even get a scholarship. Saya didn't know what a scholarship was, but when she heard that a grant would mean the gift of a whole trip to America, her tuition, even her board and lodging, she became very excited.

"But you must get excellent marks in school," said Mr. Everett.

"I do . . . I do. . . ."

That was one more reason why she must remain best student of the year.

Saya bent over her copybooks again. The paper was poor and scratchy. It was yellow but nevertheless precious. New copybooks were seldom obtainable in school, and down in the silk weavers' quarter there had been none available at all for a long time. Sometimes Saya cut off the edges of newspapers to have something to write on. The school paper was no better than newsprint. Writing pressed through to the back. The pencil point kept getting snagged in hard wooden splinters embedded in the paper. The splinters would rip out, and erasing was almost impossible. In spite of this, Saya always wrote on both sides of the page because she didn't have enough paper to write on.

Her pencil strokes faded away in the light of the oil lamp. Saya noticed one character that looked wrong. In order to check the correct way to write it, she pulled out the big dictionary her father had given her. She had to slide up very close to the two oil lamps to be able to read the small print.

When I go to America, she suddenly thought, I'll take Bo with me. Then before he goes to sleep I'll tell him the story of the cranes at dusk.

But by that time Bo will be so big, of course, that he won't want to hear any more fairy tales.

At one time Saya's father used often to come and sit by her bed and tell her fairy tales before she fell asleep. The story of the cranes at dusk was also one of his. Saya had merely embroidered it for Bo. Nowadays when she was with her father she preferred to talk to him about God and the devil.

The previous Sunday in church, the pastor had told them about the devil and that the devil must exist in order to make God shine forth that much more brightly.

Why the God of the Christians, who is supposed to be all-powerful, should need the devil wasn't clear to Saya. God is light, and the devil is the darkness; light is all that is good, darkness is all that is evil.

Saya's father had told her that light and darkness, good and evil, could each be transformed one into the other. Saya couldn't quite understand this either.

If God is all-powerful, why then is he not simultaneously light and darkness, Saya thought? Why didn't he see to it that evil vanish from the world?

Why do the Christians have an all-powerful God and at the same time the devil?

Saya had learned in school that Christians had also fought wars with each other. They had actually used the term "religious wars."

In Japan there had never been religious wars. In Japan, Shinto and Buddhism had never made war on each other.

But the pastor had said that Christian society was superior because of Christian brotherly love. The all-powerful God, Jesus, and brotherly love, the pastor had said, made Christian society better than any other, especially the Japanese.

Saya had told her father this, but he wasn't convinced. He had said that even God and Jesus couldn't maintain human society in a constant state of brotherly love. Brotherly love was a beautiful ideal that had to give way every day to reality. To engrave so great but basically unfulfillable a commandment on the souls of men was more likely to encourage hypocrisy.

"Do you mean that the pastor is lying?" Saya had asked hesitantly.

"No, it's just that he won't acknowledge that there are a great, great many contradictions between the words of the Bible and human reality. Anything that does not fit into the biblical ideal, he attributes to the work of the devil, instead of recognizing that God has created men with an infinite multiplicity of levels in all their emotions and desires."

"Should I stop going to the Christian church because maybe all that isn't right after all?"

"No one knows what is right, and for that very reason it is a good idea for you to continue to go to the Christians and listen to what they have to say."

Could there really be a land where time never ends? That is where all the birds assemble when they grow old, from the tiny, iridescent hummingbird to the great white crane. Twittering birds perch on all the branches . . . finches, titmice . . . the earth sings . . . from the clouds comes a strange music of intoxicating beauty. . . .

Could there be such a land, Saya wondered, with no difference between day and night, no difference between spring, summer, autumn, and winter, no year, no time?

There is no such thing as time.

There is only light, nothing but light, never-ending music, never-ending perfumes, never-ending sequences of color.

On their way there, the cranes fly past Mount Fuji and

compare the white of their plumage with the white of the snow. They compare the black edges of their wings with the black of the volcanic ash. They compare the red of their feathered crests with the red of the glowing volcanic pit.

There is no such thing as time, thought Saya.

Why is there no time?

Time is said to stand still. Like a clock that has stopped.

> There is no worry.
> There is no quarreling.
> There is no sickness.
> There are no tears.
> There is no aging.
> There is no death.

The oil lamp flickered again. Saya realized how tired she was and put out the light. Quietly she slipped in under the quilt beside Bo. She touched Bo's forehead. It was still very hot. His breathing was shallow and rapid. For a moment Saya considered calling her father, but then she fell asleep.

 19

CAREFULLY, SO AS NOT TO WAKEN ANYONE, THE GUJI
pushed aside the heavy wooden windscreen with which
he had closed the front door for the night and stepped
out into the cool morning. It was still dark, but in the sky
the first light glimmered. The shrine's roof carved a black
line in the sky. The bare branches of the trees formed a
frame of black filigree.

It was the first day of spring.

Quietly the Guji closed the inner shoji of the front
door behind him and walked across the graveled
forecourt. With one hand he pulled his dark gray outer
kimono closer about his shoulders, for a light wind was
blowing. The wind bore the strong, sweet scent of *hakubai*
blossoms that blended with the smell of damp earth and
moldering leaves.

On the wide stone steps the Guji paused and regarded
the shimmering hakubai blossoms that looked like white
paper in the gray early light. Turning around, he could
see far below the dense shadow of the house. He felt
relieved that Ryo, after a day without fever, had slept

right through the night without coughing. Ryo was obviously over the worst.

The Guji recalled the preceding nights and realized that his wife hadn't had much sleep either. She looked tired, worn out.

The staff surgeon's wife had come twice. The first time she had stayed the whole afternoon to help, but at some point he had heard raised voices in the house. The Guji didn't know what the dispute was about, but he hadn't been surprised that it had come to an argument. He knew his wife well enough to realize that she couldn't get along even with her best friend as soon as they tried to undertake something together other than the exchange of compliments over tea or the contemplation of ikebana creations. So the second visit of the staff surgeon's wife was merely to drop off some new medication that her husband had given her for Ryo.

From the east, traces of color were spreading across the sky. A faint redness glowed over the paling darkness of the night. Slowly the Guji climbed the last few steps and walked toward the altar building that loomed up against its background of trees. He came here each morning at this hour.

He had stopped asking himself why he had been so imprudent in his choice of a wife, having put that behind him long ago. He thought of Saya, of Ryo and Bo. After that he could no longer wonder whether it had been a mistake for him to marry this woman.

He had accepted the situation the day he realized that nothing would ever change her. No persuasion, no waiting—no patience, no amount of countereffort.

His *I-Ching* insights would have enabled him to discover his wife's true nature in time to avoid making a mistake, but on first meeting her he had told himself he must rely on his emotion—his emotion only, and not on the sober, dissecting analysis of the *I-Ching*.

Her demeanor had been very appealing. She was a young and beautiful woman, and he was attracted by her elegant, reserved manner. She had appeared to be accommodating and adaptable. She was clever. The Guji had imagined that life with her would run harmoniously. She had impressed him.

The fact that she had been able to impress him was due solely to his own carelessness. It had been his mistake, his mistake entirely, that he had chosen to rely only on his emotion.

Had it been tenderness? At heart he still felt tenderness for her because he knew she needed him. She was helpless without him. It was pity that remained—pity for her. For him there remained only loneliness.

The Guji knew that there was no escape from his loneliness.

He had to continue on his path. His reward was an ever-deepening understanding of human nature. With increasing clarity he perceived the correlations to be deduced from the hexagrams of the *I-Ching*. More and more plainly a pattern emerged of the interactions that cause men either to harm or to benefit each other—relationships through which men either inflict pain on each other or draw closer together.

He saw the river of time. He saw how every human destiny was embedded in that stream. He could predict illnesses. He could help people who consulted him about their problems. He could tell them what was best for them. He could advise them. Over the years, many had come who bore the burden of tormenting loneliness. The Guji understood them.

He also understood others who complained that they had married the wrong woman or the wrong man. He saw how many marriages were shattered from within. He was familiar with the reproaches that spouses leveled at one another. He saw how in each person hopes mingled with disappointments. He saw the time patterns imprinted on every life. He saw the avoidability of some decisions. If at certain points of intersection in their paths people had only handled their own emotions with more caution, they would have spared themselves a great deal. He saw how carelessly decisions were often made, but also how difficult it was to see into the heart of another person.

Under the altar roof it was still night; only the three little milk-white porcelain bowls—one for salt, one for water, and one for rice—showed up a shade paler against the dark background of the wooden altar steps. The altar itself also appeared only as a dark, looming structure to which the branches of the evergreen sakaki reached out. Whenever there was a puff of wind or a bird settled on a sakaki branch, the leaves scraped gently against the wood of the altar. On the upturned surfaces of the sakaki leaves glittered the dewdrops that had collected during the night. From time to time a dewdrop fell, causing faint vibrations that passed from leaf to leaf.

The Guji watched the gentle shifting of the light reflections. From somewhere out of the forest came the voices of birds. One of them was a nightingale, but when it started to sing its clear voice broke off.

"You must practice some more," said the Guji.

Soon after that, a jay sounded its warning. Its rasping cry drowned out all other, subtler sounds. A cat was slinking along beside the fence. It was trying to move carefully, but the white patches on its fur betrayed it. At one spot in the fence where two pickets were missing, the cat disappeared as silently as it had come.

From below came the first sounds of the city, the screeching of streetcar wheels.

The gate creaked on its hinges as the Guji opened it and passed through into the inner domain of the altar building. Here in this solitude, close to nature, he felt protected. He saw the dark green, shining leaves of the sakaki bushes with the dew of the night upon them. He saw the pine trees stretching out their heavy branches far beyond the outer fence of the courtyard. The buds of the wild cherry trees looked juicy and about to open. He saw the ferns thrusting through the earth with their furled fronds protected by a clay-colored, parchmentlike sheath.

The dark brown of the cedar pillars supporting the altar roof, the plain altar made of the same wood—none of it seemed to have been created for eternity. No gold, no silver—only here and there a bronze fitting overlaid with the patina of the years.

Perhaps that is why there are those billions of deities in Shinto, thought the Guji, so that new concepts of divinity can be added as they develop in the course of history. Thus all paths remain open. Because there are no sacrosanct scriptures, they do not have to be rewritten. Or paraphrased. No one can take it upon himself to say, "My God is the only God."

The first sunbeam of the first day of spring fell precisely onto the middle of the altar. The cedarwood suddenly glowed reddish brown. Light even shone from the inside of the altar, refracted from the close latticework. The grain of the cedarwood showed up strongly, carved out by the wind and the moisture of many summers. The sunlight also touched the bronze fittings, giving them a strange, dull green luster.

Actually, the Guji thought, Shinto places very heavy demands on the staying power of human beings. The renunciation of belief in the Beyond is not easy to endure. Life is limited to the here and now. There is no evasion into an allegedly better world after death. There is no escape from life, no escape into the dream of the Beyond. All responsibility—all happiness—all suffering is compressed into the time span that is being lived through here and now.

There is only the certainty that each life is a rounded, unique event in nature, that nature takes back that life and only the memory remains.

The Guji was still standing before the altar. The full light of the sun was now shining in. He could feel its warmth on his back.

From somewhere far behind him he heard footsteps on the gravel, swift, flying footsteps.

He heard Saya's voice.

He heard her calling him. Her voice was filled with terror. He turned around.

The sun dazzled him.

He saw Saya fling herself at him. He just had time to open his arms and catch her.

"Bo . . . ," stammered Saya, "Bo . . . has stopped breathing . . . Bo is . . . Bo . . . is dead."

 20

TIME HAD LOST ITS HOURS. THE HOURS HAD NO MORE MIN-
utes. There were only thoughts, thoughts that circled
back on themselves and from which there seemed to be
no way out.

And there was wind, glaring sunlight, clouds in the
azure sky.

And there was a timetable for school, and every day
two ladlefuls of hot soup at noon.

And there were the same faces in class—Yuri-chan,
Mi-chan, Hana-chan—all so carefree.

And there were branches of opening cherry blossoms
arching over the stone stairway. A new homeroom
teacher. Homework. Evening shadows. Stone stairway
again. English lessons. A hurried meal. Reproaches.
Dreamless sleep.

And there was cold water. Gray silence. Gray morning
light. Only a bowl of hot tea. School again, breaks between lessons, bells ringing.

Saya carefully placed one foot ahead of the other on the long flight of steps over which a carpet of fallen cherry blossom petals had spread. A continuous shower of petals fell from the tunnel of pink-and-white blossoms that overhung the steps and completely screened out the blue of the sky. Saya bent down and threaded more and more petals onto a long thread to make a chain. Each step she took left its trace on the soft, fragile carpet. Saya's eyes followed the falling petals as they twirled and danced in the air. When they reached the ground, they soon became indistinguishable from all the others already carpeting the steps.

"Where are you?" Saya said softly as she bent down to pick up the most recently fallen petal with her needle.

"Where are you?" she repeated. She thought of the toys still lying in Bo's room and of his little getas with the new blue straps. Saya had seen them standing there only yesterday. There was still a little earth clinging to them, and where Bo's feet had been the wood was shiny.

Was he missing his toys?

Perhaps he would now be playing trains with her abacus in the grooves of the open shoji and singing in his piping voice—*shu-shu-tu-tu* . . . *shu-shu-tu-tu.*

Under the dense arching tunnel of blossoms, a delicate twilight reigned over the steps. Now and again a drifting petal would cling to the vermilion fence bordering the stairway. Many of the black tips of the pickets already wore white caps.

Wherever there was a gap in the vault of blossoms, sunbeams entered and drew pale, flickering spots on the steps. When falling petals drifted through these sunbeams, the light would catch them.

Old Nakamura and his wife were coming up the steps. Between them walked a young man wearing a military tunic with no buttons.

"Our son has returned," old Nakamura said to Saya when he was close.

"Our Saburo is home again," said his wife with shining eyes.

Saya looked at Saburo and remembered his face. Saburo nodded.

"That's a pretty blossom chain you're making," he said and stroked Saya's hair.

"Yes," she said. Her eyes followed the three of them as they carefully wended their way up to the shrine over the carpet of cherry blossoms, while new white petals drifted down from the arching branches to cover the fresh footsteps.

Saburo's face had seemed pale and haggard to her. Manchuria, Saya thought, how cold was the winter there?

The teacher who had taken over their class at the beginning of the new term was also a returned veteran, like Saburo, but he had come back from an English prisoner-of-war camp in Singapore and was deeply tanned.

Saya was glad she was no longer in Mrs. Nakarai's class. Under Mr. Arase, the new teacher, there was an entirely different feeling in class. He reminded Saya a little of Mr. Everett because he had the same steady, frank eyes. None of those ingratiating airs of Mrs. Nakarai who, in spite of her feigned gentleness, possessed only a craving for domination.

"What a good thing we've got rid of Nakarai," said most of the girls.

Mr. Arase knew how to inspire the class with enthusiasm and how to get the best out of every girl. He encouraged them to ask questions, to use their own heads. He didn't pretend to know everything. Sometimes he said, "I don't know that." Then the next day he would explain whatever he hadn't been able to explain the previous day.

In school Saya sometimes forgot that Bo was dead. She let the lessons carry her along and actually the only thing she dreaded was the last bell, that announced the end of the school day. That meant it was time to go home.

Petal by petal, Saya added to her chain, threading them with a needle. The chain had already become so heavy that Saya had to support it with one hand. The weight of the petals, pink-edged and milky white and with the feel of soft velvet, but cool, pulled on the thread and on her needle. One end of the thread cut into her finger.

Saya now saw her father only in the evenings. As always, when she came home from her English lesson he would be standing down below at the great torii, waiting for her. He never brought a lantern, even when, as often happened, it was so dark that many stars were visible in the sky. He stood motionless, silent, frequently leaning against the massive pillar of the great torii.

Each time Saya saw him standing there she wanted to do what she had always done before Bo's death: skip up to him and call out "Otosan!" But her throat seemed to close over, and her legs refused to skip. All she could do was quicken her pace a little and softly say "Otosan" when she reached him. Then he seemed to awaken from faraway thoughts.

Without a word he would give her his hand and walk up the dark steps with her. His hand was cool. It now felt like nothing but skin and bones.

Her father would pause for a moment before the fox altar. Usually the light was already burning in the paper lantern that was becoming brittle with age. With quiet, infinitely sad eyes, her father would look into the dark

hollow space of the altar where the lantern's feeble light
did not penetrate. Then he would turn around without a
word and walk on. Sometimes he would also stop somewhere on the long flight of steps as if he needed to rest
from the long climb.

"Otosan . . . ," Saya would then say to him softly,
but he never answered. He would merely place his slender, cool hand on Saya's shoulder or on her hair, drawing
her gently to him. After a while he would walk on in his
intimidating silence. At the top, outside the house, he
would let go of Saya's hand and walk with dragging
footsteps toward his study while Saya had to go to her
mother.

Saya stopped short as she was about to pick up the
next petal from the ground with her needle. A beetle that
was hiding under it scurried away. Saya had almost im-
paled it on her needle. She thought about how many
humble little creatures there were on the blossom-cov-
ered ground, and how many of them she had killed with
every step she took. Each evening when she walked up
the steps with her father, she probably killed many creatures under her feet without knowing it.

Were there gods, too, who in passing stamp on a sleeping child without knowing it, so that next morning that
child doesn't wake up again?

Saya sat down on the steps.

Exactly one year ago, at this very same spot, she and
Bo had threaded a thousand cherry blossom petals into a
long, sweet-smelling chain. With his plump little hands
Bo had tried to catch the petals as they drifted down like
snow. Each time he caught a petal he had crowed with
delight.

"Here," he had said, showing Saya the petal lying on
his palm. "Here . . ."

He had stood quite still while she carefully picked up the white petal from his palm with the point of her needle.

When the chain was long enough, Saya had placed it around Bo's neck and threaded two more short chains for him that he wore round his wrists. Singing together, they had then both gone up the steps again, home, and for the rest of the day Bo had insisted on keeping on his blossom chains.

An emerald-green lizard darted along beside the vermilion fence, across the rock and over a few rounded stones. It flitted across the downy cherry blossom carpet and paused at a sun-warmed spot where a bit of the gray rock showed through. The lizard's slender, lustrous body contrasted with the gray rock and the white cherry blossom petals strewn over it. When the lizard turned its head, Saya could see the rapid, shallow breathing of its throat.

"Bo is dead," Saya told the lizard.

The lizard darted away. Saya looked at the empty spot until the picture became a blur.

She thought of Mrs. Yasumi, whom the death of her son had driven mad. Saya had seen her sitting in her dark room in front of her loom, talking to the blue silk into which she had woven a thousand white cherry blossoms. Saya had never before known anyone who had gone mad. Mrs. Yasumi was always talking about the cloud into which her son's soul had been transformed, or she would say crazy things that nobody understood.

Suddenly it occurred to Saya that maybe her mother had also been driven mad by Bo's death. Whenever Saya came home, she found her sitting in the same posture at the table, looking at the wall. With her narrow face cupped in her hands, she would say, without looking at

Saya, that Saya's father was responsible for Bo's death.
Bo had had to die in order to prove that there was nothing behind all that Chinese science their father was practicing.

"Hundreds of people come to him," her mother whispered to Saya in her low, husky voice. "Hundreds—but
my dear little Bo has proved with his death that I have
always been right."

Saya put her arms round her mother and shook her.
"You mustn't think such things . . . mustn't say them.
Father is just as sad as you and I are."

Her mother straightened up and looked sharply at
Saya. "Why do you always take the wrong side?" she
asked. "Who bore you? Who nursed you? Who brought
you up? Soon you will be eleven. For eleven years I have
done everything for you with a pure heart. I went without food for you. I sewed my fingers to the bone for you.
And what has your father done for you? To whom do
you owe more gratitude—to him or to me?"

"But I love you both," Saya said with an effort. She
felt so miserable that she could hardly speak.

Saya looked up into the cherry blossom roof overhead
from which the slow, steady stream of petals was still
drifting down onto her. They settled on her hair, on her
knees, her hands, on the completed blossom chain she
was holding.

At Mrs. Graham's, Bo had seen an egg lying on the
kitchen table.

"Pingpong!" he had crowed gleefully as he stood on
tiptoe. With his short little arms he could just reach the
egg.

"Pingpong!" he had cried as he tossed it across the
room. When it broke and the yolk spread across the floor
in a pool of egg white, he clung to Saya in alarm. He

didn't know what an egg was. He had never seen an egg, never eaten an egg.

"Pingpong?" Bo had asked in bewilderment. "No Pingpong?"

The Nakamuras were coming down the steps again.

"You're still here!" said old Nakamura.

"Yes," said Saya.

Mrs. Nakamura brushed the petals out of Saya's hair. Saburo squatted down on the step beside Saya.

"I just heard," he said haltingly, "about your little brother. . . . I'm very sorry. . . . I'm alone too, now that both my older brothers . . . you know . . . the war. . . ."

Saya nodded.

Saburo tried to cheer her up by pointing out that she still had another brother. Ryo.

The Nakamuras continued down the steps, all three side by side. Although Saburo was already a grown man and much taller than either of his parents, he walked between them.

Saya was thinking that a child should really always walk between its parents.

She was thinking how nice it was for a child to walk between its parents.

In her memory there wasn't a single instant where she could see herself walking on any street or any path between her mother and father. Invariably her mother had insisted that Saya walk close beside her. When in spite of this she exchanged glances with her father or laughed with him, her mother would give them a withering look and yank Saya back to her side. Afterward she was always bad-tempered.

The Nakamuras had disappeared beyond the bend in the steps below.

Saya stood up and slowly walked down the steps. She turned into the lane that led across to Kita-oji where Bo's grave was in the wide precincts of the Zen temple.

From a few of the houses came the clacking of looms. Somewhere a yarn-winding machine was whirring.

"Are you coming to play with us?" a child asked.

"No," Saya called back. She was carrying her cherry blossom chain that lay heavily in her hands—velvety and cool—over to Kita-oji. As she stood at the edge of the wide street, a jeep with four American soldiers drove by. They waved at Saya and laughed.

After the jeep had passed, Saya quickly ran across Kita-oji carrying her petal chain. She walked through the wide gate in the high stone wall. Beyond lay the precincts of the Zen temple. Through tall, slender pines there was a view of a curved temple roof. The path consisted of huge white stone slabs, five child's paces across, embedded in sand. Sand flanked the path on either side and was in turn bordered by walls. More temple roofs rose beyond. Saya ran past some black-robed monks. They wore straw sandals and walked in single file. Then came the intersection where Saya had to turn right.

Straight ahead was the great temple whose abbot her father had sometimes met for discussions. Saya could see the mighty temple roof towering above the tallest pine trees. She thought of the abbot and how, on the day when Bo's ashes were buried, he had stood by her father's side. Does he know where Bo's soul is now, she wondered?

The path became narrower. The stone slabs became smaller. The walls moved closer. Then came the narrow gate through which Saya had to pass. From there it was only a footpath that led on—past the gardener's cottage where the birdcage made of thin bamboo sticks hung below the eaves. The gaudy red parrot clambered about on the bamboo sticks, squawking raucously as Saya passed by. The ground was muddy. Privet hedges bordered the path.

At the very end of the temple garden, near the back wall, were the four-hundred-year-old graves of Oda Nobunaga and his followers. Moss grew on the gravestones.

That was the site of the new little gravestone, gray on the muddy ground. Some gravel had been strewn round it.

Saya placed the cherry blossom chain around the gray stone.

"Where are you?" she asked. She listened, but only the wind answered softly, rustling in the privet leaves and in the dry yellow grass that covered the surrounding earth. In many places, new green grass shoots were already appearing.

"Where are you?" Saya asked once more.

The characters for Bo's name that had been chiseled into the gravestone remained mute.

With her finger she tenderly followed the outline of the characters.

She sang Bo's favorite songs, softly at first, then louder.

She felt the first raindrops as they fell. The wind freshened. The rain became heavier.

Saya moved as close as she could to Bo's gravestone to protect it from the rain. The stone was cold. Saya sang at the top of her voice. The rain ran down her face. It soaked her dress. It dripped from her hair.

"You will catch cold," a voice said to her. A monk was standing there in his straw sandals, with a big umbrella that darkened the sky. Saya meekly allowed herself to be led away by the monk.

When she looked back once more to Bo's grave, she

saw the cherry blossom chain encircling the gravestone
in the rain.

"You will catch cold," the monk said again. With a
coarse, rough cloth he wiped the moisture from Saya's
face and rubbed her hair dry. The parrot squawked as
they passed.

Saya shivered.

"Come along," said the monk, quickening his pace. On
reaching the main building he led Saya under the wide
overhanging roof.

"Your father will scold you if he sees you wet through
like this," said the monk.

Outside the rain came down like a curtain.

"My father never scolds me," said Saya.

She was familiar with the great temple building. She
had often come here with her father on his visits to the
abbot, or she had accompanied the abbot back here when
he had been up at the shrine on the hill.

"Is the abbot here?" Saya asked.

"Yes," said the monk, "I'll take you to him, but first
you must put on some dry clothes."

Saya followed him through the dark, silent halls,
across the soft, springy tatami mats, across smooth, shining wooden floors. Other monks joined them, their faces
showing concern when they saw Saya shivering with
cold.

"Hurry, hurry," they said.

After taking off her wet dress and putting on the black
monk's robe, Saya felt warmer right away. The sleeves
were much too long, and the hem of the robe dragged on
the ground. The monks smiled when they saw Saya.

The abbot said, "You need not worry about your little
brother Bo. He is in that place where one day we will all
go, in the Distant Land."

Saya sat in her big monk's robe on the big floor cushion in the big hall where light from the gray, rainy sky barely penetrated.

"Where is the Distant Land?" she asked.

"Far, far away from the troubles and suffering of this world."

"But there's nobody there Bo knows. He will be very unhappy."

"No one is unhappy in the Distant Land," said the abbot in his quiet, deep voice that died away in the great dark hall. "Buddha is there and accepts all those who come to him. For the children there are innumerable Bodhisattvas. They play with the children, sing with them, dance with them, and show them all of the Distant Land, that is as vast as time itself, that never ends."

 **21**

TANAKA, THE LITTLE WHITE-HAIRED PRIEST WHO FOR YEARS
had been helping the Guji with his various administrative tasks, had moved from his office toward the rear of the administration area up to the front. He now sat in the anteroom to the Guji's study. There he had set up his desk and stacked the most important files on the bookshelves. White-haired and wrinkled, he sat behind mountains of paper piled up on his desk.

When people came who wanted to talk to the Guji, he sent them away. "The Guji cannot see you now," he would say in a soft voice, with a look of concern.

All day long, old Nakamura and his son Saburo were working in the tops of the pine trees round the forecourt. They had to keep shifting their ladders. Tufts of pine needles showered down unceasingly, forming random heaps on the tarpaulins spread on the ground. From time to time the two men would first shake the heaps of needles on the tarpaulins into one pile, then tip them into a reed basket that Saburo strapped onto his back. Finally he would carry the basket into the forest, empty it, and spread the needles out over the ground so that they mingled with the fallen leaves. On his return from the forest he would bring fallen branches with him. These he piled up at the edge of the forecourt, to be sawed into handy lengths of firewood at some later time.

Then he would climb up his tall ladder again. He and old Nakamura worked without talking much. From time to time came the snap of gardening shears, but the two men did most of the work with their hands, on which they wore elbow-length mittens that left their fingers free. With their fingers they stripped off the dry needles left over from the preceding winter. With a skillful twist of the hand they would break off tufts of needles wherever they grew too close together.

Gradually the silhouettes of the pine trees acquired the lightness that is sometimes seen in old woodcuts. Apparently nothing had changed. There was no sign of where Nakamura and his son had worked throughout the day. Nevertheless, the pines suddenly seemed more graceful yet without having lost their natural wildness.

The bright light of the May sun fell through the papered shoji in the Guji's study. Throughout the last few weeks he had done virtually nothing but look through his old notes, sheet by sheet. He had gone back year by year and looked at every single correlation diagram that he had noted down in the past for people who had come to consult him.

He saw the lines of correlation and the mathematical structures from which so much could be deduced about those people—about their dispositions, their inclinations and talents, about their spiritual and physical constitutions, as well as about their organic weaknesses, about their susceptibilities to certain diseases—gossamer spun in time and space from the vast number of possibilities that determine the wave pattern of life.

Had Bo's early death been predictable? This was the question that tormented him. It gave him no peace. It pursued him day after day. It seeped into his sleep. It engendered a profound sense of guilt in him. If he had been able to foresee the possibility of Bo's early death on the basis of Bo's correlation diagrams, he might have been able to save Bo. He should have studied the diagram of Bo's life more carefully and still more thoroughly.

But Bo had not seemed to be in any danger. His correlation lines revealed no recognizable indications of sudden early death. No indication of organic weakness. At least the Guji had not been struck by anything that might have caught his attention.

Nor had the doctor been able to find anything.

"It does happen, but very seldom," he had said resignedly after his long conversation with the Guji, "that children die for no apparent reason—while fast asleep. No one can explain it."

The only indication, from a medical point of view, was that this sudden death in sleep invariably carried off only little children. The borderline was at three or four years of age. Bo was three, thought the Guji, just a little older than three. He could not understand why so grave a failure on the part of nature was not to be deduced from the correlation diagrams.

Now, when it was too late, the Guji saw that, within the enormous multiplicity of potential mathematical linkages, there were still some other lines that could be followed up and that he had never followed up. Perhaps, he told himself, one of these lines holds the key.

Sheet by sheet he had gone through his old notations, tens of thousands of correlation diagrams. He searched, he compared, he consulted his *I-Ching* books containing the mathematical approaches to solution.

He knew there were cases where the forces of human interaction could become crucial for a life hovering on the borderline between extinction and survival. Many children go through such phases where the spiritual force flowing to them from their mother or father can have a life-sustaining or life-destroying impact. And vice versa: He knew of numerous cases where the demands made by children on the vital force of their parents—father or mother—could be so intense that a threat to the parents' life might ensue.

Slowly, one by one, new insights were stripped bare. Slowly the Guji gained additional confidence in the analysis of the problems resulting from human interaction and affecting more than one physical entity.

But he came no closer to answering the question as to the nature of the indefinable force that had snuffed out Bo's life in his sleep.

Every morning, in the hour before sunrise, the Guji stood before the altar. The nights were growing shorter. The air was growing clearer. It was filled with birdsong. The azaleas were in bloom. The new leaves on the sakaki branches still retained their fresh, pale green. The ferns uncurled their fronds and cast off the brownish yellow sheaths under which the shoots had emerged from the earth.

When people from the silk weavers' quarter approached the shrine in the early morning and saw the Guji standing before the altar—frail, motionless, with rounded shoulders and inclined head—they would bow silently.

Many times he would also stand before the altar during the day or withdraw into the inner altar area, where he found solitude. In the rooms of the adjoining sacristy, where the musical instruments for the shrine festival and the sacramental implements for the altar service were kept, it was cool. There he liked to sit down and let the silence exert its influence on him. Time after time his mind went over Bo's correlation diagrams.

Without looking up from his papers, Tanaka told the two visitors that the Guji could not see them today.

"Nevertheless, we would like to see him," said the older of the two, placing his visiting card and that of his companion in front of Tanaka.

"Oh, I beg your pardon," Tanaka murmured and stood up. He bowed. "I did not recognize you as you came in."

"Please tell the Guji that we are here," the visitor said politely but firmly.

"If you would be so kind as to have a seat," Tanaka said, somewhat flustered. He ran up the great broad stairway to the shrine to look for the Guji.

"Some important visitors have arrived," he said. "The official spokesman for the Shinto priesthood is waiting down below with a companion." Tanaka murmured the names.

"Very well, I'm coming."

The conversation began with the usual comments on the general situation.

"I am sure that is not the reason for your visit," said the Guji.

"No," said the spokesman with the suggestion of a bow. "We are here for a different reason, and that is that we, by which I mean the Shinto priesthood, are concerned that you, as Guji of a venerable national shrine, should deem it proper to send your daughter to the Christian church."

The Guji said nothing.

"Every Sunday, so we are told," said the companion who had come from Tokyo, "your honorable daughter shows her face in the Christian church, thus arousing unfavorable sentiments in many Japanese people. It is an affront, so to speak, to public morality, you understand?"

"And that is why you have taken the trouble to come here?" the Guji asked.

"At a time like the present," said the spokesman in a more conciliatory tone, the asperity in the Guji's voice not having escaped him, "where uncertainties are great and where Japanese sentiments are exposed to strong pressures, the example of a Guji who sends his daughter to the Christians has an unsettling effect. Would you not agree?"

The Guji was sitting at his desk. Before him lay his open *I-Ching* books and a few sheets of matrix calculations.

"I know it is unusual," he said in his quiet voice, "and that it may be felt to be unsettling, but for our minds to be unsettled is something we all need. Our time is open. Shinto should also be open."

"But Shinto is in danger."

"It is ridiculous to say such a thing," the Guji replied in a gently mocking tone, "just because an eleven-year-old child with questions in her heart attends the Christian service."

"One might forbid her."

"Have you so little confidence in Shinto?" the Guji asked.

"The Christians are exerting great pressure on us, as you know."

"I know," said the Guji, "Shinto is not in danger. Shinto lives from itself."

"The majority of our priesthood think otherwise," said

the spokesman. "We must do something about it—each must do his part. That is why we have come to see you."

"I would appreciate your leaving now," replied the Guji.

"And you promise that your daughter will no longer be allowed to go . . . ?"

"No."

"But if the Christians ensnare her, you—excuse me for saying so—you as Guji will be exposed to ridicule. We would like to prevent that."

The Guji did not reply. He had risen to his feet and had slid open the door to the anteroom where Tanaka, white-haired and worried, was hunched over his desk. The Guji went to the door of the anteroom and slid that one open too, so that the sun flooded into the room and the tatami mats shone golden-yellow. Outside bloomed the long row of azaleas.

"Religion is the question about life and about death," said the Guji, as the spokesman for the Shinto priesthood and his companion stepped reluctantly through the door, "but no one knows the answer. You do not. I do not. The Buddhists do not. The Christians do not. We are all searching for an answer. We do not even know whether there is an answer."

Saya was dreaming of the great white crane flying on his wide wings high up in the air. He flew so high that the light of the setting sun caught the undersides of his wings. He flew over endless forests, over mountains, rivers, and lakes. He flew over Mount Fuji, whose snow-capped peak was as white as the crane's plumage. He flew into the rising dusk. He flew under the light of the stars, in the silvery light of the moon.

"Bring Bo back," Saya said softly, "bring Bo back."

The great white crane winged its way like a silver

shadow through her dreams. In her sleep her hand reached out to the place beside her, but Bo was not there. The only thing her hand rested on was the cool, empty surface of the tatami mat.

"Where are you?" she whispered.

The pastor had said that Bo was long since in heaven. "He took part in the Christmas nativity play as a little sheep on the stage, and you always brought him regularly to church on Sundays—we can be sure that God has given him a place in heaven, for God's love belongs in a special way to all the children of this earth."

"But where is he in heaven?"

"Far, far away—there where the angels sing, where there is eternal light, where Jesus lives and God has his throne."

"But I can't see him."

"He is with Jesus. Stop worrying. Your little brother is in good hands. Believe me, he is in heaven."

Mr. Everett had also said that Bo was in heaven, and that he was sure to be happy there. "He is looking down on you," Mr. Everett had said.

"Then Bo can see that I'm crying, so he can't be happy."

"That's why you shouldn't cry."

Mr. Arase, her new homeroom teacher, had told Saya that many of his friends and comrades had fallen in the war, some of them beside him, within reach of his hand, and there had been no time to close their eyes.

"Whether they have become clouds in the sky, moss in the hills, or sea grass in the ocean—that I don't know," he had said. "I only know that I am alive and that I must try to live also for my dead friends and comrades. You must do that too for your little brother—work twice as hard, learn twice as much, demand twice as much of yourself. I've heard that you used to act with the school theater group. Start doing that again."

"I can't face it."

"Oh yes you can."

"Bo, where are you?" Saya whispered into the darkness. The night had many sounds. The beams of the house shifted and groaned. Crickets chirped somewhere. When Saya got up and quietly pushed aside the shoji, she saw the moon bathing the graveled court in silvery light. The azalea blossoms that glowed with a pink radiance during the daytime now had a strange blue-white sheen.

Saya ran barefoot across the gravel and up the stone steps. The air was warm. The curved roof of the shrine cut a black piece out of the night sky. Under the roof of the altar building, the only recognizable objects were the three porcelain bowls for rice, salt, and water shimmering on the altar steps.

"Bring Bo back to me," Saya addressed the altar imperiously.

"Bring Bo back to me," she cried, stamping her foot on the ground. "I want to see Bo!" she shouted, her voice growing loud and shrill. "I want to see him!"

Whimpering she sank to the ground. ". . . see him just one more time."

That was how her father found her.

He bent down over her and stroked her hair.

"Otosan," she whispered, "where is Bo?"

Her father was silent.

Saya felt his cool hand. Her father drew her gently to him. His nearness was soothing.

"Where is Bo?" she asked once again.

Her father was silent. After a while he softly began to

hum a tune—the song that Saya had most often sung with Bo.

Saya listened without a word. She wondered why her father had chosen to sing this particular song. It sounded so gay, as if it didn't belong here.

Then—hesitatingly—she joined in. She sang although her voice almost refused to come. Somewhere she heard Bo's artless little voice.

He was singing with her, inside her.

Then the song was over, and silence returned. Saya, weary now, nestled closer to her father.

The three porcelain bowls shimmered milk white. Where the shadow of the altar roof ended, the moon drew dark shapes of branches and leaves on the bluish ground.

Saya heard the eloquent stillness of the forest. She heard the bell chant of the gekko—gok . . . gok . . . gok. . . . She heard the crickets chirping away somewhere—chinchiro-rin . . . chinchiro-rin . . . chinchiro-rin. . . . She heard the wind—srrr . . . srrr . . . srrr. . . . She heard the moon softly parting the clouds in the sky—hyuu . . . hyuu . . . hyuu. . . . She heard the sparkling of the stars—pikka . . . pikka . . . pikka. . . . And from a great distance she heard the call of the cranes—traaa . . . traaa . . . traaa. . . .

Her father lifted her carefully onto his back and carried her home. The gravel crunched at every step. Saya leaned her head against her father's slender neck. She could feel the pulse beating under his skin.